Norwyck stopped in his tracks and rubbed his eyes to clear them.

A wave of dread overtook him as he looked upon a body lying prone in the sand. Long dark hair cloaked a narrow back, but did naught to hide pale, feminine buttocks.

A woman.

Anger was the first emotion he felt. A woman had been aboard that ship, and Bart's conflicting emotions warred within him. The knight's code had been deeply ingrained, so 'twas impossible to look upon her bruised and battered body without pity. No woman should meet such a violent and terrifying end.

Yet he had experienced a woman's treachery, and he would lay odds that *she* had somehow been responsible for the shipwreck.

He crouched beside her and touched one shoulder, pushing her over. He did not know what he expected, but it was certainly not to cause a paroxysm of retching and coughing.

God's blood, she was alive!

Norwyck's Lady

Margo Maguire

HARLEQUIN®

TORONTO • NEW YORK • LONDON
AMSTERDAM • PARIS • SYDNEY • HAMBURG
STOCKHOLM • ATHENS • TOKYO • MILAN • MADRID
PRAGUE • WARSAW • BUDAPEST • AUCKLAND

ISBN 0-373-29237-6

NORWYCK'S LADY

This edition published by arrangement with Harlequin Books S.A.

® and TM are trademarks of the publisher. Trademarks indicated with
® are registered in the United States Patent and Trademark Office, the
Canadian Trade Marks Office and in other countries.

Visit us at www.eHarlequin.com

Printed in U.S.A.

Please address questions and book requests to:
Harlequin Reader Service
U.S.: 3010 Walden Ave., P.O. Box 1325, Buffalo, NY 14269
Canadian: P.O. Box 609, Fort Erie, Ont. L2A 5X3

This book is dedicated to Julia, Joe and Mike.
No mother could be more proud.

Chapter One

The north coast of Northumberland
Late autumn, 1300

The air was still, but the North Sea surf crashed violently upon the beach, as a result of the morning's terrible storm. Dark clouds hovered over the northern cliffs and over Norwyck Keep, threatening another burst of rain.

Bartholomew Holton, Earl of Norwyck, stalked up the beach, oblivious to the weather. His tall, powerful form was garbed in his usual dark tunic and hose, though he'd worn a cloak in deference to the harsh weather.

He cared not for clothing, or fashion, especially not now, while circumstances at Norwyck weighed so heavily upon him. His elder brother William's untimely death had made Bartholomew earl. His new responsibilities disconcerted him, and his wife's treachery and subsequent death preyed upon his heart and mind.

Felicia Holton had done the unthinkable. She had

betrayed Bartholomew's elder brother, delivering him
to their Scottish neighbors to the north, the brutal and
barbaric Armstrongs.

'Twas nearly a year now since William, Earl of
Norwyck, had died at the hand of Lachann Armstrong,
and Felicia herself had lost her own life soon thereafter
in childbed, bearing an Armstrong bastard.

Bartholomew continued down the beach, brooding,
heedless of Norwyck's massive walls looming above
the shore. He sorely missed his brother. He had never
dreamed of being lord of this place, for Norwyck had
always been Will's legacy. William, lighthearted and
fair, who seemed always to know what was expected,
how to handle every situation. He'd had the respect of
every Norwyck knight, including their father's old ad-
viser, Sir Walter.

Upon his return from the wars in Scotland, Bartholomew's only wish was to retire to the demesne
granted him by King Edward, enriched by the lands
that were part of Felicia's dowry. All he'd been able
to think of was the life he'd have with his sweet Felicia, and the children that would soon follow.

Aye, Felicia. His lying, murderous, whoring wife.

Bart kicked at a piece of flotsam that had washed
ashore. 'Twas dark wood, and had once been highly
polished, but Bartholomew paid it no mind as he
scowled and continued down the beach, stepping
around other bits of debris that had washed up in the
storm.

A sudden wind whipped at his cloak and he grasped
the edges in annoyance. Sand filtered into his shoes,
but he took no notice. He hunched his shoulders
against the wind and walked on.

Eight months since Felicia's death. It had been eight

months since he'd learned of her treachery, her betrayal. And still Bartholomew did not know how she'd managed to lure William into Lachann Armstrong's trap. Or why.

True enough, Bart had hardly known Felicia when their betrothal contract and marriage had taken place. She'd been a lass of seventeen; he had barely reached manhood. They'd been married a mere six months when Bart had gone off to Scotland with King Edward's archers and his mighty cavalry.

And for two long years, he'd been away from home.

Bart had been foolish enough to hope his wife had been with child when he left. But that had not been the case. Still, 'twas no matter. They had many years in which to raise a family, and upon his return from Scotland, Bart threw himself into the task of wooing his wife. This was no hardship, for Felicia was beautiful and accomplished. Within weeks, she was pregnant.

Little did Bart know that the bairn had been planted in his absence. The boy-child, born only six months after his return, gave proof to Felicia's lie. Her hateful words during the throes of her labor only verified it.

The broad expanse of beach that ran adjacent to Norwyck Castle began to narrow as Bart walked north, and he was soon forced to walk among large boulders and shallow tide pools, with thick reeds and grassy growth sprouting from the wet sand.

More debris was here, too, and it finally caught Bartholomew's attention. Among the flotsam were several odd items—table legs, a sealed chest with brass handles, two wooden spoons, a sealed barrel.

Awareness struck and Bart stopped in his tracks to gaze out at the roiling sea. A ship must have sunk in the storm. 'Twas quite common for ships to have difficulty navigating these waters, yet only one vessel had ever gone down here in all of Bartholomew's twenty-eight years.

He'd been a raw youth, not yet in his teens, when he'd walked this beach with his father and William, looking for survivors.

There had not been any. They'd found plenty of bodies, but no one had managed to get to shore alive. He assumed this wreck would be just as bad.

Bart almost welcomed this turn of events, for it took his mind off the dark and dismal thoughts that preoccupied too many of his waking hours. He began walking again, and discovered the first body, that of a man whose clothes—what were left of them—were in tatters.

Bart rolled him over and verified that he was dead, then quickly moved on, looking for survivors.

The speed of the wind increased, and the waves crashed ever more violently upon the shore, but Bartholomew continued along the beach, caught up in the macabre scene splayed out before him. More debris and bodies were caught behind rocks and trapped among the weeds.

Not one victim was alive.

Still Bart walked, in spite of the storm that was moving in. He turned over bodies and stepped past the shattered fragments of the lives that had been lost. When he returned to the keep, he would send a contingent of men to recover the corpses and bury them. He would direct the priest to—

He stopped in his tracks and rubbed his eyes to clear them. A wave of dread overtook him as he looked upon a body lying prone in the sand. Long, dark hair cloaked a narrow back, but did naught to hide pale, feminine buttocks.

A woman.

Anger was the first emotion he felt. A woman had been aboard that ship, and Bart's conflicting emotions warred within him. The knight's code had been deeply ingrained, so 'twas impossible to look upon her bruised and battered body without pity. No woman should meet such a violent and terrifying end.

Yet he had experienced a woman's treachery, causing him to hold naught but harsh and bitter feelings toward the weaker sex. In truth, Bart would lay odds that *she* had somehow been responsible for the shipwreck.

Approaching her warily, he barely noticed her feminine form—the tapered waist that flared to smooth, full buttocks, the long, shapely legs and delicate feet. He saw only the ugly bruises and nasty scrapes that marred otherwise perfect skin.

He crouched beside her and touched one shoulder, pushing her over. He did not know what he expected, but it was certainly not to cause a paroxysm of retching and coughing.

God's blood, she was alive!

Bart positioned her so that she could cough the water out of her lungs, but she remained limp and unconscious. When she fell back into his arms, he pulled the tattered remains of her clothes from her body and somehow managed to cover her with his cloak.

He glanced around. More bodies were out there, and the storm was closing in. If the woman were to have any chance of survival, he had to get her to shelter quickly. And the only shelter to be had was at Norwyck Castle.

He lifted the woman into his arms. She was naught but deadweight, wrapped in his damp woolen cloak. But Bartholomew had a swordsman's powerful build, and the legs of a horseman. 'Twas no difficulty to carry her. He shifted in order to get a firm hold on her, then started back down the beach toward the path that led to one of the castle gates.

Servants and children were in the great hall when Bartholomew kicked open the heavy oak door and strode in carrying the woman. There was silence for a split second, then everyone began chattering at once, all asking questions simultaneously.

"What's happened?"

"Who are you carrying?"

"Is she dead?"

"Can we see?"

He went to the table and, using one foot, yanked a chair far enough away to give him room to sit down with his burden still in his arms.

"Hush, all of you," he said. He was not only the new earl, but the elder brother and sole guardian of his four younger siblings. They were half siblings, actually, for his own mother had died when he was just a lad. His father had remarried and had a second family.

The twins, Henry and John, were fourteen years old. Then came Kathryn, who was eleven, but thought she was the lady of the hall. Eleanor was last, a mere six years, as inquisitive and mischievous as two children her age.

"There's been a shipwreck," he said, leaning back, resting his arms. "This is the only survivor that I found."

Everyone began talking again, and Bart gestured for one of the footmen. "Send a maid to see that a chamber is made ready for her, Rob," he said. "Then get some men and go down to the beach before the storm rolls in, and see if there are any more survivors."

"Yes, my lord," the man said.

"Listen, all of you," Bart said, turning his attention back to his siblings. "I don't know anything about the shipwreck, only that there is debris all over the beach, as well as several bodies."

"Are you sure this one's alive?" Henry asked, giving Bartholomew's burden a sidelong glance.

"Will we keep her?"

Bart looked down at the inert body in his arms. Her head lolled against his upper arm, extending her neck. A pulse beat there—too fast, but it seemed steady enough.

"Yes, she's alive, and no, we will not keep her, Eleanor," he said to his wide-eyed sister. "If she survives, we'll send her on her way."

He wondered where the woman had been bound when her ship sank. She could have been headed for Scotland, or on a southbound ship that had been blown off course. There was no way of knowing, of course, until she regained consciousness.

"She's beautiful," Eleanor said with awe.

"You won't be falling in love with her as you did Felicia, will you?" Kathryn demanded, with arms crossed over her bony chest. She was a delicate child whose world had been shaken by William's and Felicia's deaths.

Bart scowled and let out a puff of air in derision, dismissing his sisters' words. He hadn't the slightest interest in the woman's appearance, nor would he fall in love with her. Not in *this* century at least. He was through with women.

The earldom would pass to Henry, the elder of the twins, and through him, to his sons.

Refusing to look too closely at the woman in his arms, Bart stood abruptly and made his way toward the main staircase, with his sisters and brothers following. He reached the first landing as two maids stepped out of the stairwell leading to the east tower.

"The tower room is ready, my lord," one said.

"Naught else would do, my lord," said the other, a widow named Rose, whom Bart remembered for her patience with his sisters. "The lower chambers are not yet fit for more guests."

The bishop of Alnwick and his large entourage had just left Norwyck, and the usual guest chambers were not ready for further use.

Bartholomew said not a word, but followed Rose, whose candle lit the way up a circular stone staircase to the most beautiful chamber in the keep. 'Twas the place most favored by Bart's stepmother, a circular room with four tall, peaked windows, one facing each direction. The children liked coming up here, so the maids always kept it fresh.

When Bart entered, he saw that a basin of clean water had been placed upon the stand near the bed. The bed curtains were pushed aside and the blankets pulled down. A long linen sheet lay on top, presumably to be discarded once his filthy cloak was removed from the woman's body. Then she would be naked again.

He gritted his teeth and turned to his siblings. "Everyone out. Now."

They protested, but did his bidding anyway, grum-

bling as they closed the chamber door behind them.
Bart set his burden carefully down on the bed. He
should have had Rose stay to help him, but neglected
to call her back when she quit the room with his siblings.

He picked up one of the candles and lit a lamp near
the bed. Then he turned to look at this woman survivor.

Her hair was nearly dry now, a matted and snarled
mass of a lighter brown than it had seemed before. As
he pushed it away from her face, his mouth went dry.

Dark eyelashes formed thick crescents over high
cheekbones. Her nose was straight and her mouth
wide, with full lips slightly parted. Her neatly dimpled
chin came to a delicate point over the elegant lines of
her neck. Her skin was perfection, smooth and fine.

She winced and made a small noise, then moved
one hand fitfully. Unable to keep himself from touching her again, he smoothed the hair away from her
forehead and saw that a large purple lump had formed
at the side, with a deep, bloody gash cut through it.

'Twas no wonder she was unconscious. The blow
that had caused this wound had to have been mon-
strous. He dipped a clean cloth in the basin of water
and began to cleanse the cut, stroking gently, mindful
that the slightest touch would cause her pain.

She moaned and turned away, though she remained
unconscious. Bart continued washing. He believed the
gash should be stitched, but he could not help but
think of the terrible scar that would result. The wound
was closed and dry for now. Mayhap if she remained
quiet, it could be left alone.

Bart hesitated to open the cloak that covered her,
having already glimpsed what lay beneath. He was not

about to subject himself to the kind of reaction the sight of her naked body would bring. Yet he did not want her exposed to anyone else—not even Rose.

The woman began to tremble, and Bart cursed. He had no choice but to get her out of that cloak and under the blankets. He had to warm her.

Delaying the inevitable, he stepped away from the bed and lit the fire that had been laid, fanning it until it flamed cozily, throwing its warmth into the room. Briefly, Bartholomew considered calling Rose back to deal with the woman, but dismissed the idea once again, refusing to consider his reasons too carefully. Cracking his knuckles, he turned back to her.

The cloak had stiffened in the salty mist, but he managed to peel it away, leaving part of it underneath her. She had scrapes and bruises all over. Using a cloth to brush the dried sand from her flesh, Bart forced himself to ignore the lush fullness of her body as he touched her.

She continued to tremble, so he worked quickly. She moaned again and tried to shift away from Bartholomew's touch, but was too weak to manage it. He finally turned her to her side, folded the sand-filled cloak and sheet under her, then lay her on her back again and pulled it out the other side.

He covered her with the bedclothes just as a tap sounded upon the door. Tearing his gaze away from the unconscious woman, Bart went to answer it.

"Bartie?" Eleanor said as she stepped into the room. "Is the lady going to be all right?"

Bartholomew couldn't help but ruffle his little sister's bright red hair. She was the only one who could get away with calling him "Bartie."

"I don't know, Ellie," he said, following her to the woman's bed. "She's badly hurt."

Eleanor touched the woman's hair. She frowned and pulled her lower lip between her teeth. "Will she die up here in Mama's tower?" she asked, looking up at her elder brother.

Bart clenched his jaw. He hadn't given that possibility a thought, never considering how it would affect his brothers and sisters. "Nay, little goose," he said. "She'll not die in Norwyck Keep if I have aught to say about it."

Eleanor looked back at the lady. Her gaze was thoughtful, wistful. "She is very pretty," the child said. "Will she wake up soon?"

"Ellie, I have no more answers for you," he said as he raked the fingers of one hand through his hair. He'd seen men injured like this during the campaign in Scotland. Some of them never awakened at all, and the thought of this lady's certain death did not settle well with him. "Run along and find Sir Walter for me. Have him send for the healer in the village."

"She's starting to move a bit more," Alice Hoget said, placing a cool poultice on the survivor woman's head. Night had fallen, and a terrible storm with it, yet the victim remained unconscious. How long could this go on? How long would it be necessary for her to remain at Norwyck?

"What do you think?" Bartholomew asked. An odd restlessness possessed him. He paced the length of the room while Alice examined the woman and did what she could, which was frighteningly little.

"What I think is that she took a blow to the head and was thrown overboard," Alice said in her frank manner. "'Tis a wonder she made it to the beach alive. She's lucky she didn't drown."

Bartholomew scowled and resumed his pacing. 'Twould have been better if he'd let her die out there on the beach. Less trouble for him. And no doubt less trouble for the woman whose wounds would likely kill her, anyway.

Yet he hadn't been able to abandon her to the elements. Even though he no longer had any fondness for women, the thought of leaving her on the beach had never even crossed his mind.

"What I mean is—will she recover?"

"No bones broke, only a rap on the head." The old healer picked up the lamp, then lifted the unconscious woman's eyelids. "Look," she said. "The blacks of her eyes shrink with the light. It means she'll be coming out of it soon."

"How do you know that?" Bartholomew asked.

"Experience," she replied as she gathered her things together. "Seen plenty of people knocked senseless. 'Tis not unusual for a body to remain in this state for a day or more."

"You mean she could stay this way for more than a day?"

"Aye, m'lord," Alice said. "Though this one's showing signs of coming 'round."

Bart scowled at Alice, then turned his sour expression on the woman in the bed. Alice ignored him as she collected her things and shuffled out of the chamber, leaving Bartholomew alone with the stranger…and his dismal thoughts.

He ceased his pacing and sat on a chair near the bed. The sooner the woman came to her senses, the better, he thought. Then he would send her on her way to wherever she'd been going when her ship had gone down. Likely she'd been en route to one of the southern harbors, but had been blown off course by the storm. That very thing had often been known to happen, though the ships did not usually sink.

Bart picked up one of her hands. The nails were nicely shaped, and the skin was soft. This woman could be naught but a lady with hands like these. Her face was finely shaped, too, and Bart was certain that someone would soon come looking for her.

The sudden, distant clanging of the church bell had him on his feet in an instant. 'Twas not time for services, and there was only one other reason for the bell to ring: the village was under attack.

Without another glance at the unconscious woman, Bart left the chamber and fairly flew down the steps. On the first landing, he met a footman who'd been sent to summon him.

"My lord, Armstrong men are raiding the village!"

"Go out to the stable and see that my squire has my armor and horse ready," Bart said as they quickly descended to the main hall together. "I'll be there directly."

Eleanor sat tearfully at the great table in the hall, with John's arm around her. Kathryn stood stoically near the fireplace. Henry, thrusting his chest out, approached Bartholomew as he crossed the hall. "I'm coming with you," he said.

"Nay," Bart replied. His brothers should have been sent out to foster at a neighboring estate, but circumstances in recent years had prevented it. Therefore, their training was lacking. He would not send the boys out to battle until they were ready. "Stay here and defend the keep and your sisters. The servants will look to you for direction.''

"But, Bart—''

"That is my final word, Hal,'' he said, as he crossed the great hall toward the main door. He stopped short when he reached it, and turned back to his younger brother. "I intend to bring back the head of Lachann Armstrong. Make sure there's a stout pike in the courtyard to put it on.''

Chapter Two

Lightning slashed across the sky and thunder crashed all 'round them. Only the whoreson Armstrongs would mount an attack in this kind of weather. They'd managed to torch a few cottages and rout half a herd of cattle into the hills before Bartholomew and his knights met the attack, with a ferocity that quickly had the Armstrongs retreating to their own land.

Trudging through a heavy downpour, Bart's men chased the Scots across hills and muddy dales, but the cowardly Armstrongs managed to melt away into their hidey-holes. Bart had had enough of battles to last a lifetime, and he wished the Armstrong would desist with his warring ways.

Yet, ever since William's death, the Scottish laird had made it his personal mission to destroy Norwyck. Bart assumed 'twas to pay for his and William's part in the recent Scottish wars.

To Bart's supreme disappointment, the Scots disappeared entirely by dawn. Bartholomew had no choice but to turn back without his enemy's head, though he'd managed to cut down a goodly number of the raiding Scots.

He had not given a thought to the woman in the east tower, but as he dismounted before the stone steps of the keep, he wondered in passing if she had awakened yet from her stupor.

The light in the chamber was dim, but that did not account for her blurred vision. Naught was clear, not even her hand when she studied it up close. What was wrong? What had happened to her eyes?

"Oh my!" someone cried. "You're awake!"

English. The woman had spoken English, and for some reason, the sound was strange and unfamiliar. Yet she understood the words.

"Would you like a sip of water?" the woman asked, leaning over her. She was able to make out light hair and a dark gown, but the facial features were unclear.

She nodded and accepted help in drinking from a mug.

"I'll just go and tell Lord Norwyck that you've come 'round," the servant said.

"L-Lord…Norwyck?" she queried, trying out the English words.

"Aye," the voice replied. "You're in the keep at Norwyck Castle. Lord Norwyck himself carried you here from the beach."

"Norwyck…carried me?" She swallowed dryly and furrowed her brows, only to wince at the pain it caused. Naught made sense to her. Norwyck. Norwyck Keep. 'Twas wholly unfamiliar.

"Aye, he did. When you washed up on shore." The servant was suddenly gone, leaving her alone with her thoughts.

They were surprisingly vacant.

She could not think why she'd have "washed up" on a shore. She had been... *Where?*

Her stomach did a flip when she realized that she could not remember anything specific. There were faces, and strange places, but she could not name any of them. Her memory was gone, and her sight was poor. What *was* she to do?

Panic seized her. Her heart pounded and her breathing became erratic. She could not even remember her own name! She did not know where she'd come from, or how she had gotten here.

Swinging her legs over the side of the bed, she felt a wave of nausea nearly overcome her. Even so, she could not lie here and wait for someone to take care of her. 'Twas not in her nature to be so passive, though how she could be certain of that, she did not know. It just did not seem right to remain abed and wait for answers.

Light-headedness made her falter, but she moved away from the bed in spite of it. She was bruised and sore all over, with a knot at the side of her forehead and a gash along her shinbone. At least these seemed to be the worst of her injuries. The hazy vision alarmed her, too, but she had no way of knowing whether she'd always had poor eyesight. She doubted it, since it seemed so strange to her.

Almost as disturbing as her injuries was that she was naked. She was fully and completely exposed, and there did not seem to be any clothing within reach. Squinting, she extended her arms to feel for any objects in her path, nearly tripping over a chair in her attempt to reach what she thought was a gown draped over a chair.

'Twas just a woolen shawl.

The sudden sound of footsteps and voices came to her, and she knew she could not make it back to the bed quickly without tumbling over something. She grabbed the shawl and held it up before her just as the door opened.

Bart stopped in his tracks at the entrance of the tower room, holding back his brothers and Eleanor, who had come to see the wounded woman.

"Go back down, and I'll come and get you when...er, when I..." He swallowed.

"Come on, Bart," Henry said, pushing at his brother's back. "Let us through."

"Nay," he replied, frowning as the woman stood gazing at him blankly. Her body was partially covered by the wool shawl that usually rested upon the back of one of the chairs, leaving most of her body bared to his view.

Awake, she was exquisite. His eyes raked over her, from the delicate bones at her shoulders to the swell of her barely concealed breasts, then down to hips that were not entirely covered by the shawl, to sweetly dimpled knees and slender ankles.

His siblings shoved him from behind. When he finally found his voice, he ordered them away. "Go! Go and...and I'll be down shortly." He turned and slammed the door, barring it, and ignoring the pounding that came from the other side.

'Twas naught compared to the pounding in his skull, in his chest, in his groin. She was beauty and grace, angelic and dangerously seductive.

Tearing his gaze away, he cursed under his breath. He knew better than to allow a comely form to cloud his thoughts. She was a woman, no more and no less. Fully capable of the most devious treachery.

He would allow her to stay until she was steady on her feet. But then she had to go.

"Wrap the shawl more securely, if you don't mind," he said coolly as he walked toward her.

She fumbled with the heavy wool as she stepped back, and lost her footing. Bart lunged and caught her before she fell, and lifted her into his arms.

Her naked flesh felt absurdly enticing. She had only covered the front of her body—and not very well at that—leaving her back entirely bare. Her skin felt smooth, warm.

Her eyes were an unusual light green, edged in blue, framed by dark lashes. Bart did not believe he'd ever seen eyes like hers before, but they were unfocused, confused. Her predicament touched him. To have survived such an ordeal, possibly to have lost her family in such a terrible way, was unspeakable.

Inuring himself against any feelings of pity, he set her on the bed and tossed the blankets over her. Whatever had happened was done. It had naught to do with him. He would allow this woman to remain at Norwyck until she was well enough to travel, then send her on her way.

When she began to tremble, Bart looked away.

"My lord?"

"You're at Norwyck Castle," he said, keeping his back to her. "Your ship went down in our waters."

"My...ship?"

"As far as we know, you are the sole survivor," he said, turning back to pierce her with his stony gaze. "And you are...?"

She moistened her lips. "I...I...cannot remember," she said simply.

Bart stared at her mouth, unable to comprehend the meaning of her statement. Oh, he well understood what she'd said, but he did not know quite what she meant.

"You cannot *remember?*"

"N-nay, my lord," she said. She fought to keep a tremor from her voice, but Bart refused to be taken in by that manipulative wile. 'Twas one his late wife had used to great effect. "I awoke without knowledge of who I am or w-where I belong."

Bart chortled without humor. How was it possible that she did not remember who she was? She must think him a fool to believe such a tale.

He walked to the eastern window and gazed out to sea. He did not care to look at her now, not with that impossibly vulnerable expression in her eyes, nor the lies on her tongue.

"So. You have no idea who you are, or from whence you came," he said. "What, exactly, *do* you remember?"

She hesitated long enough that he was just about to turn to her, but then she murmured, "I remember...only s-snatches of things. A face, a garden...children. I... I—"

Bart pushed away from the wall and turned to her. "You'll pardon me if I find your story difficult to believe," he said derisively. He crossed the room, looking back at her only when he'd reached the chamber door. "You will need clothes. I'll have a maid bring something suitable to you. When next I see you, mayhap you'll have a more believable tale to tell."

With those parting words, he was gone.

She turned away from the door and blinked back tears. Not only was she unable to remember anything of substance, but something was terribly wrong with her eyes. The lord's attitude was quite obviously hostile, as if her turning up at Norwyck had somehow offended him or caused him undue hardship.

Well, she would just remove herself from this place. There had to be someone who could direct her to a more hospitable dwelling, a place with a less frightening master. As soon as she had clothes to wear, she would get as far from Norwyck as possible.

If only she could remember. She wracked her brain trying to place the images that came to mind, but was unable to make anything coherent of them. The face of a woman…some blond children…a field of flowers…

Someone entered the chamber, and she looked up to see the shadowy form of a child. A child with bright red hair, certainly not one of the children she'd seen in her mind.

"My lady?" the girl said as she approached the bed.

She cleared her throat. "Yes…"

"I am Eleanor," the child said, "sister to Bartholomew."

She must have looked quizzically at the child because the youngster clarified, "Bartholomew Holton, Earl of Norwyck."

"Oh," she replied numbly. Bartholomew was the bad-tempered man who'd just left her.

"I've brought you some… What is it?" the child asked.

"My eyes."

"Your eyes are beautiful, my lady," the girl said

as she placed something on the bed. "So clear and bright."

She shook her head, sending sharp spears of pain through her skull. Lying back on the bed, she swallowed back a wave of nausea. "Nay, they are not clear. I cannot see."

"You are blind?" the child asked, astonished.

"Not quite," she replied, "but I might as well be. Everything I see is hazy. Blurred."

"Like when I squeeze my eyes almost closed and look at you?"

"Something like that."

"How terrible," the child replied, placing a small hand on her forearm. "How do you manage? I mean if you're—"

"I do not know," she said. "I don't know if I've always been like this, or if... Nay. This malady seems too unfamiliar. I could not have suffered it before...."

"I do not understand, my lady."

She hesitated. Would a child—even this child, who seemed so bright, so interested—ever understand?

"I—I seem to have lost my memory."

Silence filled a long, empty interval, and she could feel the little girl's eyes upon her. Finally, the child spoke, her voice alight with wonder and puzzlement.

"You've lost your... You mean you cannot remember—"

"I cannot remember anything," she whispered in reply.

"Did the wreck take your memories away?"

"I suppose so, though I have no way of know—"

"Your name! You do not even remember your name?"

She fought back tears. "Nay. I do not know who I

am. Or where I belong.'' She did not even know if English was her own language. It seemed familiar to her in an odd, distant way.

Eleanor made a small sound, then walked around to the other side of the bed. ''Will you ever remember it?'' The girl's voice was full of astonishment and sympathy.

She felt the child's interested gaze upon her.

''I do not know.''

''What will we call you, then?'' the child asked.

She bit her lip and tamped down the panic that threatened to overwhelm her again. Who was she? She tried to think of a name that seemed to fit, but could not. Naught seemed familiar, and trying to force the memory only made her head hurt more. ''I have no idea.''

''Then we'll just have to give you a new name,'' the child said excitedly. ''I will share my name with you. We'll call you Eleanor.... Nay.'' It sounded as if the girl was frowning. ''That would be too confusing, with two of us. I know!'' The voice brightened. ''We'll call you after King Edward's wife—Marguerite!''

''"Tis as g-good a name as any, I suppose,'' she replied, though it, too, sounded utterly unfamiliar.

''Oh, I forgot!'' Eleanor said. ''I brought you some clothes. Bartie sent a maid to do it, but I came in her stead.''

''I thank you, Lady Eleanor,'' Marguerite replied, somewhat buoyed by the girl's exuberance. ''Tell me, is there a shift or chemise I can put on now? I seem to have…lost all my clothes somehow.''

Eleanor sorted through the stack that she'd brought,

and held up something long and white. "This will do," she said. "Shall I help you?"

"Yes, please," Marguerite said. The friendliness of the child continued to surprise her, especially after her brother's antagonistic behavior, and Marguerite felt fortunate that there was at least one gracious person at Norwyck Keep. She did not know if she'd ever needed a friend before, but 'twas clear she needed one now.

Bart took a long swallow of ale as he stood by the fire in the great hall. He'd finished removing his armor, but still wore the soaked and stained undertunic and hose he'd had on all through the night of battle. The rain had not let up, and still there were bodies lined up under a tarp on the beach. Huge piles of debris as well as valuables were under guard down by the sea, and a half-blind woman with no memory lay wounded in his tower.

If she could be believed.

He doubted it. He had to give her credit for a gifted imagination, though. Who would ever have thought of such a ploy? A lost memory.

He shook his head and laughed grimly. She would not be able to keep up the farce for long. 'Twas likely her ship was a Scottish one, and she was afraid to admit her identity.

Bart turned when he heard footsteps approaching. 'Twas young Kathryn, who seemed to suffer most after William's death, and from what she understood of Felicia's betrayal.

"Bartholomew," she said, her expression grave. "Eleanor is in the tower room."

"I told her to stay out—"

"Yes, but does she ever listen to anyone?" Kathryn asked disdainfully. She tossed her long blond braid behind her, then followed her brother as he crossed the hall and started up the stairs. "She will not mind me, but goes about, doing as she pleases."

"She's young, Kate," Bart said, trying to rouse an interest in his sister's concerns. Yet the only thing he cared about was that Ellie was in the woman's room. The stranger could be a Scottish assassin, for all he knew. Odder things had happened in recent months, and Bart was not about to take a chance with Eleanor's safety.

He reached the tower room and threw open the door.

"Bartie!" Eleanor cried.

"What did I tell you about coming up here?" he demanded.

The woman slipped back under the blankets, while Ellie crossed her arms and slammed them down over her chest. Annoyance colored the glance she threw at Kathryn, even as her red curls quivered with anger. "I was just helping Lady Marguerite—"

"Ah, she has a name, has she?"

"Nay. We just gave her the queen's name," Ellie replied. "To use until she remembers her own."

He looked over at "Marguerite." Her lips were pressed tightly together, and from the rapid rise and fall of the covers on the bed, he could tell she was breathing heavily.

"You two leave," he said, "and I'll help *Lady Marguerite.*"

"But, Bartie—"

"No arguments, or you'll dine on bread and water for a week," he said menacingly, though 'twas a fa-

miliar warning. Bart threatened Eleanor so often that
it had become something of a jest between them.

"Lady Marguerite needs my help!"

"I'm afraid she will have to do without it," Bart
said as he glanced toward the beautiful lady in the bed.
"This time, she will have to be satisfied with mine."

Chapter Three

Marguerite had barely pulled the soft chemise over her head when her chamber door had burst open and Lord Norwyck had stormed in.

She shifted under the covers and pulled the flimsy cloth down over her legs. This way, at least, she did not feel quite so vulnerable.

"Lady Marguerite, eh?"

"Eleanor suggested it, since I still cannot remember my own name."

"Shall we call you 'your highness', or will 'my lady' do?"

"Are you always so caustic, my lord?" she asked haughtily, "or do I have the sole pleasure of evoking your ire?"

"Liars always have that effect upon me," he replied, "even beautiful ones."

Marguerite wished she could see his features clearly. She could only tell that he was tall and broad shouldered, and his hair was dark. His voice was deep and resonant, his accent pleasant, and there was a softness to his tone when he spoke to his sisters.

'Twas distinctly harsh when he spoke to her.

A bright flash of light from within seared her eyes. Closing them tightly, she flinched with the pain. Nausea roiled in her belly and she swallowed repeatedly, unwilling to embarrass herself before Lord Norwyck.

"God's bones, woman," he said, plucking a bowl from the table near her bed, "haven't you got the sense to seek a basin when you—"

She turned and retched into it, barely conscious of his hand upon her shoulder, gently pulling her over. She did not think it possible to feel any worse, and still live.

She fell back and suppressed a groan. Suddenly, a cool cloth was upon her lips, then soothing her brow. Tears seeped from her eyes.

He remained silent, and if not for his touch, Marguerite would not have known he was there. She did not want to feel any comfort from this stern, unyielding man, yet the warmth of his hand on her chilled flesh sent shivers through her. Mayhap he was not as grim as he wanted her to think.

"I'll send a maid up to sit with you," Lord Norwyck said. His voice was devoid of emotion, and Marguerite was glad she had shown none, either. She was sure those tears had only been the result of her violent retching, not because of the fear or helplessness she felt. She did not really need his presence or any reassurance from him to know she would survive.

When she heard his footsteps retreating, and the sound of the chamber door closing, Marguerite nearly convinced herself she felt relieved.

Weary after the long night of battle and chase, Bartholomew left Marguerite in the tower and returned to the great hall.

'Twas insanity to allow her appearance of vulnerability to affect him. She was just a woman, clearly a deceitful one at that. Bart knew all about falling for a dishonest woman. 'Twas not something that would ever happen again.

He crossed the hall and made his way to the study, a warm and cheerful chamber at the southeast corner of the hall.

"My lord." Sir Walter Gray stood as Bartholomew entered the room.

"Don't get up, Sir Walter." The white-haired knight was as weary as any of the men who'd fought all night.

Walter had lived at Norwyck more than thirty years, serving as steward for Bartholomew's father. He was something of a revered uncle to the Holton sons, and had helped to manage estate matters after their father's death, while Will and Bart were fighting in Scotland. Sir Walter was Bartholomew's most trusted advisor. "The last of the men have returned from their northern foray."

"Any luck cornering Lachann or his son?" Bart asked as he dropped into a chair across from the older man.

The old knight shook his head. "They gave chase all the way to Armstrong land, but were rebuffed by archers when they approached the keep."

"Did we lose any men?"

"Not this time."

"There must be some way to take Braemar Keep along with the Armstrong and his bastard son."

"If there is, we have yet to find it," Walter said. "'Tis always well guarded by the best Scottish archers."

Bart made a rude sound.

"There is naught more to do today, my lord. Why don't you seek your bed now, and rest? Armstrong is not so much a fool as to attack two nights running."

"You wouldn't think so," Bart said as he got to his feet. "But his methods have been unconventional these last few years."

"To say the least, my lord," Walter replied.

Bart knew the man blamed himself for not seeing through Felicia's deception. After all, Armstrong's son, Dùghlas, had seduced and impregnated her while Walter had been in charge of the estate. But Bartholomew did not blame him. Felicia's affair had been conducted in secret while Walter managed the estate and the children. It might even have begun before Bartholomew had left for Scotland.

"Still, I cannot believe the scoundrel will come back tonight," Walter added.

"You may be right, but I do not trust the Armstrong to behave reasonably or predictably," Bart said as he rubbed his hand across his jaw and his morning whiskers.

Against all convention, Laird Armstrong had corrupted Felicia. He'd set his son, Dùghlas, to seduce her. Then he'd somehow convinced her to deliver William into his trap without so much as a sword being drawn. The man was as devious as a freebooter. "See that guards are posted at every gate," Bart said. "I want sentries in the hills north of the village. If the Armstrongs come again, we'll need ample warning."

"Aye, my lord," Walter said, "I'll see to it."

"I'm going to sleep for a couple of hours," he said, then he stopped and turned back to Walter. "Send someone for Alice Hoget later. I'd like her to look in on the lady in the tower…while I am present.''

Walter frowned. ''Is aught amiss, my lord?''

''I do not know,'' Bart replied. ''The woman says she cannot remember anything…naught of her past, not even her name.''

When Walter did not respond, Bartholomew continued. ''I want Alice's opinion. I want to know whether such a thing is possible.''

''Aye, my lord,'' Walter replied. '''Tis passing strange, though not unheard of. Alice will be here when you awaken.''

Unpleasant dreams plagued Marguerite's afternoon nap, and she awoke unrefreshed. She supposed the images in her dream must mean something, but she could not imagine what. The faces, the places…all were unfamiliar to her.

The worst parts of the dream had awakened her. She'd felt as if she were drowning, as if her very life was being squeezed out of her. She'd sat up in a panic, her heart pounding, her head aching. Yet still she could remember naught of her past.

The door to her chamber opened suddenly, and a wizened old woman appeared. Gazing at her, Marguerite realized then that her vision had improved significantly. She could see the old lady almost clearly.

''Well, yer looking better than ye did last time I saw ye.''

''You know me, then?'' Marguerite cried hopefully, placing a hand over her heart as if she could quiet its hopeful patter.

''Nay, m'lady,'' the woman replied. ''The only time I've ever seen ye was when ye were lying here in this bed, insensible. I'm Alice Hoget. I'm the healer in these parts, but mind ye, I'm no surgeon.''

"Oh." Marguerite's shoulders slumped and tears filled her eyes. She had hoped—perhaps unreasonably—for a ready answer to all her questions. But 'twas not to be. She blinked back the tears and sniffed before she noticed a tall, dark figure standing in the doorway behind Alice.

Her heart sank when she realized 'twas Lord Norwyck.

Now that she could see more clearly, she was struck by his handsome features, even though they were mitigated by a thoroughly bad-tempered expression.

His eyes were dark, nearly black, and shadowed by thick, dark brows. He was possessed of a strong chin and jaw, the muscles of which even now clenched in disapproval of her. His lips were full, yet sculpted, his nose straight and aristocratic. His black hair brushed his shoulders.

There was no softness to his features, yet Marguerite had experienced his kindness, no matter how gruffly it had been cloaked.

"Lord Norwyck says ye've lost yer memory."

Unable to find her voice at the moment, Marguerite nodded.

"Can ye remember aught?"

"Only a few faces, bits of a storm," she said. Her voice was shaky and she struggled to control it. "'Tis a strange sensation to…to *feel* that there is a memory there, but be unable to bring it out."

"Aye, it must be," the old woman said. "But I've heard of it—this malady of memory loss."

"You have?" Marguerite cried, in spite of Lord

Norwyck's approach. "Will it pass? Will I soon re-mem—?"

"Hold, lass," Alice said. "I cannot tell ye. I know too little of it. Lie back, though, and let me look at the gash on yer poor skull."

Marguerite did as she was told, suddenly aware of her lack of proper dress. She slid down into the bed, quickly pulling the blanket up to her shoulders.

"Lord Norwyck says yer eyes aren't right, neither."

"That's right, but my vision has improved since I awoke this afternoon," Marguerite said, striving to ignore the lord's looming presence. "'Tis still not entirely clear, but much better than 'twas."

"That's a good sign, then," the healer said. "I expect yer memory will return soon, too."

"Oh, Alice, do you think so?" Marguerite said, grasping the old woman's hand in her own.

"Well, I can't be sure," Alice replied, "but I'd say there's hope, at least."

"That's all I've prayed for," Marguerite said quietly.

Alice extricated her hand from Marguerite's and patted her shoulder. She turned to Lord Norwyck, who stood just behind her. "Naught more can I do, m'lord," she said. "I'll be happy to come if there's any change, but I expect these scrapes and gashes to be healed within the fortnight."

"And her memory?"

"No promises there, m'lord," Alice said with a smile. "'Tis up to the good Lord to restore it."

Bart followed the old healer to the door and partway down the stairs. "What do you make of her?"

"In what way, m'lord?"

"Do you think she speaks the truth?"

"Ye mean, about her memory?" Alice asked. "Well, I wouldn't know about that. She seems sincere enough, and I'd hate to think of one so fair as a liar...." She hesitated, and Bart knew she thought of Felicia. "But I have no way of knowing."

Bartholomew had to agree. The woman seemed ingenuous enough, but the most accomplished liars were capable of fooling anyone. He returned to the tower room and found the lady out of bed.

"Oh!" she cried, whirling away from the long, narrow window that overlooked the beach and the sea beyond. "I did not realize..."

"Realize what?" She was unbelievably beautiful, Bart mused, with her lush hair cascading around her shoulders and her lovely eyes focused upon him. Her body was covered in a filmy silk chemise, but it clung to her, somehow making her more alluring than if she'd been naked.

"Realize th-that you would be coming back."

"Making it necessary to continue with your little sport?"

"My s-sport, my lord?"

Bart had to admit she was fairly convincing. 'Twas no wonder old Alice had been taken in by her pretty face, her woeful tale. Hardening his heart against any sympathy he might feel, he approached her.

"Tell me what you recall of the storm and the ship you were on."

"Naught, my lord," she said. "But I dreamed while I slept this afternoon. That I was drowning."

Which revealed exactly nothing. Bart gazed into those pale green eyes and sought the truth. She appeared to be naught but a guileless maiden, yet he knew better than to trust appearances. His *innocent*

Felicia had duped not only him, but William and Sir Walter, as well.

"That's all?" he asked coolly.

"Nay," she replied. "I saw faces...the same faces that appear in my mind sometimes while I'm awake. Yet I have no idea who they are."

"Very convenient for you."

"I—I do not understand why you should mistrust me so, my lord," she said, clearly unnerved by his proximity. He moved even closer. He would frighten the truth out of her if necessary. "I have naught to gain by feigning this malady."

"Nay?" he said as he closed the distance between them. "Then you have no allegiance to Laird Armstrong or his ally, Carmag MacEwen?" he asked quietly. His face was a mere breath away from hers. Another inch and his chest would touch her breast.

"These names mean naught to me," she whispered.

He was close enough to kiss her, and every muscle and sinew of his body urged him to abandon his questions and do so. He tipped his head and leaned forward, intent upon tasting her. His eyelids lowered slightly.

The chamber door burst open with a crash, spilling argumentative children into the room. Bartholomew raised his head and, with a calm he did not feel, turned to look at the intruders, his young siblings.

"Eleanor. Kate," he said, enunciating each name carefully. He crossed his arms over his chest and willed his pulse to slow as Eleanor ran to him. "What is the purpose of this intrusion?"

"She does not mind me, Bartholomew," Kathryn began. She cast a scathing look at her sister, who now clung to Bart's legs.

"I tried to stop them, Bart," John said sheepishly. "I never intended for them to bring their argument all the way up here."

"Where is your nurse?" Bart asked.

"We have no need of a nurse, Bartholomew!" Kate declared, placing her hands upon her hips. She had become a rigid little tyrant in the past few months, often resorting to tears when she did not get her way. Bart had hoped she would ease back into childhood, now that the worst seemed to be in the past, but it was clear he would have to deal with her.

Yet how would he go about it? She might have recovered from the death of their father, but for Felicia *and* William to have followed within the year—well, 'twas too much for the child.

"Ellie," he said, turning his sister loose from his legs. "Can you not listen to Kate when she speaks to you?"

"Nay, Bartie! I don't want to!"

Obviously. "Eleanor, Kathryn has only your—"

"She is a bully!" Ellie cried. "She thinks she is Mama, or Papa, but she's not!"

Kathryn screeched and lunged for Eleanor, but John held her back. Bartholomew pushed Eleanor behind him.

"Kate, I will see you in the nursery momentarily," he said, averse to continuing such a display before Marguerite. "John, will you see that she gets there?"

"Aye," John replied, his voice sounding odd.

"But—" Kathryn began.

"*I will speak to you downstairs,*" Bart said firmly, and John pulled his sister's arm and drew her out of the tower chamber. "And you..." He crouched down to look Eleanor in the eye. "You must stop giving your sister so much trouble. She's only trying to look after you."

"She doesn't need to," Ellie said, looking down at the floor and pushing out her lower lip. "She's not my mama or my nurse. Besides, I'm big now. I can look after myself."

The child's head barely reached his waist, yet she thought she was big. He'd have laughed aloud if Lady Marguerite had not been there to witness it.

He took Eleanor by the shoulders, turned her around and gently pushed her toward the door. When he saw that she'd gone down the first few steps, he turned back to Marguerite. "Do not think that I've finished with you."

He followed his sister out of the room, closing the door behind him. Marguerite picked up the shawl and drew it 'round her shoulders, then collapsed in a chair near the fire. Confusion prevailed in her mind. Between the images of vaguely familiar people and places, and Bartholomew Holton's formidable presence, she could not sort through her thoughts in any coherent manner.

She knew she should be frightened of the overtly hostile earl. She trembled in his presence and her heart pounded so loudly she believed he might even hear it. Yet her reaction was not one of fear. 'Twas one of...fascination.

She was *attracted* to the man.

Marguerite slid her lower lip through her teeth and frowned in consternation. She'd been the victim of his animosity ever since awakening to this nightmare of doubt and confusion, yet she knew he was not inherently wicked or mean. His demeanor toward his sisters had made that abundantly clear. Though he nearly managed to hide it, his tender feelings for the little girls showed every time they appeared.

His loathing was directed solely at her. And she did not understand why.

Marguerite drew her legs up under her, vowing that until she had a better grasp of her situation and why Bartholomew Holton was so antagonistic toward her, there would be no softening of her heart toward him.

Chapter Four

Morning dawned bright and sunny. Marguerite gazed out the window of her chamber and realized that her vision was completely clear. She could see a vast expanse of sandy beach, and make out several gulls flying high above the waves.

She sent a silent prayer of thanks that her vision had been restored. Now if only her memory would return…

On the opposite wall, another window overlooked a courtyard. Marguerite crossed the room and gazed down, anxious to see if all was clear there, too.

She saw a number of Norwyck's knights on a practice field beyond the courtyard, engaged in swordplay. Several of the men were on horseback, and one in particular worked at a quintain at the opposite end of the courtyard. His movements were powerful, yet agile, striking quickly and mightily, then ducking the reprisal.

Marguerite knew at once that this man, wearing naught but a light undertunic that was damp with his exertions, was Bartholomew Holton. His hair was bound at his nape, and she sensed without seeing that his facial expression would be fierce.

A shudder ran through her and she whirled away from the window. Her unruly response to the young lord was unacceptable. The man had no liking for her, and she had no business having the kind of reaction he kindled in her. Besides, 'twas entirely possible she had her own young man or a husband waiting somewhere for her. Mayhap even children.

The thought of children gave her pause. Marguerite ran her hands down her bodice, across her breasts and to her belly. Had an infant once nestled in her womb? Suckled at her breast?

She did not think so, though she could not be certain. The children whose faces came to her at odd times must have some significance to her. Who were they? Why did she see them every time she closed her eyes?

Rather than dwell on a puzzle that served only to upset her, Marguerite pressed one hand to her heart and turned her attention elsewhere. She let her gaze alight upon the furnishings of the circular room.

The bed, she already knew, was a comfortable one, with rich linen fittings and warm woolen blankets. Two chairs flanked a stuffed settle near the fireplace, where a fire blazed cozily. There were two large wall hangings that Marguerite was able to see clearly now, beautiful, colorful tapestries depicting happy times.

A short, stuffed bench sat before the wash table, and a small mirror hung on the wall above it.

Two closed trunks perched against the wall opposite the bed, and upon inspection of the first, Marguerite discovered a cache of gowns, shifts and hose—among them the clothes Eleanor had brought up the day before. At the bottom were shoes, which Marguerite took out. When she tried to slip her feet in, she discovered a collection of jewels in the toes.

There were rings and chains of gold, with an assortment of colorful gems set into them. Marguerite weighed the pieces in her hands. Eleanor must have put them here, she thought. The child was well-meaning and eager to please, and just young enough that she would not understand the value of such jewelry.

Marguerite put the treasure into the toe of the hose, then placed the sock carefully at the bottom of the trunk. She would see that the gold and precious gems were returned to their rightful place as soon as she was able. In the meantime, she opened the other trunk to see if any more treasures awaited.

Inside were two musical instruments, a psaltery and a gittern. For some reason Marguerite could not fathom, these instruments seemed more precious to her than the gems she'd hidden away in the other trunk.

Carefully, she lifted them out and set them on the bed. Each instrument was beautifully made, from the highly polished wood to the tightly woven strings. Marguerite brushed her hand across the strings of the gittern, causing a discordant sound.

The instruments, the strings, the sounds, seemed familiar. She knew the gittern needed to be tuned, and she tightened or loosened the pegs accordingly. Afterward, when she strummed, it sounded right to her ear, though something was missing.

She did not have time to ponder the question, though, for the door to the chamber opened and Eleanor came in. "You have Mama's gittern!" the child said as she approached the bed.

"Oh, 'twas your mother's?" Marguerite asked. "I'm sorry. I'll put it—"

"Nay, can you play it?"

"I...I don't know."

"Try."

Marguerite took the neck of the instrument in her left hand and strummed the strings with her right, as she had done before Eleanor had come in. She placed the fingers of her left hand over different strings and elicited various notes when she did so. As she strummed the instrument, a pleasing sequence of sounds filled the room.

She knew how to play!

When Eleanor clapped her hands, Marguerite looked at the child in astonishment, then back at the gittern.

"Play another!"

"I...something is not..." Marguerite said, frowning. She was completely puzzled. She felt entirely at ease with the instrument in her hands, yet something was wrong.

"I know!" Eleanor turned, reached into the trunk and pulled out a small object. "Kathryn calls this a plec... A plec—"

"A plectrum," Marguerite said, though she could not say how she had come up with the word. It had just suddenly appeared upon her tongue.

"Aye," Eleanor said. "And when Kate tries to play, the sounds she makes..." The child wrinkled her nose and shook her head.

Marguerite took the quill from the child and began to play a tune, using the plectrum. The instrument now felt much more natural in her hands, and Marguerite sensed that she must have played many times before.

When she noticed the calluses upon the fingertips of her left hand, there could be no doubt that she was a practiced musician.

"I forgot," Eleanor said. "Sir Walter sent me to see if you are hungry. Are you able to come down and break your fast with us in the great hall, or would you rather have a tray up here?"

Marguerite hardly knew how to respond. She'd been cloistered in this tower room ever since awakening without her memory, and she felt strangely timid about leaving. "I don't think your brother—"

"Bartie is training on the practice field with the rest of the knights," Eleanor said, unconcerned. She lifted the lid of the trunk that contained the clothing, and pulled out a bundle of dark green cloth. "He will be out there for hours."

Marguerite set down the gittern and took the gown from Eleanor. 'Twas a lovely creation of velvet, with contrasting panels of gold and white silk. "Did this belong to your mother?" she asked the child.

"Nay. To Bartie's wife."

"His...wife?"

"Aye," Eleanor said. She stuck out her lower lip and looked away. "She died in spring."

So *that* was the reason for Bartholomew's hostility. His beloved wife had died, and here Marguerite was, an interloper in what must have been Lady Norwyck's tower room. 'Twas no wonder he was not disposed to be friendly toward her, and Marguerite did not think 'twould be prudent to wear the late Lady Norwyck's clothes.

"Mayhap your brother would be disturbed by seeing me in his poor wife's gown."

"Why?"

"Well, it might remind him of her."

Eleanor seemed to consider this for a moment, then shook her head. "Nay," the girl said. "He never saw her in it."

Marguerite's expression must have been a startled one, causing Eleanor to explain. "This gown was made while Bartie was away, fighting the Scottish wars," she said. "When he came home, Felicia was with child, so she never wore it."

"A-and she died…in childbirth?"

"Aye," Eleanor said. "And the bairn with her."

"How terrible," Marguerite said, aghast at Eleanor's revelation. "Your brother must have been devastated."

"Aye," Eleanor remarked. "And he said that if he ever got his hands on the Armstrong bastard who fathered the bairn, he'd kill him."

Marguerite and Eleanor descended the stairs and saw that the other children were already at table, breaking their fast. "My lady," John said as he looked up. Smiling, he came to the foot of the stairs, took her hand like a true gentleman and escorted her to the table. "I'm glad you decided to join us."

"Thank you, John," Marguerite replied, relieved by a moment of normalcy in this strange place.

Henry was tearing into his meal, completely oblivious to her presence. Kathryn was there, too, but she stopped eating and placed her hands in her lap. Her displeasure with Marguerite's presence could not have been made clearer. No one named Sir Walter was present.

"Good morning to you all," Marguerite said brightly.

"Sit here, my lady," John said. "Next to my place."

"Thank you, John," she said as she took a seat. From the corner of her eyes, she observed Kathryn rolling her eyes with disdain.

"I'm off to the training field," Henry said as he wiped his mouth and stood.

"But Bartholomew forbade you to—"

"Stuff it, pest," Henry said as he circled the table. "I do as I please."

Kathryn bit her lip to keep from responding, but Marguerite could see that Henry's defiance, as well as the rude name he'd called her, did not sit well with his younger sister.

"There's bread and fish," Eleanor said, ignoring her brother and handing Marguerite a platter laden with food.

"And cider," John added, filling a mug for her.

"Thank you both," Marguerite said as she applied herself to the food before her. Sitting here among the Holton children felt right. This was as it should be, she thought, with the children around her....

A clear, but fleeting memory filtered through her mind, and she saw three bright blond heads bent over their bowls, children eating hungrily, happily.

The memory disappeared before it really took hold in her mind, and Marguerite could not recapture it, though she concentrated hard enough to make herself light-headed. Frowning, she bit her lip and refrained from groaning in frustration.

"My lady?" Eleanor asked as she placed one hand on Marguerite's arm.

"Oh, 'tis naught," she replied, giving the child a

quavering smile. "My head…'tis just a bit sore is all."

"Mayhap you should return to your bed," Eleanor said, her voice full of concern.

"I'll be fine," Marguerite said, "though a walk outside might help." She thought the fresh air might serve to clear her head, and possibly bring back the memories that were so elusive.

"Shall we go and see Bartie?" Eleanor asked, following Marguerite's lead in pushing away from the table.

"I think not," she replied. She doubted that Bartholomew would appreciate her arrival upon the practice field. He barely tolerated her presence in the tower. "Mayhap to the beach? Where your brother found me?"

Kathryn slapped one hand upon the table. "Bartholomew will be angry if you go outside the walls."

"Just to the beach?"

"You know what he said, Eleanor," Kathryn said angrily. She addressed her sister, as if it had not been Marguerite who had spoken. "No one is to leave Norwyck's walls. Not with the Armstrong threatening us at every—"

"Well, our men routed the Armstrongs when they last attacked, did they not?" John asked.

"Yes, but—"

"'Tis no matter, Kathryn," Marguerite said, unwilling to ruffle anyone's feathers. "I'll walk in the garden if that's permissible."

Kathryn shrugged. "It should be all right," she said grudgingly.

"We'll come with you," John said, arising from the table.

"Nay, John," Marguerite said. She needed to be alone to try to sort out her thoughts. She touched Eleanor's head gently, and addressed them both. "I'd like to go by myself this time."

Both children looked disappointed, but they accepted Marguerite's declination graciously.

"Shall I find you a shawl?" Eleanor asked, regaining her usual enthusiasm.

Marguerite smiled. "That would be lovely."

Bartholomew handed his helm and sword to the young page, while his squire unfastened the heavy breastplate and pulled it off him. Then he bent at the waist and unbuckled his own cuisses and greaves while he gave Henry's argument his full attention.

"But, Bartholomew, 'tis well past time for me to begin my training," the lad said. "I'll never become a knight if you do not give your consent."

Henry's argument was a valid one, but Bart would rather keep his brothers at Norwyck, safe behind its stout walls. If he sent them out to foster, they'd be subject to all sorts of dangers. Here, at least, he could keep them protected. Safe.

Bart handed the last of his armor to his squire and turned to Henry. "I'll give it due consideration, Hal."

"Not good enough, Bart," Henry said, digging in his heels. "I am ready. You know I am."

Bart put his arm across his brother's shoulders and started walking. "You are that anxious to leave us?"

"'Tis not that," Henry said. "But how will I ever become a man, make something of myself as you and Will did? If you do not send me out to foster—"

"Hal, I did not deny your request," Bart said. "I merely said—"

"That you'd consider it. Aye, I know," Henry said. "Please, Bart. I want to become a knight, like you. Like William. I want to come back and fight the damnable Armstrongs. Mayhap one day I'll be the one to bring Lachann Armstrong's head to Norwyck."

"Mayhap," Bart said quietly. After all that had occurred, he'd hoped his younger brothers would be content to remain at Norwyck. Clearly, that was not the case. At least not with Henry. John gave no sign of wanting to leave, but 'twas possible the lad just kept his own counsel. He tended to be less outspoken than his twin.

Bart let his arm drop, and continued walking toward the hall. The chilly air cooled his overheated body, right through the light tunic and hose that he wore. He was looking forward to a bath and a shave, and did not want to think about his brothers leaving.

As they neared the keep, Bart caught sight of a woman walking toward the postern gate, a small, rusted entryway from the beach that was so rarely used, he'd forgotten it. 'Twas Marguerite.

"Go on ahead," he said to Henry. "I'll return later."

Angry with his lack of a decisive answer, Henry did not protest, but stalked away as Bartholomew headed toward Marguerite.

Her skirts were green, and she was wrapped in a dark woolen shawl that concealed her form from her neck to her hips. Her head was uncovered, and her honey-brown tresses were attractively confined in soft, artful plaits that set off the delicate bones of her face.

Bart chastised himself for beginning to believe the woman's story, only to find her attempting to slip away from Norwyck. Where was she going, and who did she plan to meet? He sped up his pace in order to catch up with her before she could pass through the gate.

"Where are you going?" he asked roughly, grabbing hold of her arm.

She winced in pain as he pulled her around to face him, but Bart refused to take note of her discomfort. Chivalry be damned. He had no intention of letting her play him for a fool.

"T-to the garden," she replied, pulling away from him.

Her hesitation betrayed her. True enough, Norwyck's expansive garden lay adjacent to the wall, but Bartholomew was certain she would not have stammered had she spoken the truth.

He made a rude noise. "I don't know why I bothered to ask."

"I—"

"Get back to the keep, madam," he said. "And do not venture—"

"Nay!" she cried, standing firm as she crossed her arms over her chest. "I have no intention of returning to the keep until I've had my walk."

"'Tis not for you to defy—"

"Nor should you try to hold me prisoner!" she said, her eyes flashing angrily. Her chin trembled and she swallowed once, drawing his eyes to the muscles working in her delicate neck. The pulse at the base of her throat throbbed rapidly. "I have done naught to you or yours, my lord, and I wish you would stop your...your vile insinuations!"

Without hesitation, she flipped the end of her shawl over her shoulder, turned and strode away.

Bart dropped his hands to his sides and stood

speechless for a moment, watching as she stepped onto the garden path. Her back was straight, and she held her head high, though he could see that her poise was hard-won. She was not nearly as confident as she would have him believe, and her boldness intrigued him.

He went after her.

Quickly catching up, he took hold of her arm again and whirled her around. Her chest rose and fell with each rapid breath, and her eyes were dark with anger. Her cheeks were now flushed with color, and her mouth parted in surprise. Without thinking, Bartholomew lowered his head and pressed his lips to hers.

Marguerite was shocked by the heat of his mouth and the sound of need that emerged from deep within him. She was suddenly awash with her own needs, her own cravings. She was drowning again.

The kiss was no light brushing of lips, but a meeting of flesh that quickly intensified as her body melted into his. His heat enveloped her, his scent tantalized her. His mouth was warm, but softer than she ever would have imagined, knowing how hard and unyielding he was.

An exquisite ache formed in Marguerite's lower body, and it seemed the only way to soothe it was to press even closer to him. When she moved to do so, he suddenly broke away.

Still dazed, Marguerite did not resist when Bartholomew took hold of her hand and pulled her alongside him, farther into the garden.

'Twas late enough in the season that the trees were mostly bare of their leaves. All of the flowers had ceased to bloom, leaving withered stalks and tangled, brown underbrush along the path. The garden was colorless and bleak, but Marguerite noticed naught but the pounding of her heart and the heat of Bartholomew's hard, callused hand around her own.

When they were deep in the garden, Bart stopped next to a massive oak tree at the edge of the path. The only color in his face was the slight flush in the hollows of his cheeks. He looked altogether too formidable, and when he let go of her hand, Marguerite took a step backward, causing a collision between her backside and the tree.

He followed.

Without speaking, he pressed his hands against the trunk on either side of Marguerite's head. Fire was in his eyes, and determination in the set of his head. He studied her face, gazing at her cheeks, her eyes, her nose, and then at her mouth.

Marguerite trembled under his scrutiny, unafraid of him, but distinctly alarmed by her own attraction to him.

Without warning, he took her mouth again.

With both fists, she grabbed the damp linen at his chest and pulled him to her, taking possession of his lips, his teeth, his tongue. Shivering, she felt his hands drop to her shoulders, then down her back and lower, dragging her body into closer contact with his.

Marguerite let go of his tunic and slid her hands up the hard muscles of his chest, even as he overwhelmed her senses with his mouth, his touch, his very size. He tasted male, if that was possible, and so very potent he made her dizzy.

Every nerve in her body hummed. Her blood boiled and her bones seemed to melt under his sensual onslaught. Her lack of memory made no difference now, when the present was all that mattered.

He jerked abruptly away from her. "I must be mad," he said. He encircled her wrists with his hands, imprisoning them against his chest even as he stepped back.

Marguerite swallowed and gazed blankly at his chest as she worked to compose herself. He was not the only one suffering a kind of madness. She had allowed herself to succumb to her attraction for Bartholomew, in spite of her anger, in spite of her uncertainty of who and what she was.

She let out a shuddering breath and looked up.

His dark eyes still smoldered with heat, and his jaw was clenched tight. His breathing was not as steady as usual.

Her own certainly was not. Nor did her heart maintain its normal rhythm. Every inch of her skin felt as if it were on fire, and the tips of her breasts tingled uncomfortably. She swayed toward him, unwilling to end their ardent encounter.

After but a moment's hesitation, Bartholomew swept her up in his arms and carried her farther into the garden. He did not stop until they'd reached a small, wooden hut, hidden behind a thick row of evergreens. He shoved the door open with one foot and carried her inside.

There were no windows, so the only light inside emanated from the open door. Marguerite eased her arms from around Bartholomew's neck and slid down the length of his body to the floor. He cupped her face and kissed her once, quickly but deeply, then turned away, leaving her shaken and with a growing sense of uncertainty.

Marguerite was hardly aware of his actions as he lit a lamp and closed the door. Being alone with Bartholomew in this isolated shed at the far end of the garden was as daunting as it was exciting. And Marguerite knew she could not stay.

Bartholomew did not trust her, nor did he believe her claim of memory loss. She would never allow such intimacy while he held such a low opinion of her.

She clasped her hands before her and cleared her throat. "M-my lord," she began. "I…" She bit her lip and watched him as he came back to her.

"Do not think, Marguerite," he said, nuzzling her ear. He moved his lips to her throat. "Just feel…."

She swallowed, and felt all too much. Her body was overcome with the sensations he was able to elicit with barely a touch, and she felt herself falling all over again.

"My lord," she breathed. "I cannot… This is unseemly…."

"I want you." He pulled the shawl away from her shoulders and let it drop.

"I…I—"

His hands slipped down to cup her breasts, and Marguerite felt the tips hardening in response. The only thing that could possibly feel more glorious would be his hands on her naked flesh.

"You want me, too."

She swallowed hard. "Wh-what if I have a husband, my lord?" she asked tremulously. "Or a betrothed?"

The seductive touches at her throat and breasts stopped abruptly, and Bartholomew drew himself up to his full height, sliding his hands up to her shoulders. "Have you?"

Marguerite blushed. She shook her head. "I do not know," she whispered. "I don't believe anyone has ever t-touched me this way, but I cannot be sure."

"It changes naught," he said roughly. "How can you cuckold a husband or lover if you cannot remember him?"

"I do not know, my lord," Marguerite retorted as she worked to compose herself, "b-but I would not betray a husband if indeed he exists."

"But you…" Bartholomew turned away, dragging his fingers through his hair in frustration. She heard him mutter something under his breath, but could not make out the words. He walked toward the door, then stood facing it as he plowed his fingers through his hair.

"I am sorry, my lord, if—"

"I want you in my bed," he said, turning to her again. His hair was more disheveled now, and his eyes were dark, dangerous to her peace of mind. "I want you naked, willing. Come to me when you've decided what you want."

Chapter Five

"Bartie!" Eleanor cried when she met Bartholomew on the garden path.

"What is it, Eleanor?" he growled. His young sister had managed to take him off guard, and that was highly unusual.

"Are you angry?"

"Nay," he said, more harshly than he intended.

"But you look—"

"What is it?"

"I came to find Lady Marguerite in the garden," Eleanor replied, abandoning her line of questioning. "I thought you were on the practice field."

"Lady Marguerite told you she was coming here?" he asked, focusing on Eleanor's first statement. "To the garden?"

"Aye, for a walk," she replied. "She said she hoped 'twould help to clear her head."

As would a walk outside the walls, he thought. Just because she'd told Eleanor that she was going to the garden meant naught. 'Twas just as likely she'd lied to Ellie about her destination.

"Did you see her?" Eleanor asked.

"Hmm?"

"Bartie," Eleanor said with exasperation. "Are you listening at all? I asked if Lady Marguerite is in the garden."

"Aye," he replied absently. "But I think it unlikely her head has cleared."

He left Eleanor in the path and returned to the keep.

It took a long time for Marguerite to regain her balance after Bartholomew left her. She picked up her shawl from the floor and left the shed, closing the door tightly behind her. She stood quietly for a moment, with her hands on the rough wooden door.

"Come to me when you've decided what you want," he'd said, as if there was no question that she'd want to become his mistress.

A tremulous sigh escaped her. She could not deny the attraction that pulled so strongly between them. She craved the sensual pleasures of Bartholomew's promise, but knew she could not engage in such intimacies without involving her heart.

And she knew Bartholomew Holton would never do the same. He guarded his heart like the fiercest sentry at the castle gates.

She would be no more to him than his leman, a woman who gave her favors to the lord in exchange for her keep, and any other gifts he might bestow. 'Twas an arrangement that would crush her spirit.

The sound of a child's song interrupted Marguerite's deliberations, and she turned to see Eleanor, skipping and singing as she made her way up the path. Marguerite stepped away from the shed and greeted her.

"Do you feel better now?" Eleanor asked.

Marguerite smiled. "Aye, I do. Especially now that you're here to show me all the best places in the garden."

"I know a much better place," Eleanor said, her eyes sparkling with excitement. She took Marguerite's hand and pulled her in the opposite direction from which she'd come. "Shall we go and watch the men who are building our wall?"

"Nay," Marguerite said. "First you must tell me about the jewelry you left in the shoes in the trunk."

"Jewelry?"

Marguerite looked askance. "Aye. You knew very well that I would find those necklaces and rings among the clothes in the trunk."

"I thought you would like them," Eleanor said, clearly aware that further denials would achieve naught.

"That is not the question," Marguerite replied as she walked along beside Eleanor. "Whose jewelry is it, and where does it belong?"

"They are the Norwyck jewels," she said. "Bartie keeps them in a casket in his chamber."

"Then you must take every bit of it back to your brother's room when we return to the keep."

"Very well," Eleanor said petulantly, but she quickly brightened. "But shall we go and see the wall now?"

Marguerite followed along in good humor. She had seen very little of Norwyck through the tower windows and wished to see more. "What wall?"

"Around the village," Eleanor said as she hiked up her skirts and pulled herself up onto a low branch of a tree. "Bartholomew says that is the only way to protect the village from the Armstrongs."

"Ah, and 'tis a good idea, too."

"He just hasn't figured a way to keep the Armstrongs from stealing the sheep and cattle from the hills," Eleanor said as she climbed higher.

"Aye, but keeping the village safe is of greater importance," Marguerite remarked as she watched Eleanor swing her legs from the limbs overhead, wondering at the same time where the girl's nurse was.

"Still, our wealth comes from the sheep."

"You're quite informed for one so young," Marguerite said. In truth, the child was an amazing dichotomy of youthful mischief and a mature understanding that seemed beyond her years.

"Aye," Eleanor replied breezily as she reached up and climbed to a higher branch. "Someday I will grow up and be the lady of a grand demesne. Nurse Ada says I must learn all that I can here at Norwyck before I marry a great lord."

Marguerite stifled a smile. "Why don't you come down here and tell me who you have in mind?"

"No one." Eleanor sighed. "But Bartie will find a suitable husband for me." She climbed down and jumped to the ground, then took Marguerite's hand and continued up the path. "Kathryn will wed first, but Bartie will find a much better husband for me after he learns how with Kathryn."

Marguerite laughed and asked Eleanor to tell her about Norwyck's wall.

"Bartie says that every cottage must be within the wall. We'll even have two wells inside, one in the castle and one in the center of the village!"

That was a definite advantage. Norwyck could withstand a siege as long as they had a water source. Food would be another problem altogether, but if the villagers stored their grain and kept chickens and pigs in their yards, 'twould not be quite so bad.

Marguerite had no idea how she knew all that, but did not question it when they reached the site where masons were erecting a gatehouse, using large stones gathered from the hills and fields. She was amazed by the extent of Bartholomew's project, but knew it made perfect sense to defend Norwyck this way.

It seemed to Marguerite that he was a prudent and vigilant overlord, actively working toward the safety and well-being of all who lived within his realm.

There was a great deal of activity here. Dust flew and tools clanged as voices carried across the site. Men pulled carts laden with the stones that would make up the wall, and tipped them out on the ground near the masons. Others stood on ladders, laying rock and patching small holes with mortar.

Eleanor took great delight in showing Marguerite around, dashing here and there, speaking to some of the men at work. Marguerite had to direct the child away from potential hazards several times, but Eleanor continued to scamper everywhere, running on both sides of the wall. She tipped over one bucket of water, and stuck her foot in a mass of wet mortar.

"Eleanor!" Marguerite cried. Though she had no real authority over the child, she knew she had to get the girl away from the work site before she caused a serious disaster.

A burly man in a coarse brown tunic caught Eleanor's arms before she could fall into the mess.

"I am duly impressed with the wall, Eleanor," Marguerite said, looking up gratefully at the giant who'd rescued the child. She grasped her hand and pulled her away. "But we should take ourselves back to the keep."

"Aye," said the burly man, wiping Eleanor's shoe, "your brother wouldn't want ye here, m'fine young lady. Besides, we've got some problems."

But an exuberant Eleanor slipped away again.

"M'lady." The man turned to Marguerite. "Lord Norwyck has been sent for, and he'll be on his way in a moment. 'Twould be better if he did not find his sister here."

Nor did Marguerite want him to find *her* here, either. She gave a quick nod to the fellow and turned to go after Eleanor. She would insist that they return to the keep *before* Bartholomew arrived.

But Eleanor delighted in her game, running away from Marguerite and attempting to hide behind a precariously stacked pile of rocks. Marguerite worried that the child might upset the pile and injure herself. 'Twas obvious Eleanor was not going to come away easily, so Marguerite had to think of some way to entice her.

"I'll wager I can beat you back to the keep," she called. "I'll even give you a head start."

Eleanor laughed aloud and came away from the rock pile, allowing Marguerite to breathe again. "Nay! I'll make it there first!" the girl cried, then ran away through the village lanes toward Norwyck Keep, while Marguerite watched her.

"I'll give ye due credit, m'lady," the big man said behind her. "Ye handled her better than most."

Marguerite turned to face the man, and saw that Bartholomew had arrived and stood beside him. He still wore the sweat-stained tunic and hose she'd last seen him in, and he remained silent, quietly observing.

Marguerite did not know how long he'd been standing there, but he said naught.

She gave a slight bow, hoping he could not hear the wild beating of her heart, then turned and walked away.

Bart was going to have to find a younger nurse for his sisters. One who was more capable of governing them than poor old Ada could do. The family's old nurse had declined in the past year, and Bartholomew would not have his sisters making the poor woman's life miserable.

As he stood watching Marguerite's fading form, his mouth quirked into the semblance of a smile. She had handled Ellie like a master—better than even *he* could do, and he'd been the only one who'd had any control over the girl since William's death.

"M'lord?" Big Symon Michaelson brought his attention back to the matter at hand.

"What seems to be the trouble?"

"Er...the bailiff and the reeve are about to come to blows, m'lord."

This was not the first time the two men had clashed during the building of the wall. Norwyck's Bailiff Darcet was a strict little man whose opinions and judgments often seemed overly harsh to the villagers, and Bart himself had had occasion to question his competence. On the other hand, the reeve was intimately familiar with the situations of every family in the village, and he exempted the village men or women from work accordingly.

Until now Bartholomew had kept the peace by keeping the two men separate. But the wall-building was an important function, one he could not keep ei-

ther from attending. He just wished he could manip-
ulate them as well as Marguerite had managed
Eleanor.

He followed Big Symon to the gatehouse and spent
an hour solving the dispute to everyone's satisfaction,
when all he wanted was to go back to the keep, get
cleaned up and consider the best way to seduce Marguerite into his bed. He wanted her with an intensity
that was entirely foreign to him. Even without knowing who she was, or what lies she'd told him, he felt
a desire that was unparalleled.

That did not mean he would trust her. He would
provide shelter and board at Norwyck, but 'twas not
necessary for him to believe every tale she told. She
was beautiful, and enticing, and that was enough
for him.

Chapter Six

All day long, Marguerite experienced fragments of visions that made no sense, and left her feeling unsettled and uneasy. Try as she might, she could not remember who the blond children were, nor could she place the manor house with all the flowers surrounding it. She had no doubt that these images meant something, but she could not figure out what.

So preoccupied was Marguerite that 'twas after the evening meal before she remembered the jewels in the trunk in the tower room. But Eleanor had been confined to her chamber for the time being, as a penalty for evading Nurse Ada and causing so much disruption at the site of the wall construction. Marguerite would have to wait until the child was freed from her punishment before she could get the jewels back to Bartholomew's chamber.

Supper was a quiet affair, and Bartholomew did not join them, since he was out on patrol with a company of knights. Only John made any attempt at conversation, while Henry attacked his meal silently. Kathryn excused herself as soon as she was finished eating, and

Marguerite followed soon afterward, feeling troubled and lonely.

She went up to the tower and discovered that a fire was already burning cozily in the grate. She would have sat down and gazed out at the sea while she tried to sort out her thoughts, but night had fallen and 'twas dark outside the tower windows. She lit a lamp and stood alone in the center of the room, feeling chilled in spite of the fire.

She finally knelt by the trunk where she had hidden the jewels, taking each piece out to admire it in the flickering light. 'Twas awkward having them in her chamber, but there was naught she could do about it now. She would see that they were all returned to Bartholomew's chamber as soon as possible.

Marguerite put the precious pieces away, then prepared for bed, kneeling first to pray for the return of her memory. Then she prayed for Bartholomew, that God would return him safely to the keep after his patrol, and finally added his siblings and all of Norwyck to her intercessions.

She undressed down to her shift and washed, and was just about to blow out the lamp and climb into bed when her chamber door opened and Bartholomew stepped inside.

As always, Bart was struck by her beauty. Unclothed as she was now, or fully garbed, she enticed him as no other had ever done.

"M-my lord?" she asked tremulously.

He stepped into the room, unsure why he'd climbed up here now, still smelling of horse and sweat, when he'd told *her* to come to *him* when she was ready.

"Is there…"

"My sisters need looking after," he said, clasping

his hands behind his back. The idea had come to him just now, when he realized he needed some reason, some excuse to have barged in on her this way. "I thought perhaps you..."

"Perhaps I...?"

"Would take them on," he said, taking one step toward her. "Only until I find a proper nurse for them."

"But I don't belong here, my lord," she said. Her voice was quiet, naively seductive. She reached for her shawl and covered her gloriously bare shoulders.

Bart swallowed and moved closer. His fingers burned to touch her; his mouth longed to taste her. 'Twas a kind of madness he could neither understand nor control.

"As soon as I remember where I belong, I must leave Norwyck."

"Have any memories returned?"

She shook her head. "Nay, not really. A few faces, a manor house...that's all."

"Then it may be some time before you remember who you are...where you belong." He, too, could play this game.

Her eyes glittered with moisture, and Bart wondered if she'd produced those tears for his benefit, to play upon his sympathies.

She could not possibly know that he had none.

"I...I suppose I could look after Eleanor," Marguerite replied. She slipped away from him and moved to the fireplace, unaware that the light from behind outlined her legs and hips in detail. Bart's mouth went dry. "But Kathryn will not take kindly to my supervision."

He cleared his throat. "I saw how you handled

Eleanor today,'' he said. ''I have no doubt that you can manage something with Kate.''

''Your confidence is humbling, my lord,'' she said.

And her apparent naiveté was all too beguiling. Was that part of it? Had she been sent by Lachann Armstrong for some nefarious purpose, mayhap to seduce him, as Felicia had been seduced by his son?

Bart almost laughed at the thought. If anyone at Norwyck were to be seduced, 'twould be Marguerite. And soon.

''Will you do it?'' he asked. ''Watch over my sisters?''

She bit her lip. ''Aye, my lord,'' she finally said. ''I'll try.''

''All is quiet, my lord?'' Sir Walter asked, meeting Bartholomew at the foot of the stairs in the great hall.

''Aye,'' Bart replied. ''No raiders in the hills tonight.''

''It's turned cold, though.''

Bart nodded. His feet and hands had been nearly numb when he'd returned to Norwyck's courtyard after his patrol. But his visit in Lady Marguerite's chamber had warmed him significantly.

''My lord…young Henry asked me to speak to you with regard to his fostering.''

Bart rubbed the back of his neck. He hadn't expected his brother to ask Sir Walter to intercede for him.

''The lad's fondest desire is to become a knight,'' Sir Walter said. ''There must be an estate where he can go and squire, my lord. I would not deny him this, if I were you.''

''Nay,'' Bart said with a sigh. ''I know he should

go, as should John. 'Tis just that the past months have been difficult…for all of us…."

"Aye," Walter said. "You could not bear to part with them."

Bartholomew would not deny it. He had needed the presence of his young brothers to help soften his grief when William had been killed. But 'twas past time to let them go.

"'Tis true," Bart said as he poured warm, mulled wine into a thick earthenware mug. He offered it to Walter, then poured his own and sat down in one of the big, comfortable chairs before the fire. Everything continued on at Norwyck, different, yet just as it had before, with Will gone and Felicia's betrayal. There were quiet nights in the hall, teasing banter with his siblings.

And now there was Marguerite.

"I have yet to meet the lady you brought back from the shipwreck," Sir Walter said.

"I've asked her to look after Eleanor and Kate until she regains her memory."

Walter frowned as if he had not heard Bartholomew correctly. "She still does not remember?"

"Nay. And she still wants me to believe she cannot remember who she is, or where she's from."

Sir Walter scratched his head. "I've seen that once, my lord."

"What? A bump on the head—"

"Nay, the loss of memory," the knight replied. "When I was a lad, no older than your brothers, a man in our village fell from a tree while he was picking apples. He was knocked unconscious, and when he came to his senses, he had no knowledge of who he was."

Bart frowned. "Did he ever remember?"

"Aye, I think so. He *must* have," Walter said, frowning at Bartholomew. "Mustn't he?"

Bart had no idea. But the fact that Walter had witnessed the same kind of memory loss suffered by Marguerite lent credence to her story. Still...just because she might have told the truth about her memory did not mean they had to believe anything else she had to say. She was a woman, and therefore capable of any manner of deceit.

"My lord..." Sir Walter seemed hesitant. "You know that I had my doubts about Lady Felicia for many months after you and Lord William left with King Edward for Scotland."

"'Tis pointless to belabor it now, Walter."

"I just want you to know that I did what I could to control the lass," he said. "'Twas my opinion, back when your father made the betrothal agreement with the lady's father, that she was not to be trusted. She had too many opportunities to ally herself with the Scots while she was in France."

Bartholomew had considered this possibility over and over after Felicia's death in childbirth. He wondered if she'd begun her liaison with Dùghlas Armstrong while she was in France, well before their marriage.

'Twas altogether possible, since the Armstrongs had relations in France, and Felicia had spent several years there. But since Bart was not on speaking terms with the Armstrongs, he did not know if Dùghlas had spent any time in France while Felicia was there.

The two men let the matter drop as they sipped their wine. They had discussed William's murder and Felicia's betrayal until they both were sick to death of it. Bart did not need to hear Walter's suspicions again to know that Felicia had never been worthy of his trust.

He vowed never to make the same mistake again.

She was drowning.

She struggled to keep her head above the water, but the waves overcame her and dunked her again and again.

"Marie! Tenez!" cried a man nearby. She could hardly make out his features, for he was soaked, and repeatedly swamped by the violent waves of the sea. But he was young and handsome, and his hair was light.

Several times she tried to reach out to him, but something always prevented it. Then, all at once, she had hold of his hand and he was pulling her toward him.

"Ici! Prenez ma main!"

She grabbed him, but her hand slipped out of his—

"My lady!"

A heavy weight pressed the breath from her chest and she struggled for air. The mast had come crashing down and the sea was swallowing her! She thrashed against the water that was pulling her down, and tried to call out to the man whose hand she'd just lost. She thought her heart would burst with terror. She could not catch her breath, and she wept with the effort it took.

"Marguerite!"

She opened her eyes. 'Twas Eleanor upon her chest. Marguerite was not drowning, nor was there a light-haired man calling to her...in French. What was it he'd said?

"You were having a bad dream," Eleanor said, as Marguerite tried to recapture the visions of the ship going down. Somehow, the dream should help her to remember. It *must!*

Another voice intruded. "My sister was so thrilled to have you looking after her, she could not wait to come up and see you," Bartholomew said dryly. He stood leaning on the doorjamb, his arms crossed over his chest.

Marguerite had some difficulty catching her breath and gathering her thoughts. First the disturbing dream, and now Bartholomew...standing so tall and masculine, watching her with dark, hooded eyes. She knew he had barely restrained the urge to take her in his arms the night before, and Marguerite had hardly been able to think of anything but the way his mouth had felt upon hers, his hands caressing her body.

The man in her dream had never had such a tumultuous effect on her. Marguerite did not know how she knew it, but she could not have been more certain.

"What shall we do today?" Eleanor asked as she slid off the bed. Marguerite pulled the blanket up to her neck. "Will you teach me to play the gittern?"

"I—"

"Or take me to the garden and watch me climb—"

"Eleanor," Bartholomew said with a warning in his tone. "You can easily be confined to your quarters again."

"Nay, Bartie!" Eleanor cried, rushing over to her brother to implore him to have mercy.

Marguerite could not resist a small smile. "If you two will give me but a moment, I will dress and join you in the hall. Then we can decide what to do to-day.''

Anxious to do whatever was necessary to speed the process, Eleanor shoved past Bartholomew and scampered down the stone steps. He remained as he was for a moment, leaving his eyes locked on Marguerite's. The promise in his gaze made her tremble. And when he turned and left the chamber, she flopped back on the bed and attempted to calm her wildly beating heart.

When she realized 'twas no use, she climbed out of bed, worried that she would feel edgy all day.

''What are you doing with that?'' Henry asked when he came into the great hall, dressed in old clothes and smelling as if he'd brought the entire stable with him.

''She is playing Mama's gittern,'' Eleanor said, wrinkling her nose.

Marguerite would have preferred to take Eleanor and her music to the solar rather than making a spectacle of herself here, but she'd hoped to garner Kathryn's interest. So far, the elder sister had gone to great pains to avoid Marguerite throughout the day. But from the time she had started playing the beautiful gittern, Kathryn had come through the hall twice.

Since early that morning, Marguerite had seen Bartholomew only at a distance, and the space between them gave her some relief from the tension she felt whenever he was near. The farther he stayed away from her, the less likely she was to succumb to his allure.

''You can play my mother's gittern?''

'''Twould seem so, Henry,'' Marguerite replied.

"Though I cannot tell you how I remember the music."

"'Tis your fingers that remember," Eleanor said ingenuously.

Marguerite heard a snicker behind her, but ignored it. She knew 'twas Kate's reaction to her sister's innocent remark.

"Play a tune, then," Henry said.

Marguerite took the neck of the gittern in her left hand and put her fingers into position. Closing her eyes and making her mind go blank, she used the plectrum to pick out a tune. Then she began to hum.

John added his voice to hers, putting in a word or phrase as the song continued. When it was finished, Eleanor clapped her hands with delight. "Mama used to play that song for us!"

"'Tis a popular tune all over Britain and France," Bartholomew said as he stepped away from the staircase. He was freshly washed and shaved, and Marguerite did not think he'd ever looked quite so handsome as he did now.

"Aye, but 'twas a favorite of Mother's," John said.

"True enough," Bartholomew replied. "So, you remember how to play," he said to Marguerite.

"Aye." She nodded. The song had sent a sharp stab of bittersweet longing through her, and she had to struggle to find her voice. "I do."

"You...play very well," he said, the compliment sounding awkward on his tongue. "Play another." He sat in a chair opposite her and pulled Eleanor onto his lap.

Surprised by Bartholomew's kind words, Marguerite managed to continue playing, to the delight of the children, and many of the servants, who came into the hall to listen. Kathryn only walked through a few times, the scowl on her face never softening.

Yet there was a flicker of interest in her eyes that made Marguerite believe that the girl wished she could be part of the group, but had too much pride to join their frivolous activity. Besides which, 'twas Marguerite who was at the center of it all, and Kate had decided from the first day to dislike her.

Marguerite caught Bartholomew's eye and tipped her head slightly toward Kathryn. It took a moment for him to understand what she intended, but he finally caught on.

"Kate," he said. "Come and sit here with us."

"Nay, Bartholomew," she replied, walking away from the group. "I have work—"

"It can wait," he said. "Why don't you sit here by me, and show Lady Marguerite your own talents with the gittern?"

"I think not, Bartholomew," she said indignantly. And she left the hall.

Marguerite tried not to let Kathryn's rebuff worsen her mood. She played another tune, and another. For some reason, she'd had fewer "memories" today, as if her dream that morning had somehow shocked the visions right out of her.

In a way, she did not miss those snippets of memory. All they did was confuse and upset her. The images of those children and the feeling that something was horribly wrong disturbed her. What if they were her children? What if they were at home in the lovely flower-strewn manor, waiting for word of her, while she sat here in Norwyck's great hall, entertaining other children with her music?

Pain and uncertainty suddenly choked Marguerite,

and she felt a burning at the back of her throat. Her hands trembled and she was no longer able to play. Biting her lip to keep it from trembling, she stood up, set the gittern against the back of her chair and stepped away from the group.

"I'm…I—" She could not think what to say, but turned and fled from the hall. She did not think about where she was going, but blinked back tears as she moved, and eventually found herself in a quiet, dimly lit chapel at the opposite end of the keep.

There were several long benches against the walls, and Marguerite sat down on one of them. She leaned back against the cool stone wall and took a long, shuddering breath.

She did not know what had come over her. The sense of grief and loss had suddenly become overpowering, but Marguerite did not know why. For whom did she grieve?

'Twas a question she would not be able to answer until she regained her memory, and that did not seem likely to happen very soon. It had been days since Bartholomew had brought her to Norwyck. Outside of the improvement in her vision, there'd been no other change in her condition.

Why couldn't she remember?

'Twas frustrating. Memories were right on the verge of her consciousness, but she was unable to get any kind of a hold on them. They escaped her like sand filtering through her fingers, every time she tried too hard to remember.

She wiped away tears that she'd shed without even being aware of them, and was startled by the sound of clapping at the far end of the chapel.

"Excellent performance," Bartholomew said, continuing his mocking applause as he walked toward her. "Worthy of the greatest mummers in all of England."

Marguerite refused to dignify his insult with a reply. She stood and turned away so that he would not see the evidence of her tears. He would only make sport of her pain, and Marguerite knew 'twould hurt the worse, especially now that she knew how tender he could be with his sisters.

If only he had a bit of kindness to spare.

"What?" he said. "No retort?"

She swallowed and forced a calmness that she did not feel. Then she turned to face him.

"My lord," she said, clasping her hands together. "This is n-not working well. I cannot stay. If—if there is an abbey or nunnery nearby, or a—"

"You wish to leave Norwyck?"

Marguerite cast her eyes toward the floor. "I...I wish only to know who I am, from whence I came. I want to know if the children whose faces I see when I close my eyes are my own. I want to know if the light-haired man in my dreams is my husband."

"What light-haired man?" Bartholomew growled.

"I dream of him drowning," she said, her voice trembling and timorous. She turned quickly away so that he would be unable to see the emotion on her face, and composed her voice before speaking again. "We struggle to reach each other in the water, but just as we touch, our hands are wrenched apart. I know that he is desperate to get to—"

"You are no man's wife," Bartholomew interrupted abruptly.

Sniffling, she felt anger take over. She whirled to face him. "*Really?* And pray, by what method can you tell?"

He grasped her upper arms roughly. "This method." Scowling, he swooped down and captured her lips in a searing kiss. 'Twas a mating of mouths and teeth and tongue that stole Marguerite's very breath. Air surged out of her lungs, and fire replaced it.

She had no will or desire to resist him. Her hands found their way to his waist and she held him in place, her body trembling with a raw hunger that seemed so foreign, yet so alarmingly familiar with Bartholomew.

His body was solid and hard, and Marguerite's excitement grew as he closed the gap between them, making the evidence of his desire plain. At the same time, his tongue swept through her mouth, and she responded with an eagerness that shocked her.

His hands slid across her back. One moved to cup the back of her head, the other swept downward, past her waist to her hips, pressing her against him as he moved.

Marguerite gasped and broke the kiss. Stunned, she looked up into Bartholomew's eyes as he continued to press his hard length against her. His gaze was hot and knowing. "Have you need of any more proof that you are no man's wife?" he rasped.

Marguerite whimpered when she felt him move against her again. He pressed his lips to her jaw, trailing hot kisses down her neck to her throat.

"I want you," he said.

Marguerite shuddered again, worried and very frightened because *she* wanted *him,* too. But when his hands moved to span her waist, then traveled up to touch her breasts, she pulled away. She looked wildly about her and remembered they were standing in the chapel. In a church!

She could not find her voice to answer him, and 'twas a good thing, too. For she did not know what words would have come out of her mouth.

She was torn in two. Part of her longed to stay, to explore him in wonderfully wicked ways. The other part knew she could not, should not.

On wobbly legs, she stepped away from him.

When he would have reached for her again, she stopped him. "This is unwise, my lord," she said shakily, taking another step back.

"Whoever said wisdom was the most prized of virtues?"

Marguerite swallowed. She had no answer for that. She only knew she needed some time and distance in order to determine what to do.

Chapter Seven

Several days passed, with Marguerite coming no closer to discovering who she was. She and Eleanor passed the time with music and sewing. They took long walks in the garden and played games in the courtyard, always staying clear of the castle's workers.

There was no repetition of the incident with Bartholomew in the chapel, though Marguerite often saw him in the bailey, or on the practice field. He joined the family for meals in the hall whenever he could, and on those occasions, Marguerite felt his hot gaze upon her. He did not return to her chamber in the tower, though Marguerite spent many a restless night trying to forget the smoldering looks he sent her way.

Late one afternoon, as the sun shone brightly over the keep, Marguerite and Eleanor dressed in warm cloaks for a walk in the garden. They were headed in that direction when Eleanor asked for a change in plan.

"May we go and visit Big Symon?" Eleanor asked.

"Only if you promise to stay clear of the workers."

"Oh, yes!" she cried, taking Marguerite's hand. "I won't go near them. I just want to see the new wall and how much more is done!"

They followed the path and left the castle proper, then walked on until they reached the edge of the village. Men were laying stone and mixing mortar, just as they'd done the one other time Marguerite and Eleanor had visited the site. Marguerite kept Eleanor's hand in her own, steering her far from the wagons full of stones, and away from the piles of rock stacked upon the ground.

She did not want to deal with any near disasters today.

As they walked around, looking at the wall, men doffed their hats in respect and went on with their work. Big Symon was atop the wall, and he gave them a friendly wave.

"There ye are, m'little lady," said a gruff voice behind them.

"Master Alrick!" Eleanor cried, clearly delighted to see the old fellow. His lined face was framed by wispy gray hair, and his small eyes sparkled with intelligence.

"And what's this?" Alrick asked. "A ribbon in yer ear?"

Using sleight of hand, he seemed to pull a ribbon from Eleanor's ear. Eleanor shrieked with glee while the man's blue eyes twinkled gaily.

"Do another!"

"Well, I'm not so sure as I know another," he said. But as he spoke, he took a rope from his pocket, circled Eleanor's waist with it and tied it securely. He glanced up at Marguerite and winked at her, then looked back at Eleanor. "Try to pull it loose," he said.

The girl tugged, but naught happened.

"Aw, m'little princess," he said, taking hold of the

knot. "Ye should do better than that!" And the rope
fell away, as if it had not been tied.

Marguerite could not tell how he'd done it, but the
trick had delighted Eleanor, and 'twas obvious that
Master Alrick had often entertained the child with his
sleight of hand.

"More!"

"Alas, m'lady," Alrick said, removing his cap and
bowing deeply, "I must get back to work, or Master
Symon will surely have my hide."

"Oh, but—"

"We thank you for your time, Master Alrick," Marguerite said, taking Eleanor's hand. "And for showing
us your extraordinary talents."

Alrick bowed again. "'Twas my pleasure, m'lady."
Then he left them to join the men working on the wall.

"Have you seen enough?" Marguerite asked
Eleanor.

"Nay!" she cried. "Mightn't we walk to the other
side of the wall? See how 'twill look to the Armstrongs when they come raiding?"

"Eleanor—"

"Please, Lady Marguerite!" the child said, pulling
on her hand. "We will not go far beyond, just around
to the outside. And 'tis daylight. Naught will happen."

Marguerite had to agree with her. The castle and
village were on high ground, and the Armstrongs
would be hard-pressed to get away with an attack now,
in daylight, with so many Norwyck men around.

They walked to the end of the wall, then went
around to the north side of it, leaving the enclosure.
Hills sloped away from the village and castle, blending
into more hills beyond the dell at the bottom. Marguerite knew the North Sea lay to her right, at the

far end of the castle, though she could not see it from here.

'Twas a pretty setting, and when they walked a short distance down the hill and looked up at the castle, she was struck by its towering majesty. Norwyck was a magnificent stronghold.

"Look! 'Tis Bartie!" Eleanor cried.

Marguerite turned around and saw riders in the valley below. They were knights in dark hauberks, riding powerful warhorses, with their swords at their sides. One of the knights carried the Norwyck banner, bearing the shape of a blue lion on a white background.

Several men herded cattle behind the line of knights. Marguerite put one hand up to shade her eyes and saw that there were more men, much farther behind, herding sheep. She returned her gaze to the horsemen up ahead, who had turned to follow a winding path up the hill to the castle. Eleanor was right. Bartholomew was in the lead.

Marguerite tamped down her feelings of excitement when she saw him, and composed herself. She had striven to conceal his potent effect on her, and had no intention of letting him see it now.

"He is even more handsome than William ever was," Eleanor said wistfully. "I hope he finds me a husband just like—"

"Who is William?"

"Our eldest brother," Eleanor said. "We never speak of him…at least, not aloud. It makes everyone too sad."

"I'm sorry," Marguerite said. "What…happened to him?"

"The Armstrong killed him when Felicia lured him away from the castle."

"Felicia?" Marguerite asked, frowning. "Bartholomew's wife?"

"Aye," Eleanor replied. "Bartie was really angry with her. He said that Will would never have gone down to the valley unless Felicia had needed his help."

This was hardly an adequate explanation, but Marguerite could get no more from the child before Bartholomew and his men arrived at the wall. All of them appeared battle-weary, and many of the men were wounded. Bartholomew motioned his knights to ride ahead, then stopped and dismounted near Eleanor and Marguerite.

He was covered with grime, his hair slicked back with sweat. His hauberk accentuated the strong planes of his chest and shoulders, and the narrow span of his hips and waist. Weary lines settled across his face, but the light of victory shone brightly in his eyes.

"Bartie!" Eleanor cried as she wrapped her arms around his legs. "Did you go raiding the Armstrongs?"

"We only brought back what was ours. What are you doing so far from the castle?" he demanded, peeling her off.

"We came to see the wall," she replied, sensing a jovial mood beneath his stern mien. "But we went no farther."

"See that you don't," he replied, lifting the child into his arms. "I would not wish to lose you, even if you are an imp and a troublemaker."

"Put me down, Bartie," Eleanor protested, squirming. "You are sweaty and smelly."

Bartholomew laughed, warming Marguerite's heart

with the rich, deep sound. She realized she'd never
heard him laugh, and had barely even seen him smile.

And she was afraid. This different, lighthearted Bartholomew had a better chance of seducing her than the
stern, passionate one.

"Nay, wench," he said, tossing his petite sister up
onto his shoulders. Her legs straddled his brawny
neck, while she laughed with delight. "You must suffer the brute who risks life and limb to keep you safe!
Is that not so, Lady Marguerite?" he asked, spearing
her with his dark gaze.

"Eleanor does not appear to be suffering, my lord,"
she said, ignoring the double entendre.

"Ah, but does she appreciate the finer qualities of
her lord and protector?" he asked as he gathered the
reins of his mighty warhorse in one hand, keeping the
other upon Eleanor's wool-clad legs.

"Mayhap she does, my lord," Marguerite said, falling into step next to him, "but has not yet found an
appropriate way to express it."

"Yes I can!" Eleanor said, giggling. She leaned
over and put her fingers across her brother's eyes.
"You are a loggerhead, Bartie!"

'Twas so unexpected that Marguerite laughed aloud,
while Bartholomew sputtered with feigned indigna-
tion. This was a side of Bartholomew that was so utterly charming, Marguerite had to turn away or be
completely taken in by his appealing manner.

He was jolly and playful with his sister, and for a
moment Marguerite could see the boy he must have
been, before war and betrayal and tragedy had struck
Norwyck. She wondered about Eleanor's earlier
words. What exactly had Felicia done?

Marguerite could hardly credit that Bartholomew's

wife would betray him with another man. *And* cause his brother's death.

What kind of charlatan had the woman been?

What kind of fool?

If the child's stories were to be believed, then 'twas no wonder Bartholomew was distrustful, especially of women. Marguerite doubted she would learn any more from Eleanor, for the child knew only what she'd overheard. By the very nature of the betrayals, Marguerite was certain the adults had kept much from her.

Still, Eleanor was not one to let much get past her. Marguerite could imagine the child listening at keyholes or hiding behind furniture to discover all she could. Mayhap she could get a bit more from Eleanor if she asked the right questions.

A loud crack, then an earthshaking rumble and the sound of men's panicked voices cut through the air. Marguerite turned toward the wall in time to watch in horror as the last section of it came crashing down, rocks and mortar, dust and men.

Bartholomew acted quickly. He swung Eleanor down to the ground and tossed the reins to Marguerite. "Tether him," he said as he took off at a trot toward the fallen men.

Eleanor followed her brother, while Marguerite looked for a post or a tree to which she could tie the huge beast. When she'd secured the animal, she went after Eleanor.

They did not need another disaster.

Bart sent a man to fetch the healer, then knelt over Big Symon, whose body lay inert and unconscious upon the ground. His leg was quite obviously broken, but there were other injuries, too.

"M'lord, we should get him home!"

"Nay, do not move him," he replied. "Not until Alice Hoget looks at him."

"Aye, 'tis wise, m'lord," said another man.

A soft, feminine form was suddenly beside him, with her thick, woolen cloak in her hands. She covered Symon with it, smoothing it over his body and tucking the ends under him to keep him warm.

Bart looked up at her, but she kept her eyes upon the injured man. They showed naught but fear and concern for his recovery. Her hands were so small, so smooth. Yet they moved with care and efficiency.

"B-Bartie?" Eleanor said. Her face was pale and her eyes shimmered with tears. "Is he…dead?"

"Nay, Ellie," Bart replied, taking her into his arms. "But he's in bad shape. Alice will come and do what she can for him. Then we'll…we'll just have to pray for his recovery."

Bart felt shaken himself. The work on the wall had been going so well, with their main problem being that of supplies. Symon had had to send men farther and farther afield to collect the large rocks that made up the wall, and lately there'd been arguments between the reeve and the bailiff over the mixture used for the mortar.

Bart glanced at Marguerite and saw her brushing away her own tears furtively. She stood abruptly, sniffed and walked toward another of the fallen men, whose forehead was bleeding.

She crouched down and spoke quietly to the fellow, putting one hand on his arm, then spoke to an uninjured man standing nearby. He quickly brought Marguerite a wet cloth, and she mopped the blood from the deep cut on the injured man's forehead. The fellow blushed with all the attention being given him by the beautiful lady, but Marguerite's straightforward attitude prevented any real embarrassment.

Her hair, at first covered by the hood of her cloak, was now loose. Time seemed to stand still as Bart watched her slip one fine lock of that rich mass of honey-brown over her ear. He could think of naught but the taste of her skin below that ear, her scent when he aroused her with his kisses.

Stifling his own groan, Bart turned his attention to Symon's moan of pain. He thought it a good sign that the man was coming 'round, even though the leg was in bad shape. Alice would know what to do.

"Symon?" Bart asked.

"Aye," the big man growled. "What's happened?"

"The wall collapsed. You and several others fell," Bart replied.

Symon grimaced in pain when he tried to move. "M'lord, is there something sharp poking into m'leg?"

"Nay, man," Bartholomew replied. "'Tis broken. You broke it when you fell."

The color drained from his face, even from his lips, and Bart knew what was coming. "Ellie, go and stay with Lady Marguerite," he said as he gently shoved her away. He quickly turned Symon's head so the man could vomit without choking.

"Tsk, tsk, Symon Michaelson," said a female voice. "What have you gone and done to yer leg."

'Twas Alice Hoget, with her satchel of herbs and potions. Bartholomew could not have been happier to see any woman.

But with that thought, he glanced toward the place where Marguerite had been, and discovered that she and Ellie were no longer there. Frowning, he looked around and saw that she now stood next to the mountain of rubble that had once been Norwyck's wall.

She suddenly dropped down to her knees and frantically began to throw rocks from the pile. At the same time, she cried out, "Lord Norwyck! *Someone!* Come help!"

Leaving Symon in Alice's capable hands, he hurried to the place where Marguerite knelt.

"'Tis Alrick!" she cried when Bart got near. "He's under all this rubble!"

He saw the old man now, most of him crushed under a ton of rock and mortar, heard his moan. Calling for more assistance, Bart wasted no time in moving in beside Marguerite and hauling debris off the fallen man, while Eleanor stood crying beside them.

"Hold on, Alrick," he said. "We'll get you out...."

Others joined the rescue effort and soon the man was free, though his body lay battered and broken upon the shattered rocks. His breaths were shallow and rattling. Blood and bruises covered him, and he was unconscious.

Bart looked up to discover Marguerite watching him with watery eyes as she hugged Eleanor to her breast. Her chin trembled as she struggled for control. "Get Alice Hoget over here, Matheus," he said to the man next to him.

A few minutes later, Alice crouched down beside him.

"M'lord," she said. "Symon's wife is on her way. Would ye waylay her a bit? Ye know how fretful she is. She'll be more hindrance than help until the men can move him to his cottage. I'll do what I can here, but..."

Bart nodded. He glanced around, looking for Marguerite, and located her beside the wall, talking to yet another injured man. She had to be chilled, wearing only a thin gown and kirtle. It could not possibly keep her warm enough in the wintry air. What had she been thinking, giving her cloak away as she had?

Bart turned quickly. He would not allow himself to be overly concerned about her warmth or well-being. If she wanted to give away her cloak and every other stitch of clothing she wore, then she was welcome to do so.

A group of housewives scurried toward him, Symon's wife among them.

"Mistress Anne," he said, waylaying her.

"My Symon...is he h-hurt bad, m'lord?" The woman's face was blotchy, her eyes red from weeping, and she hadn't even seen the damage yet.

"Aye, he is," Bart replied. "Some of the men are going to carry him to your cottage," he added reassuringly. "Mayhap you should return home and see that all is ready when he arrives."

She did not seem capable of understanding what he'd said, but one of the other women took her arm and led her away.

The village wives cared for their injured men. There were buckets of clean water and cloths for cleaning the bloody scrapes, and the women had brought cloth for bandages, too. The worst injury besides those of Alrick and Symon was a broken arm, which Marguerite tied to the man's chest to keep him from moving it.

When Bart looked her way again, he saw that she was absently rubbing her hands up and down her arms in an attempt to keep warm.

Damnation!

Bart was half tempted to ignore her discomfort. Instead, he stalked over to his horse and yanked the pack down, drawing out a blanket. He carried it to Symon, pulling Marguerite's cloak off and replacing it with the blanket. Then he carried the cloak to the foolish woman.

Her back was to him as he approached, and he startled her when he slipped the cloak around her. She reached up and caught it at her shoulders, meeting his hands there. Neither of them breathed for a moment as a shock of awareness ran through them.

Marguerite leaned into him and Bart felt her entire body trembling against his. He went taut with excitement and arousal.

She remained motionless for only a moment before stepping away and turning to him. "This…" she gestured around her "…my lord, this is terrible. How…why did this part of the wall give way?"

He ran a hand through his hair. "I don't know," he replied. "But I'm going to find out."

"Poor Alrick. And Symon. Is there anything more we can do for them?" Marguerite asked. "I feel so helpless."

"No," Bart replied, though he did not think she'd been helpless at all. She had discovered Alrick under the rubble, then managed to comfort several of the injured men before their wives came to tend them.

Aside from Alrick, Bart was not at all sure he appreciated seeing her hands on those other men.

He shrugged off that notion and walked back to the disaster site, looking for his bailiff, Thom Darcet, and the reeve, Edwin Gayte. The two men would have to cooperate with Sir Walter to determine the cause of the collapse. For Bart intended to get this wall finished—without further mishap. 'Twas Norwyck's main hope of defense against Lachann Armstrong's frequent raids.

Bart's only other option was to step up his own offensive, which was something he was loath to do. He'd seen enough of bloody battles to last a lifetime.

Chapter Eight

Eleanor sat perched upon Bartholomew's mighty warhorse and rode back to the keep in a grand style. Marguerite walked beside Bartholomew, who led the horse by its reins. He'd said naught since hoisting his sister onto the saddle, but walked quietly, brooding over the collapse of his wall and the injuries of the men working there.

He truly cared about those men. He cared about the protection that the wall would give his people.

Marguerite stole quick glances at him. She could not keep her heart from going out to him. There had been too much tragedy here at Norwyck in the last months, and pain and worry were evident in the lines on his face.

Bartholomew Holton was not the cruel, unfeeling warlord she'd thought him when she'd first awakened at Norwyck. Rather, he was a bereaved man, a caring brother, a betrayed husband.

"My lord!" called Sir Walter, hurrying toward them across the open bailey. Marguerite had been introduced to the old knight, and had spoken to him briefly upon a few occasions since then. He bowed to her and to Eleanor, then said to Bartholomew, "What has happened? The men said—"

"What they told you is true," Bart replied, lifting Eleanor down. "The last portion of wall collapsed, injuring several of the workmen. The worst is Alrick Stickle. He was crushed beneath the wall when it fell."

The older man crossed himself and said something too quietly for Marguerite to hear. "Is there aught I can do?" he added.

"Aye. Mediate between the bailiff and reeve and see if you can determine what went wrong with the construction."

"Aye, my lord," Walter said. "I'll see to it right away."

"And see that Alrick's wife and Master Symon's family lack for naught," Bartholomew said. "Send provisions to their cottages and see that they are given whatever help is needed."

"I'll take care of it, my lord," Walter said. He patted Eleanor's bright red head and gave a short bow to Marguerite. Then he took the reins of Bartholomew's horse and walked across the bailey toward the stable.

"What made the wall collapse, my lord?" Marguerite asked.

Bartholomew shook his head. "Bad mortar, mayhap. Or possibly the way the rocks were stacked, large atop small.... 'Twould make it unstable."

"Master Darcet and Master Gayte are always quarreling about the mortar," Eleanor said, walking between Marguerite and Bartholomew, and holding the hand of each. Her eyes were wet and her nose still dripped from weeping.

Bartholomew raised one dark eyebrow, and Marguerite detected a subtle shrug of his shoulders. Even if the two men did not agree on the mixture, Marguerite could not imagine that either one would intentionally try to weaken the wall.

"Sir Walter will determine what went wrong," Bartholomew said.

"Tell us about the raid, Bartie!" Eleanor said, changing the subject entirely. She freed one of her hands and wiped her face. "Did you get all our livestock back?"

"Aye."

"Did you kill many Armstrongs?"

"Nay."

"Did you go a'wenching?"

Bartholomew stopped abruptly. He turned an icy gaze upon Eleanor. "What did you say?"

"Henry s-said that all knights go a'wenching after b-battle and that he's—"

"Enough! *Enough!*" Bartholomew said. "'Tis unseemly talk for a maid."

Marguerite felt her face heat as Eleanor tipped her head down and looked at her shoes. 'Twas the first time she'd ever seen the child cowed. Bartholomew took her hand again and continued toward the keep. The muscles in his jaw clenched once or twice as they walked. "Henry should not be talking to you of such… There are things that only…"

He made a face of utter frustration and looked at Marguerite, realizing his mistake instantly.

"Men often do things that ladies are expected to ignore, Eleanor," she said. "Though if *I* had a husband, and *he* went a'wenching, he would not be welcome in my…abode…for a very long time."

* * *

Bart watched Marguerite's retreating form, a small smile quirked the side of his mouth. Her fire heated his blood like no other. 'Twas true that some of the men had gone wenching after the raid. But Bart had refrained, only because he could not raise sufficient interest in any of the available women.

There was only one that he wanted.

"Is Lady Marguerite angry?" Eleanor asked.

"Nay, I don't believe so," he replied.

"Then why did she go off like that?" the child said. "She *seemed* angry."

"I think she just wanted to make a point."

Eleanor ignored her brother's remark, but continued watching the ground as they walked, lost in her own thoughts. "Do you think she'll go away and… Will she talk to Dùghlas Armstrong like Felicia did?" she finally asked.

Bart stopped abruptly and looked down at his sister. How could he answer such a question? What man ever knew what a woman was thinking, or what she would do? Bart would never have guessed Felicia capable of cuckolding him while he was away fighting the Scots, yet that was exactly what she had done.

She'd gone to Dùghlas Armstrong's bed, had borne his bastard child.

"I pray not," he finally replied, in a deceptively calm tone. Marguerite was out of sight now, though Bart kept his eyes trained upon the spot where he'd last seen her. 'Twas likely she'd gone for a stroll in the garden.

"Why do the people call Felicia 'Norwyck's whore'?"

Bart stopped abruptly. He'd heard the term once or twice, but was appalled that Eleanor had, too. He crouched down in front of her. "People oft say things that are better left alone."

"What does it mean, Bartie?"

He chewed the inside of his cheek and wondered how to answer her. "It means she was too friendly with a man who was not her husband."

"The Armstrong bastard?"

"Eleanor, you must guard your tongue," he said, arising. He jabbed his fingers through his hair and wondered if Ellie's strange questions would ever cease. They began to walk again. "Certain words are not appropriate for a young lady to say, and *bastard* is one of them."

"Is Henry going away to foster?" she asked, moving rapidly from subject to subject, as was her way. Bart was glad he did not have to dwell upon her earlier questions, yet *this* was not an easy one, either.

He let his breath out slowly. "I'm considering it."

"But where would he go? Far away?"

"Mayhap not so far," Bart replied, though far enough that they would not see him for years on end.

Eleanor continued her chatter until they reached the keep. 'Twas with relief that Bart left her with Nurse Ada and went to his chamber to bathe.

And to consider the best way to get Marguerite into a more compliant mood.

She'd become quite prickly at the mention of wenching, and Bart could only surmise that she did not like the notion of *him* with another woman. 'Twas an intriguing thought.

Mayhap he should send for her to attend his bath.

Naked, he stepped into the tub, and continued to stand as he washed away the grime of battle. He was weary, but his skin was exquisitely sensitive as he ran his hands across his chest, his buttocks, his groin. He thought of Marguerite's soft hands, and all too easily imagined his reaction to her caresses.

He shuddered and tried in vain to channel his thoughts in another direction.

'Twas no use. He would not rest until he'd had her.

There had to be some way to coerce her to his bed. Though she had avoided him in the days prior to his raid upon the Armstrong laird, 'twas past time he made some progress with her. He knew she was not indifferent to him—her responses to his kisses were proof of that. Mayhap an extra mug of wine this eve would put her in a mood to be seduced.

In any case, he would not—nay, he could not—wait much longer for her to come to him. He was driven to distraction by the memory of her mouth under his, of her touch upon his skin. Thoughts of her soft, feminine body plagued him, and Bart decided he would allow her to keep her distance no longer.

He rinsed the soap from his body, then shaved, combed his hair and dressed in tunic and hose. When he left his chamber and headed for the great hall, he knew his family would already be gathered for supper. And Marguerite would be with them, not exactly indifferent to him, but not quite ripe for the plucking.

The fire blazed in the huge fireplace, all the wall sconces were lit, and light from the chandelier over the table sparkled merrily. A number of Norwyck knights were gathered, too, to celebrate their victory. Judging by the gaiety of the men, they had already begun to drink to the success of the previous night's adventure.

Bart allowed himself a smile. It had been a highly enjoyable venture, besting the Armstrong at his own game. Norwyck men had routed their missing live-stock without harming a single one of the young Armstrong lads guarding the enclosure. Bart had judged them too young to die over a few cows.

And he knew that, by their sparing them, Lachann Armstrong would be enraged. He would not like to think of his enemy stepping in and taking his bounty, with nary a drop of blood shed.

Confident of other victories tonight, Bartholomew stepped over to the additional trestle tables that had been set up in the hall, and greeted his men. Some of them drank to his success, others patted his back and offered congratulations.

When servants began to carry trays of food into the hall, Bart turned to take his place at the dais where his family would take their meal.

Marguerite was not among them.

He quickly glanced toward both ends of the table, but did not spot her. He turned around and searched every corner of the hall, but she was not to be seen.

"Our food grows cold, Bart," Henry said. "Come and sit so we may begin."

Scowling, he climbed the dais and took his place, allowing the chaplain to say the prayer. When every-one had begun to eat, he turned to Eleanor. "Where is Lady Marguerite?" he asked.

"I thought she was with you, Bartie," Eleanor replied.

Bart leaned forward and spoke to John. "Do you know where Lady Marguerite is?"

"Nay, Bart."

He turned then to Kate at his left, even though he doubted she'd have an answer for him. "Kate, do you know why Lady Marguerite is not with us?"

"Why would I, Bartholomew?" his sister replied. "'Tis not up to me to watch what she does, where she goes."

Bart felt his jaw clench. This was not at all what he had planned for the evening. Where could she have gone? The last he'd seen her, she'd been headed in the direction of the castle garden, but 'twas dark now and cold outside. Surely she had not been angered by the wenching discussion to the point of freezing herself to death.

Nay, she must have taken a tray in her chamber. That suited him just as well. When supper was finished, he would climb to the tower and let nature take its course.

Marguerite held the youngest of Symon Michaelson's seven children in her arms while she stirred the pot hanging from the hook in the fireplace. There was plenty of food for this family and the families of the other injured men, thanks to the castle kitchens.

Earlier, she'd sat quietly with Alrick's wife, and watched over the poor man with her, but there'd been no sign of improvement. When the woman's neighbors came, Marguerite had left.

Here, poor Symon was laid low with his ruined leg, but sleeping now with the aid of a powerful potion administered by Alice Hoget. The old healer had needed the help of several men to pull Symon's leg straight, and had managed to splint it with two stout boards. 'Twas a serious injury, for if the man's leg did not heal straight, he would be crippled, and hardpressed to provide sufficiently for his family.

Symon's wife hovered about, weeping and twisting her apron in her hands. She was entirely useless in helping with Symon's care, and she hardly remembered her children. So 'twas fortunate that Marguerite had stopped in after visiting the other families, to see if there was aught she could do to help.

The children were frightened for their father. Their mother's frantic behavior did not reassure them, but Marguerite did all she could to calm their fears. She set each of the older children to tasks to take their minds off their father's pain, and while they were occupied, she got their meal on the table.

The activity felt perfectly natural to her.

Each child was given a bowl of thick soup and a slice of bread. They sat silently together and ate their food, the elder ones helping the younger, while Marguerite went to Symon's wife and spoke quietly to her.

"Anne," she said. "You must feed the bairn."

Anne's nose ran and her eyes were red from weeping. "I don't think I can, m'lady."

"Of course you can," Marguerite countered, though she knew no such thing. She dragged a chair to Symon's bedside and bade Anne to sit. Then she handed the bairn to his mother and helped her arrange her bodice so that the child had access to her breast.

The activity began to calm Anne, so Marguerite remained crouched in front of her and continued speaking of her children. She stroked the infant's downy, black hair as she spoke, and allowed him to catch her finger within his tiny fist.

In so doing, she knew with a certainty that she had never experienced this kind of intimacy with a bairn. The children whose faces came to her at odd times every day could not be hers. Nay, she would surely remember if her own infant had suckled at her breast.

'Twas both a relief and a disappointment.

"Mum?" the smallest of the children asked as she slid off her stool and came to stand next to Marguerite.

Anne looked down at her daughter. "Aye, Abby," she said in a wavering voice.

"Will Papa get up soon?"

Marguerite pulled the little girl into a loose embrace. There was naught she could say about Symon's condition without lying to her. She lifted the child into her arms. "We shall pray for him, Abby, and then God will take care of him."

She carried the little girl back to the table, where the rest of the children were just finishing. Together, they cleared away the remnants of the meal and cleaned their bowls.

"Does anyone know a song?" Marguerite asked the children, while keeping an eye on Anne and the bairn.

Six frightened little pairs of eyes gazed up at her, and her heart nearly melted at their looks of dread.

"Come," she said. "Let's get your pallets ready for sleep." They went without protest to the cupboard where their blankets and straw mattresses were kept, and took them out. Spreading them on the floor near the fire, Marguerite began to hum a tune as she tucked the children into their beds.

Soon, a few of the words came to her and she added them to her song. The children joined in, one voice at a time, until they were all singing quietly together. When Marguerite saw that Anne had finished feeding the bairn, she took him from his mother's arms and sat down among the rest of the children and finished the song.

Anne remained sitting listlessly in her chair, but there was naught Marguerite could do for her now.

She just wanted to get the children calmed and settled. Then she would do what she could for their mother.

She began to sing again.

"Lanquand li jorn son lonc en mai
m'es bels douz chans d'auzels de loing..."

Little Abby slipped out from under her blanket and, with her thumb stuck firmly in her mouth, crawled over her brothers and sisters to get to Marguerite's lap. Marguerite rearranged the bairn in her arms to make space for the little girl while she continued to sing.

"e quand me suis partitz de lai
remembra-m d'un'amor de loing."

The children were all dark-haired like their parents, and had deep brown eyes, so their looks were quite different from the children Marguerite "remembered." Yet the feelings they evoked were the same. She felt calm and centered here among the little ones, even though she did not truly belong.

She continued singing quietly, and wished she had Lady Norwyck's gittern. Mayhap on the morrow she would bring it to Symon's cottage and play for the children.

Anne was certain to need help with them then.

Marguerite wondered if Symon's wife would ever manage to calm herself enough to take care of him. 'Twould take a great deal of patience and skill over many weeks to deal with Symon's injuries. Even then, he might end up crippled, after all.

Marguerite looked at the five children lying in their

beds, and the two little ones in her arms. How would they ever manage then?

It had been hours since Marguerite's disappearance. Bartholomew's knights had spread out to search, scouring the courtyards and gardens, looking in every building within the castle walls. Bart had even led a party of men out to the beach and up into the hills to hunt for her, fairly certain that the woman had fled Norwyck when the opportunity had presented itself.

His anger at her flight was deep and sharp.

"My lord," Sir Walter said as Bart rode into the courtyard and dismounted. "Any luck?"

"Nay." The word was clipped.

"Mayhap she is—"

"She is no longer my concern," Bart said, closing off any further discussion of her. In another hour, he would recall his men from the search. "What have you heard of Alrick Stickle and the others?"

"Alrick's condition is dire, but at least Symon Michaelson holds his own, my lord," Walter said. If his speech was clipped, 'twas not for Bart to notice. "I was just about to take these parcels out to the injured men's families."

Bart looked at the satchels on the ground behind Walter. They were packed with foodstuffs and other essentials. "I'll take them," he said, bending down to pick up the two heaviest. "Who gets what?"

Walter answered the question as Bart put the packs on his horse. When all was ready, he remounted.

"My lord..."

Bart turned back and looked impatiently at the old knight.

"Mayhap...I believe 'tis possible you've misjudged Lady Marguerite."

Bart sat quietly for a moment before speaking. "'Tis no matter now. She was a stranger when she arrived, and still a stranger when she left. She took naught with her but Eleanor's affection."

If Sir Walter replied, Bart did not hear it, but turned his horse and rode toward the village, forcibly banishing all thoughts of Marguerite from his mind. He did not care to hear whatever the man had to say in her favor.

He stopped in the cottages of the injured men, carrying the goods into each house, staying to visit each family. The lady of the estate should have been the one to handle these visitations, but there was no lady. Nor would there be one until Hal took a wife. Mayhap his sisters would fill the void until then, since each one was so keen to act the chatelaine.

When he reached Alrick's cottage, he found the man's wife sitting next to his bed, and Alice Hoget hovering over him. Norwyck's priest sat alongside her.

Alice looked up at Bart and shook her head, and he knew then that Alrick would not survive. Bart thought of all the years the man had entertained the children, even himself as a child, and knew his jovial presence would be sorely missed.

Bartholomew spoke a few words of comfort to Alrick's wife, then took his leave. He had one more cottage to visit.

"Coming to see Master Symon, are ye, m'lord?" Alice asked, catching up to him as he untied his horse.

"Aye," Bart replied. "How is he?"

"The leg is set," she said simply. "And his wife is fraught with worry. I've got a couple of girls to come help her with the children, but I'll walk with ye now and look in on him before I go home.''

Bart remembered Anne's reaction to her husband's injury and wondered if the woman had gathered her wits since he'd last seen her. He could not blame her for being distraught. As he recalled, Symon had a number of young children. The prospect of a crippled husband, with so many mouths to feed, would be daunting.

Bart tied his horse and gathered the parcels for Symon's family, then followed Alice as she pushed through the cottage door. All was quiet in the darkened room, but for the sound of a clear, rich feminine voice raised in song. As Bart turned and latched the door against a wintry wind, the song abruptly stopped. He looked up.

'*Twas Marguerite!*

His muscles froze in place at the sight of her here, sitting unharmed among Symon's children.

As though he and his men had not spent the last several hours searching for her.

How long had she been here? Did she have any idea how he'd worried? How he'd searched in vain? He cracked his knuckles and made a conscious effort to unclench his teeth. He did not know whether to throttle her or take her in his arms and clasp her to him so that she might never again leave his sight.

Mayhap he should do both.

Chapter Nine

"Ah, 'tis good that ye stayed, m'lady," Alice said to Marguerite as she picked up the lamp from the table. "Mistress Anne is in no condition tonight to manage on her own."

"'Twas a pleasure to help with the children," Marguerite replied. "And since there was naught to do for Alrick's wife..." Her voice was rich and clear, and caused the kind of reaction that was becoming all too familiar to Bart. Need...*acute* need, combined with some odd sensation he did not recognize.

The sight of her soft lips nuzzling the dark-haired bairn in her arms made his mouth go dry. The vision of her delicate hands stroking the tiny child's back sent a stab of longing through him that was strong enough to make him stagger. Bart had no trouble imagining Marguerite bearing his own dark-haired child.

He dragged one hand across his mouth and jaw and turned away. *How absurd.*

"Ah, Annie girl," Alice said, giving Bart a much-needed excuse to turn his attention elsewhere. "*Do* take a seat, if ye please. Yer makin' me dizzy with all yer pacing."

Mistress Anne sat herself down on a chair next to her husband's bed and chewed a corner of her lip. Her hands pulled nervously at her apron. It made Bart uncomfortable just to watch her, though 'twas better than torturing himself with visions of Marguerite.

It annoyed him to know that his anger was misplaced. The lady had spent the evening helping the people of the village—*his people*—while he was out looking to prove a point. He had intended to discredit her once he found her fleeing into the hills.

He'd been an ass.

And he still wanted her. Mayhap even more than before. His anger cooled as reason set in again, along with a severe case of lust.

The cottage was fairly spacious, though with seven children and three extra adults, the quarters were cramped. Intentionally avoiding Marguerite's eyes, Bart stepped over the children's pallets and went to Symon's bedside.

The man was insensible. His broken leg was swollen and blue, and tightly bound to two straight boards. It did not look good. Grimacing, Bart glanced up at Alice. "Will this heal?" he asked.

Alice raised her eyebrows and shrugged, clearly unwilling to speak frankly with Symon's fragile wife so near. "Who can say how the bone will mend?" she said. "Time will tell, m'lord."

"Aye, but do you think…" he began, but one look at Anne's anxious face and he changed the question. "Do you think he'll feel better on the morrow?"

"Nay," Alice replied. "He's likely to feel worse."

A sudden, piercing wail broke the quiet of the room. Bart turned and saw that the bairn in Marguerite's arms was restless. She was attempting to quiet him, but her movements were hampered by the little girl slumbering in her lap. Unless she moved the older child, she would not be able to comfort the babe.

Alice was occupied with frowning and looking under Symon's eyelids, while Mistress Anne hugged her arms about herself and anxiously watched every move Alice made.

Seeing no alternative, Bart stepped over the children and crouched before Marguerite. Without speaking, he carefully lifted the little girl, brushing his hands against Marguerite's legs in the process.

A shudder ran through her, and her eyes closed. In that moment, Bart did not doubt that he would soon linger there, touching her as intimately as a man could touch a woman. And 'twould give them both pleasure.

He swallowed hard and turned his attention to Symon's little daughter, carrying her to the only vacant pallet, gently placing her on it and covering her with her woolen blanket. As the little girl stuck her thumb in her mouth he heard Marguerite rise behind him and start to pace as she sang quietly to the bairn.

Marguerite moved around enough to calm the infant, and managed to keep her distance from him. Still, her hushed song penetrated the quiet and he clearly heard the French words that she sang.

"Let me take him, m'lady," Alice said, stepping away from Symon's bed. "Ye look fair spent, if ye don't mind my saying."

"Oh, but I—"

"Ye've got dark circles under yer eyes, and yer just out of bed from near drowning," Alice countered, taking the babe from Marguerite. "Take her back to the keep, m'lord. She needs her own bed tonight. I've got Judith Atwood's daughters coming to help Annie.

There's no more either of ye can do here before the morn.''

The old healer was right. Whatever Marguerite had been doing since leaving him in the courtyard, it had wearied her. Bart glanced at Marguerite, his eyes meeting hers, and felt a tenderness that made him uneasy. She looked away shyly.

"Go on with ye, now," Alice said, fairly shooing them from the house. "All's as well as it can be here."

Bart reached across several sleeping bodies and offered his hand to Marguerite. "My lady?" he said, more gruffly than he intended. 'Twas not easy, knowing how wrong he'd been about her.

Marguerite hesitated only an instant, then took his hand and stepped over the children. 'Twas but a moment more before they reached the door. Bart spotted her cloak hanging on a hook, and had just begun to help her with it when there was a light tap at the door. Expecting the Atwood girls, he was surprised to discover 'twas the knight he'd left in charge of the search for Marguerite.

"My lord," he said, gesturing toward Bart's horse tethered nearby, "I saw your horse, so I came to you here rather than wait—" He caught sight of Marguerite. "My lady! You found her, my lord?"

"Aye, Duncan, only a few minutes ago," Bart replied dryly. He placed his hand at the base of Marguerite's back and directed her out of the cottage to his horse before she could ask the knight what he meant.

Bart mounted his horse and reached one hand down to Marguerite as Duncan gave her a boost up. Once she was sitting sidesaddle atop Pegasus, Bart settled her into the V of his legs and encircled her with his arms to take hold of reins.

A faint flash of lightning lit the sky, and soon they heard the distant rumble of thunder.

Bart turned to Duncan. "Round up the men. 'Tis cold, and a storm is moving in. I would not have them chasing wild geese on a night like this."

"Aye, my lord," the young man replied. "I'll see to it."

Bart turned and rode in the direction of the castle, while Duncan mounted and headed toward the hills. When Bartholomew felt Marguerite shiver, he pulled her body even closer to share his heat. She smelled slightly floral, thoroughly feminine. He breathed deeply of her.

"My lord," she said, turning her face toward his, "were you...did you think I had run away?"

"It crossed my mind."

"But why would I leave here?" she asked, pulling her cloak more tightly around her. "Where would I go?"

Indeed. That was the question. "If you left Norwyck, where *would* you go, my lady?" he asked quietly. Her head was tucked under his chin and the side of her body rested against his chest.

"My lord," she said in frustration, moving her head to gaze up at him. "I still have no memory of who I am, or from whence I came...though I am fairly certain I must be French."

Bart did not respond. If she knew she was French, how much longer would it be before she remembered everything else? How much longer before she left Norwyck?

"When I sing, the French songs seem much more familiar, and the words come to me so easily."

"Your English is perfect."

"It does not feel as natural as the French."

Bart would not argue the point. Mayhap she *was* French, although that was no comfort to him. The Scots were strongly aligned with the French, and she might very well be an ally of his Armstrong and MacEwen enemies.

Marguerite shivered again and huddled closer. Her body slumped with fatigue. Bart slipped one hand about her waist and knew that Alice Hoget was correct—Marguerite was exhausted.

She must have returned to the village after leaving him and Eleanor in the afternoon. God knew what kind of tasks she'd taken up at Symon's house. Mayhap she'd made herself useful to the families of the other injured men, too.

Bart would not press her to come to him tonight. However, he had no intention of letting this opportunity to touch her go to waste.

Marguerite allowed herself to melt into Bartholomew's embrace. The night was cold and she felt chilled. His warmth blanketed her, making her feel safe and secure in his arms. He still did not trust her, but that did not seem to matter tonight. He had been worried about her, and had sent his men searching for her.

She had felt his anger earlier, when he'd first entered Symon's cottage, and though Marguerite had not understood it, she sensed that it had mellowed somehow. Mayhap he was entitled to some mistrust. After all, Felicia had committed the ultimate betrayal—adultery with Bartholomew's enemy. 'Twould take a saint to forgive her and immediately trust again.

Without haste, they rode through the village lanes. Her hood was down, and Marguerite felt Bartholomew's breath on her ear and her neck, instilling her with warmth and an awareness of the potent fire that burned within him. They reached the main gate of the castle, and Bartholomew guided his horse through the upper and lower baileys, to a large stable near the courtyard.

"I'll bed Pegasus down, lads," he said to the grooms who roused themselves upon his arrival. "But the knights will soon return from the hills. Their mounts will need attention."

Still holding her against him, Bartholomew rode into the dark recesses of the stable and dismounted. In no time, he'd lit a lamp, illuminating the area surrounding an empty horse stall.

"Slide down," he said, raising his hands to her waist.

His dark eyes burned hot, and Marguerite trembled at the seductive promise she saw deep within. She took a breath, placed her hands on his shoulders and let herself down into his waiting arms.

He did not release her when her feet touched the ground, but kept his hands at her waist. He tipped his head and brushed her lips with his own.

An instant later, his hands were gone, and so was his mouth. "This will only take a few minutes," he said, leading his horse into the stall.

More shaken by his gentle kiss than she wished to admit, Marguerite followed him and watched as he unbuckled the girth strap and lifted the huge saddle off the horse. Next, he unfastened the bridle and removed it, handing it to Marguerite, as if naught had just occurred between them.

"You can hang it on one of those hooks," he said, indicating the wall outside the stall, where a row of leather straps and bridles hung.

Marguerite reached up and put the bridle on a hook, while Bartholomew pulled off the horse's blanket, then rubbed down the animal's back and legs. He tossed Marguerite a cloth. "We'll finish sooner if you take that side," he said.

Unmoving, Marguerite watched for a moment as Bartholomew rubbed the horse's shoulder, then stroked the beast's back and side. She looked at the cloth in her hand, then raised it to the horse. It seemed a wholly unfamiliar task, leading Marguerite to believe she'd never done it before.

Still, the motion was soothing, and she could only imagine how 'twould feel to have someone rub *her* down, and knead the knots from *her* muscles. 'Twas a foolish fancy, and she must have chuckled aloud at the thought, because Bartholomew asked, "What?"

"'Tis naught, my lord," she said, working her way to the horse's rump.

Bartholomew's dark eyes pierced her. "You laughed," he said. "I would know what has caused you such mirth."

Marguerite felt her skin heat at her foolishness. She did not want Bartholomew to think she'd been laughing at him. "I thought it amusing that your horse gets more kind attention than most people do, my lord."

"Is that all?" he said, looking at her curiously. "You envy Peg his currying?"

Marguerite felt herself smile. "Nay, my lord. Of course not."

Bartholomew was quiet, and seemed lost in thought as he finished with his horse. He put the saddle and the rest of the equipment away, then took Marguerite's arm and walked out of the stable. His body was hard and tense beside her, and Marguerite wondered if he would kiss her again.

They walked silently, and when they entered the keep, Bartholomew stopped and faced her at the foot of the stairs.

'Twas nearly dark in the hall, and Bartholomew's rich, deep voice penetrated the deepest recesses of Marguerite's resistance. "Rest well, my lady," he said quietly.

She stood speechless, wanting no more than for him to take her in his arms and kiss her senseless, to carry her up to the tower and do exactly what his eyes threatened, every time he looked at her.

Instead, he made a slight bow and turned away. Within seconds, he was swallowed up in the darkness of the hall, leaving Marguerite feeling alone and bereft.

Restraining the urge to call out to him, she pivoted, picked up a candle and made her way up the solid stone steps to the tower. As usual, Rose had already stoked the fire in her chamber and turned her bed down. Still, though the room was warm and cozy, 'twas lonely up here, away from even the possibility of companionship.

Pulling the laces from her gown, Marguerite dispensed with it, sighing as she sat down on the padded bench near the washstand. A distant rumble of thunder drew her attention to the windows, as did the sight of lightning flashing in the distant sky and the sound of the wind whipping around the tower.

The storm was still far out at sea, and Marguerite felt no threat from it. At least not yet. She told herself that this tower had stood for many a year, through many a storm. 'Twould withstand this one, too.

Still, she felt restless, unnerved. She *had* to figure out where she belonged, for 'twas certain she could not remain here at Norwyck Castle with Bartholomew Holton much longer. She stood again and paced the length of the tower room and back. She had tried forcing herself to remember, but that had served no purpose other than to frustrate her.

The faces of the blond children came to her often, but never long enough for her to discern their features, or to recall their names. One of them, a little girl was...was—

A name came to her. *Cosette!* The smallest one was Cosette!

Marguerite sat back down on the bench and pressed one hand to her chest, covering her pounding heart. She'd been right. Cosette was a French name, so she must have come from France. That was it! She'd been on a voyage from France to England when the ship had gone down and she'd nearly been lost. She'd been with a light-haired man named...named...

She let out a breath in frustration. Why couldn't she remember any more?

She concentrated on Cosette. Bringing the little girl's face to mind again, Marguerite wistfully remembered the child's carefree smile. She could practically hear her voice, sweetly singing a simple French song.

Besides her memory of Cosette, there was nothing else.

Marguerite did not know how long she sat trying to retrieve her lost memories, but eventually she brushed away tears of frustration and turned to face the small mirror above her washstand. Removing the combs from her hair, she shook her head until her long tresses fell about her shoulders and down her back.

'Twas no use thinking about Cosette or the man on the ship. She did not even recognize her own face in the mirror. Marguerite knew there was no way to force the memories—heaven knew she'd tried often enough, to no avail. She picked up her comb and began working the tines through her hair while she changed the direction of her thoughts.

Master Symon came to mind immediately—his plight, and that of his family. She hoped his leg would heal well, and that he'd be able to return to wor—

A sound startled her and she dropped her comb and turned.

Bartholomew stood in the shadows of the doorway.

He did not speak, but moved toward her, his steps slow and deliberate, his eyes never leaving hers.

Gently touching one of her shoulders, he turned her toward the mirror once more, then picked up her comb and began to run it through her hair. By the second stroke, the feeling was so delicious, Marguerite closed her eyes and tipped her head slightly forward. After each stroke, his hand caressed her, from the crown of her head to the nape of her neck, becoming more bold each time.

He slid one hand under the edge of her chemise and slipped it off her shoulder, leaving it bare to his touch, his kiss.

Chapter Ten

Marguerite's eyes flew open when he touched his lips to her warm, flushed skin, and she saw her reflection, along with Bartholomew's. He glanced up just then and met her eyes as he lowered the chemise from her other shoulder.

It slipped as they both watched.

Only the upper slopes of her breasts were bared, and though Marguerite knew she should not allow Bartholomew to touch her this way, or to see her so unclothed, she was powerless to stop him when he began to knead her shoulders.

Her head fell back as his thumbs exerted pressure on the most sensitive points of her spine, as his hands compressed the muscles of her bare shoulders and back. He worked his strange enchantment, and succeeded in making Marguerite groan with pleasure.

His hands slid up and cupped her upper arms, lowering the chemise beyond decency. "You are so very beautiful," he breathed.

Marguerite swallowed, watching his reflection in the glass. His eyes dropped from where they held hers, darkening when his gaze lit on her naked breasts. His hands slid lower, until he cupped their fullness. Marguerite's breath caught in her throat as his thumbs gently teased the engorged peaks.

Thunder sounded, much closer to the castle, but neither of them noticed. Bartholomew touched her shoulder with his lips, then moved his mouth to her neck. Marguerite shivered when she heard his low growl. Her head fell back once more and her eyes drifted closed.

"So soft…"

His arms were suddenly behind and underneath her, and he was lifting her off the bench, carrying her to the bed. He tipped his head and captured her mouth with his own, searing her with his kiss.

Ever so gently, he placed her in the bed. Desperate for his touch, Marguerite reached for him, but Bartholomew evaded her, leaning over to pull the blankets up to her chin.

"Rest well, my lady," he said, brushing one finger across the sensitive skin below her eye. "When I come to your bed, you must be well rested. I will demand much of you."

The storm continued all night and into the morning hours, though 'twas not the reason for Marguerite's fitful sleep. Bartholomew was the cause.

His effect on her was a powerful one.

The room was chilly as Marguerite slipped out of bed. She wrapped her shawl around her shoulders and went to stoke the fire before dressing for the day. 'Twas still raining, and the day was bleak, yet when she looked out the window facing Norwyck's practice field and saw Bartholomew in his hauberk, the day took on an entirely different appearance.

He was easily the tallest among his men, and surely the strongest, though she knew those hands and arms could be gentle, too. She felt a flush of heat on her cheeks, recalling how he'd kissed her, touched her and spoken to her before laying her in her bed.

It should never have happened, but Marguerite was powerless against Bartholomew's advances. Besides the incredible attraction between them, her regard for him grew with all that she learned of him. His camaraderie with his knights, his concern for Master Symon and the other injured men, his deep love for his young siblings—these things only drew her closer to him.

As for his distrust of her, Marguerite could understand it, now that she knew of his late wife's treachery. No man would find it easy to trust another woman after what Felicia had done. For all his size and power, he was just a man, vulnerable to the pain inflicted upon him by those he loved most.

When Bartholomew left the field, Marguerite turned away from the window. She washed and dressed, then went down to the great hall. Only a few servants were there, and the main table was empty of all but a few candlesticks. Marguerite realized she must have arisen late.

"Have you seen Lady Eleanor?" she asked the servant, Rose, who swept cold embers from the hearth.

"Nay, my lady," the girl replied. "No one's been about for quite some time…except for Lady Kathryn. She went that way."

Following the direction of the girl's outstretched arm, Marguerite crossed the hall and turned into a dark corridor. There were several chambers here, if all the closed doors were any indication. Marguerite stopped and listened, not at all sure that she wanted to find

Kathryn. The child was prickly at best, and had no interest in any kind of friendship with her.

Still, Kathryn might have Eleanor with her, and Marguerite had promised Bartholomew she would take over the supervision of the youngest Holton.

As Marguerite stood quietly, she heard the faint sounds of music. Well, 'twas not exactly music, for the sounds were discordant and unpleasant. Yet they were made with a musical instrument—a gittern, if she was not mistaken.

Curious, she walked along the corridor, listening, then found the place from which the music came. Quietly opening the door to a chamber full of windows, Marguerite saw Kathryn sitting on a window seat, her attention completely centered upon the gittern in her hands.

She attempted to play several notes, then a chord. None of the sounds could be called music.

Marguerite moved back behind the door and knocked, then stepped in. Kathryn looked up, clearly embarrassed to have been caught secretly playing her mother's gittern.

"Good morn to you, Kathryn," Marguerite said. "I'm looking for Eleanor. Have you seen her?"

"N-nay," Kathryn said as she set the gittern aside and stepped away from it.

Marguerite glanced at the instrument and then back at Kathryn. She thought the girl might have fled the room if she had not been blocking the doorway. "There is a psaltery in the trunk in the tower room," she said. "Did your mother play that, too?"

Kathryn kept her eyes down. "She played anything with strings."

"Ah, then she was truly gifted," Marguerite said,

walking toward her. "I would know more of your mother."

Kathryn's eyes flitted up to Marguerite's, then skittered away again. She backed up to the window seat. "There is naught to tell. She died the year before my father, and…"

"And?" Marguerite said gently.

"And…she had started to teach me to play the gittern b-before she became ill."

Marguerite did not know what she hoped to accomplish, but she came even closer and said, "Tell me more of her. Did she sing?"

Kathryn swallowed. "Aye," she said quietly. Then she looked defiantly at Marguerite. "I've never heard *anyone* who could play as well or sing as sweetly as my mother."

Marguerite ignored the thinly veiled insult, taking the child's words for what they were—an expression of her grief over losing her mother. Marguerite could imagine how it had been for Kathryn after Lady Norwyck's death. She'd had two brothers away in Scotland at the time, two older brothers who were mere adolescents, and one very small sister. 'Twas likely her father had had little insight into his daughter's sorrow.

"Tell me about her," Marguerite said, sitting down across from the window seat. "I imagine she was very beautiful."

"Aye, she was!" Kathryn replied, taking her place again. She picked up the gittern as she spoke, absently holding the neck and touching the strings. "And she let me walk with her everywhere, when she planned meals with Cook, when she looked over stores with the pantler."

As she remembered her mother, Kathryn's eyes became distant and wistful, and Marguerite wondered if she'd done the right thing in encouraging the girl to evoke her sad memories.

There was naught to do now but listen, and Marguerite gave Kathryn her full attention. The thought of having such painful memories frightened her. What if she eventually discovered that she'd lost her husband when her ship sank? What if those three children were, indeed, her own? Where were they now? Would she ever see them again?

Caitir Armstrong. The name suddenly came to her as Kathryn spoke, but Marguerite could make no more of it. Why would she know of an Armstrong woman? Why on earth would that name come into her head?

"...and she p-promised to teach me to play her gittern," Kathryn said, "before she d-died."

Marguerite blinked her eyes several times to shake herself out of her strange reverie and pay attention to the young girl before her, the child who needed her attention so desperately. "Well, I...I doubt I have the talent your mother had, Kathryn," she said, "but I would be honored show you a few chords."

When Kathryn made no reply, Marguerite crouched before her and moved the girl's fingers so that they rested above the correct strings. "Now, press down," she said.

Kathryn did so.

"Take your right hand and strum," Marguerite said.

Kathryn ran her fingers lightly across the strings and a harmonic sound emanated from the instrument. Marguerite gave a few more instructions on the positioning of the fingers, and Kathryn strummed again. Once she'd mastered that chord, Marguerite showed her another, and another. Soon Kathryn was able to strum a simple song.

Kathryn avoided looking up at her, and Marguerite sensed that the girl's pride would be the most difficult obstacle to overcome in dealing with her. 'Twould never do to move too fast with her.

"You learn quickly," Marguerite said as she stood up and stepped away. She was certain there was a limit to Kathryn's tolerance, and she did not want to push her past it. "Your mama would have been proud of you."

Kathryn did not respond, but kept her eyes down and continued to practice what she'd learned, while Marguerite went to the door. "Be careful not to make your fingertips too sore. 'Twill take time for them to grow accustomed to pressing on the strings."

When Kathryn did not even acknowledge her words, Marguerite slipped out of the chamber and into the corridor, where Eleanor caught sight of her and charged away from Nurse Ada like an overgrown puppy. The poor nurse was clearly out of her element with the spirited child.

"Lady Marguerite!" Eleanor called from the far end, "I've been looking everywhere for you!"

Bart washed the mud from his body and dressed in a clean tunic. And never stopped thinking of the sight of Marguerite giving Kathryn instruction on playing the stringed instrument.

He could hardly credit that Marguerite had gotten Kathryn to allow her so close. His sister had been prickly and difficult ever since his return from Scotland, and he had hardly known how to deal with her. His only hope had been to marry her off early.

Bart had happened upon Kathryn and Marguerite in his study just now, but had remained quiet, preferring to observe their interaction unnoticed. He was still amazed.

Marguerite was a thoroughly uncommon woman. He could not imagine Felicia or any other lady having the patience to endure Kathryn's vexatious temperament, nor did he think his wife had been particularly tolerant of his other siblings.

She had certainly never abided his touch the way Marguerite had the night before.

Thinking of Marguerite's response, Bart found his body reacting just as it had when he'd touched her. His blood burned for her. His flesh ached. No amount of swordplay on the practice field had been able to dispel the image of her sensual gaze as he'd caressed her naked breasts, and it tortured him.

No woman had ever looked at him that way.

As he tied the laces of his tunic, he vowed never again to be blinded by lust, as he'd been with Felicia. Marguerite was beautiful and passionate, and he *would* take her to bed. But he would never put any trust in her, nor would he ever give her aught but pleasure.

And when she figured out where she belonged—if, indeed, she truly did not know—he would send her off with no regrets, no demands. 'Twas the only way.

In the meantime, he would send letters to several neighboring lords and see if he could find a place for Henry to foster. The lad was a bit old to begin, but there were a few men whose estates were not far, who might be inclined to take on a boy of Henry's age. Feeling more settled now, Bart left his chamber and went to the great hall.

Eleanor was there with Marguerite, and the two

were playing some foolish game with string as they sat on the floor before the fire.

"Bartie!" Eleanor called out as she saw him.

He crossed the hall and joined them. Marguerite kept her eyes on the string, which had somehow bound Eleanor's hands together in an intricate pattern. Then she used both hands to pull the string off Ellie's hands and onto her own.

Only then did she look up at him.

"Look what Lady Marguerite taught me!"

"I see," Bart said. "And how did Lady Marguerite manage to remember such a complex game?"

Marguerite shrugged, as if to deny that his words had any effect upon her, but the tightening of her lips told him otherwise.

Mayhap 'twould serve his purpose to keep his caustic remarks to himself. After all, he only wanted to bed her. What did he care who she was or where she belonged, or whether she intentionally kept that information from him?

"Bartie, I don't care how she remembered," Eleanor protested. "'Tis the best diversion from the rain."

He would give her that. "Aye, it appears to be."

"My lord, have you heard aught of Master Alrick or Master Symon this morn?" Marguerite inquired.

"I visited Alrick first thing," Bart replied as he shook his head. "He's no better than he was."

A troubled look crossed her face. "And what of Symon?"

"He's awake now, and in pain, but at least he's sensible."

"How does his wife fare?"

"The same," he said. "But her neighbors were there to help."

Marguerite gave a quick nod, causing a luxurious lock of her hair—which she'd left uncovered—to slip over one shoulder. Bart could not help but remember how warm and alive it had felt under his hands. She was exquisitely sensitive to his touch, which would make her all the more susceptible to him when he finally took her to his bed.

She was dressed in a simple blue gown that hid her most intriguing attributes, but made her eyes shimmer with the bright color of a spring sky. His hands fairly itched with the urge to untie the laces that held the bodice together, to hold the weight of her breasts in his hands as he'd done the previous night.

Her nipples had come to taut peaks so quickly, and her breath had quickened with his touch. 'Twas all he'd been able to do to force himself from her chamber and down the stairs, when his body fairly screamed to remain there and join her in the bed. He could only imagine how she'd respond when he touched her even more intimately, when he joined their bodies as one.

Marguerite continued to play absently with Eleanor, and Bart noticed that the expression in her eyes seemed thoughtful and distant. He wondered if she was thinking the same kind of thoughts as those that had plagued him all night and all through the morn.

"Bart!" Henry said as he came into the hall. "I've been looking for you."

"Aye, Hal," he said, gazing at his serious young brother.

"May I speak with you? In your study?" he added, casting a glance toward his sister and Lady Marguerite.

"Of course," Bart said, reluctantly turning away from the most alluring sight in all of Norwyck. He did not doubt that the vision in blue silk would stay with him until he saw her next.

Chapter Eleven

She had finally begun to see. Images of some past life flitted in and out of her mind all day, but it seemed that reality intruded every time she was on the verge of remembering.

'Twas going to be necessary to leave the keep and everyone within it in order to concentrate enough to bring the memories back fully. She needed a quiet place, one where she would not be interrupted.

And Marguerite felt that if she went down to the beach, the sight of the sea might help to stimulate her recollections. Yet if she left the castle walls, Bartholomew would have cause to accuse her of running away again.

She had no choice but to tell him of her intentions. She looked for him in his study, and in several other rooms in the keep, but did not find him. Deciding he must be out of doors, she headed to the stables. She found Sir Walter there instead.

"I would like to walk," she told him. "But I cannot find Lord Norwyck, and I know he would not approve of me leaving the castle without an escort."

"You've got the right of that," Walter replied with a snort.

"Well, I was hoping…" she said. "I must get away from the castle for a while. I feel as if I might remember…*something* if I get away from everyone here, go down to the sea."

"Where Lord Norwyck found you, then?"

"Exactly," Marguerite replied.

"I'll take you, my lady," he said. "If you'll just wait until I've had a word with the stable marshal…"

"Nay, Sir Walter, if you'll just find a groom to accompany me, I'm sure—"

"Please, my lady," Walter said. "'Twould be my honor to watch over you."

Marguerite did not want to inconvenience the distinguished knight, but if this was the only way she would be allowed outside the castle walls, then she was content to wait. She had a feeling that all would come back to her, once she went down to the water and got close enough to smell the sea, feel the briny water upon her skin. Nay, she did not intend to wade into it, but she was certain that close proximity would help her to remember.

Sir Walter returned from the stable wearing a heavy cloak. "Ready, my lady?"

"If you are certain I'm not detaining you from something more—"

"Of course not," he said.

"I truly appreciate your company."

"I know you do, lass, I can see it in your lovely eyes," Walter answered. "And I know how your loss of memory must trouble you."

Marguerite blushed at his compliment and found herself surprised that he understood her predicament.

Taking the knight's arm, she walked toward a rusty old postern gate, which she assumed led to the sea.

"Nay, my lady," he said with a chuckle. "We must go 'round to the main sea gate. This one's been rusted shut for an age."

"If only Lord Norwyck would be half as accommodating as you, Sir Walter," she said, "we would get on twice as well."

Walter chuckled. "Our Bartholomew has had a rough go of it since his return from the wars."

"I've heard bits and pieces from Eleanor, but she does not have the complete story."

"None of us really does," Walter said, moving steadily down the path. He gave Marguerite a supportive hand whenever the ground was rough. "I never trusted Felicia from the day she came to Norwyck, but Bart's father insisted upon the betrothal. The lass brought a fine piece of property, and with Bart being the second son…"

Marguerite nodded. "Property would be important."

"Aye. Well, they were wed but half a year when Bart and Will were summoned by the king to join him in Scotland. I'm sure the lad hoped Felicia would be with child before he left, but 'twas not to be."

Surprised by her reaction to the thought of another woman bearing Bartholomew's child, Marguerite kept her thoughts to herself, leaving Walter to continue.

"Will's company returned from Scotland first, though Bart was right upon his heels. Anxious, he was, to get home to Felicia," he said.

"Eleanor said that Felicia lured William away from the castle and that the Armstrong killed him."

"Well, we know there was a trap," Walter said.

"And we know that 'twas Felicia who summoned Will to the hillock where he was killed by an Armstrong arrow. We did not learn that she'd played a part in the trap until she lay dying in childbed. Many truths came out that day."

"Oh…" Marguerite murmured.

"Aye. You've heard, no doubt, that the bairn was not Bart's."

She nodded.

"The midwife swore the bairn was full to term," he said. "Yet she delivered him a mere six months after Bart's return from Scotland. He was stillborn."

Marguerite remained silent. The magnitude of Felicia's betrayal was overwhelming, and she could only imagine what Bartholomew had felt.

"'Twas Laird Armstrong's son, Dùghlas, who fathered the bairn," Walter said, "to make the betrayal complete."

Dùghlas Armstrong. Who was he? Someone she knew? Kin? Whoever he was, Marguerite knew that only a blackguard would seduce another man's wife. Only a coward would lure a man's brother to a place where he could be trapped and killed.

"Here you go, m'lady," Walter said somberly. "I'll just sit here on this rock and keep watch if you care to walk."

"Thank you, Sir Walter," she replied with a meager smile. "I'll not go far."

"Just mind the surf," he said. "And keep your cloak pulled up about your neck. The storm hasn't yet passed. We're likely to get more rain."

Marguerite nodded and walked down to the water. The waves were strong, and she stayed clear of them, stopping to close her eyes and inhale deeply of the sea air as the wind whipped the edges of her cloak.

Caitir Armstrong. What had she to do with Bartholomew's Armstrong enemy? For certainly 'twas no coincidence that this name was familiar to Marguerite. Who was Caitir?

And why did the name Armstrong strike such a familiar chord in her? Did she know Lachann...Dùghlas? Could she have known such despicable men and not remember them?

She turned and walked down the beach, staying within Walter's line of vision as she walked south. The crashing waves were familiar, frightening. Was this how it had been when her ship had gone down? Cold and stormy, with massive waves threatening at every moment?

She stopped and closed her eyes, willing the memory to return, terrifying though it was.

The vision of a lantern swaying precariously came to her. 'Twas hanging over the deck of her ship as it pitched violently in the storm. Thunder crashed and lightning flashed through the endless sky, and Marguerite could almost feel herself falling. The bruised scrape on her shin burned with the memory.

Men were all around, throwing ropes, holding on to rails. Yet naught could keep the ship from going down.

A man called to her. "Marie!"

"Alain!" she called back. "*Je ne peux plus m'acerocher!*"

Alain. The man was Alain, and she had cried out to him in French. Was he...could he possibly be her husband, when her heart and soul seemed so filled with Bartholomew?

Shocked by the admission of Bartholomew's effect on her, Marguerite tucked her head down and resumed walking again. She *had* to remember more than this. Mayhap thoughts of the child, Cosette, would help. Bringing the little blond girl's face to mind, Marguerite tried to remember everything about her.

She was young...mayhap no more than two or three years old, with bright yellow curls and freckles across her nose. A happy child, Marguerite thought, for in her memory, the girl was always smiling. She...

Marie. Marguerite stopped cold. The man, Alain, had called her Marie. She swallowed hard. Was that who she was? A Frenchwoman who happened to—

Genevieve. Gaspar.

The names came to her too fast, too abruptly, causing Marguerite to lose her balance and stumble. Quickly regaining her footing, she walked on, oblivious to the wind and the crashing waves.

Five people, their names familiar yet so distant, swirled through her mind as she walked. Marguerite desperately tried to make her recollections mean something. Clearly, these people were significant to her, else she would not have their faces and their names blazed upon her mind. The children—

"Where are you going?" A harsh voice assailed her.

Bartholomew grabbed her arm and turned her to face him, but Marguerite was speechless.

"You left an old man sitting out in the cold, waiting for you, watching over you while you satisfied your whim—"

"'Twas not a whim!" she cried, pulling away from him. "I had a purpose in coming h—"

"To meet with the Armstrong?"

In one rapid motion, she brought her hand up to slap his face, but he caught her wrist before she could make contact.

"How dare you insinuate that I'm no better than Felicia!"

"You—"

"Aye, I know of her perfidy, her adultery," she snapped. "Everyone speaks of Norwyck's whoring wife."

Bartholomew dropped her wrist as if he'd been stung by a fistful of nettles. Narrowing his eyes, he might have spoken had Marguerite given him a chance.

"I have naught in common with your late wife, Bartholomew," she said over the wind. "Nor did I somehow coerce Sir Walter into walking here with me. I...I—"

Abruptly, she turned away before the tears that burned the back of her eyes had a chance to fall. Storming off on her southward path, she wiped her eyes and followed the shoreline, struggling to channel her thoughts back to the memories.

But 'twas no use. Her concentration was broken. Bartholomew had ruined it for her.

Clenching his jaws so tightly, 'twas a wonder Bart did not break a tooth. As he watched her run away, his blood boiled and his skin burned in spite of the cold bite of the air. There had been few times in his life when he'd been this angry. And it seemed that 'twas his destiny of late, to be so affected by the females in his life.

When she was naught but a dark spot against the turbulent sky, he turned away and stalked back toward the sea gate. Marguerite was a dark spot in his brain, too, he thought angrily, never doing or saying what he expected, making him wrong more times than he cared to count.

Had he been mistaken about Sir Walter accompanying her? Bart hated to admit 'twas likely so. If Walter had discovered her coming to the beach alone, he would have followed her, at the very least, whether she had asked him or not.

Bart kicked a weed out of his way and continued up the path, but a loud clap of thunder startled him, stopping him in his tracks.

He turned and looked down the beach, but Marguerite had followed the curve of the land and was out of sight. The wind blew harder, carrying sand, making Bart's eyes tear, taking his breath away. The storm would soon be upon them. He wondered if Marguerite would realize she should seek shelter.

Without thinking, he reversed his direction and trotted back to the beach. He'd been wrong about her before, and 'twas possible he'd mistaken her purpose again today. Though he felt no more inclined to trust her than he had a week ago, he did not wish to see her injured in the storm. She could be blown out to sea, or a tree could fall. Mayhap even lightning—

He ran across the sand, following Marguerite's path. She could not have gotten too far ahead in such a short time, so he might be able to catch up with her before the rain came. Lightning slashed the sky above the sea, and as the thunder crashed, Bart could see the storm moving toward the shore. He whipped his cloak behind him and broke into a run.

Following the curve of the shore, he finally caught sight of her, still running on the sand. He was beyond the castle wall now, and naught but dense forest lay from this point south. If she kept on going, where would they find shelter?

He narrowed the distance between them as lightning struck ever closer. Huge, sparse drops of rain began to fall, and Bart knew that 'twould not be long before they were caught in a downpour.

"Marguerite!" he shouted above the din of the waves, the wind, the thunder.

Her steps faltered and she turned, slowing when she saw him. A multitude of emotions crossed her face.

"Stop!" he said, his anger forgotten for the moment. "Marguerite, stop running! We've got to find cover!"

He caught up to her and took her arm, then headed toward the forest, which lay inland, beyond the beach. He could only hope they would remain safe and relatively dry among the trees. "Come on."

The wind tore at their cloaks and the rain hit hard as they ran through a rocky area sparsely covered with low shrubs. Quickly they made their way into the trees, following a path that was partially overgrown with vines and weeds. Holding Marguerite's hand, Bart led them deeper into the forest with the hope that he would spot a stand of close-growing trees that would provide some cover.

"Over here!" he said.

Lightning struck nearby, and Marguerite cried out in fear. Bart gripped her hand more firmly and kept going. What little light there was had dwindled with the onslaught of the storm, making it difficult to look for adequate shelter. Besides, Bart had not explored this territory in years, not since his travels to Scotland with King Edward.

A moment later, he tripped over something. He could not tell whether 'twas rocks or a log, but the shadows were deeper here, and they were sheltered from the wind. Another crack of lightning showed him that they stood beside a broken-down hut. He pushed on the door, knocking it off its hinges, and ushered Marguerite inside.

"What is this place?"

"I don't kn—" he began. Then he looked 'round. "It must be old Jakin's hut."

Only a small portion of the roof was intact, and two of the walls were caved in. Still, enough of the structure was left to protect them from the worst of the storm raging 'round them. Bart lifted the broken door and propped it against the rotting lintel, and hoped it would hold against the wind.

"Who is old Jakin?" Marguerite asked, shivering.

Bart opened his cloak and, without removing it, enclosed her within its warmth, bringing them into contact from shoulder to knee. "He was an old recluse. My father gave him leave to fish and trap small game down here."

"W-why would he not live in the village?" she asked, her teeth chattering, her body shuddering with cold.

He felt her hands go around his waist and knew she only intended to steady herself and glean some of his warmth.

"He was not quite right in his mind," Bart replied, vaguely remembering the odd old fellow, but much more preoccupied with Marguerite's proximity. He slid his arms 'round her and pulled her even closer. "The old man had no family, and as I recall, he used to mutter to himself all the time, and shout strange things. No one wanted him near.''

"Mmm," was her reply. "'Tis sad."

"I suppose it might have been, except that he did not care for anyone's company, either."

Bart inhaled deeply and smelled the rain in her hair. Somehow, he'd known she would find Jakin's tale a sad one. She possessed an unusual compassion.

Lightning struck nearby and with the thunder came an earsplitting crash.

Bart moved them into a more secure corner of the hut.

"What was that?" she whimpered.

"The lightning must have hit a tree nearby."

Arousal, hot and thick, struck him deeply, just like the broadside of a sword. When she sighed, 'twas as if all that had transpired in the last hour had led to this. He felt regret for his harsh words and wished he'd thought before speaking.

He pressed his lips to her forehead and moved his hands down her back. He could barely see her in the shadows of the hut, yet when she tipped her head, he could see an expression of doubt and wonder in her eyes. She trembled once, and made a tentative movement of her hands at his waist.

Bart grasped her hips and pressed her lower body to his own, suppressing a groan at the exquisite pleasure of their contact. He heard Marguerite's breath catch, and he lowered his head, his mouth seeking hers. Her soft, cool lips ignited him.

The walls shook as the storm raged around them, but Bart took no notice. Marguerite responded to his kiss with an intensity that rivaled any storm. She opened her mouth to his sensual probing and moaned softly, sliding her hands up his chest.

Her touch made him wild for her. Her taste bewitched him. Her scent inflamed him.

Bart leaned into her, rocking against her in a pale imitation of the act he desperately craved. Marguerite moved shyly at first, but soon her body cradled his, meeting his every move as if she felt the same reckless need.

He tore his mouth from hers and groaned, then searched the dark corners of the hut for a place where he might lay her down.

'Twas a shambles. Most of it was wet; all of it was filthy. There was no intact surface anywhere, and the floor was running mud.

"Marguerite," he whispered in agony.

She gave a soft cry as he spanned her waist and touched the undersides of her breasts with his thumbs.

"I would take you now," he said hoarsely.

The soft, feminine sound that came from the back of her throat made him shudder. He forced himself to maintain control, to release his hold on her and put a few inches of space between them.

"Yet this hovel is no place for a man to bed a woman."

Marguerite did not reply. She slipped out from the shelter of his cloak and covered her mouth with her fingertips. Bart turned away from her and looked out at the passing storm to keep himself from reaching for her again.

'Twas still raining, but the worst of the storm had passed them by. A murky, green-tinged light lit the forest outside, and Bart knew they would soon be able to leave.

"Tonight, my lady," he said, turning to face Marguerite again. "You will sup in your tower room. And I will join you afterward."

Chapter Twelve

The fire crackled and blazed in the tower room, and Rose had prepared a tub of very hot water. She left Marguerite alone to bathe.

With teeth still chattering from the cold, Marguerite lowered herself into the tub and slid down as far as the limited space would allow. In a few moments, the heated water began to warm her chilled bones. Her shivering stopped, only to be replaced by utter chaos in her heart.

She feared she was in love with Bartholomew Holton.

'Twas not just due to the effect of his kisses or the power of his touch upon her, though those were mighty persuasions. His honesty and integrity, and the compassion he did not even realize he possessed, were other factors. She admired his desire to do what was right for his siblings and for the people of Norwyck, while he still suffered the loss of his brother and the betrayal of his wife.

When he came to her chamber later—and she had no doubt that he would—she would not have the power to rebuff him. She was afraid she did not have the will to turn him away.

Whoever Alain might be, Marguerite was certain he was not her husband. It didn't feel right. She could not imagine why he'd been on board the ship with her…unless her dreams of him drowning when their ship went down were only just that—dreams….

Rose had left her supper tray upon a nearby table, but Marguerite had no appetite for food. Her stomach was aflutter, but only because Bartholomew would soon arrive. He'd made clear his intentions, and she had no desire to thwart him.

If anything, she wanted him as badly as he wanted her.

She lay her head upon her knees and let the heat of the water surround her. The interlude in the decrepit hut had showed her how powerless she was against Bartholomew, against her growing feelings for him.

The air in the tower room shifted subtly, and Marguerite knew the door had opened. Without looking, she knew the footsteps she heard were Bartholomew's.

She lifted her head as he crossed the room and came to her. He was dressed in a startlingly black tunic and hose. No ornamentation embellished his garb, and with his dark hair and eyes, he was as comely and alluring as ever.

"Have you eaten?" he asked.

She shook her head. "Nay, my lord." Her voice sounded strange to her ears.

He went to the supper tray and lifted the cover from a crock, letting a fragrant steam escape. But Marguerite's senses were entirely engaged by Bartholomew's masculine form. She had no interest in food when 'twas he who occupied her full attention.

He took the crock and a spoon and returned to her, crouching next to the tub. He ladled a spoonful and held it to her lips. She took the bite, puzzled by his unusual demeanor.

Again he ladled a bite of the soup and held it to her mouth. Marguerite sipped the savory liquid, watching as his dark eyes became ever more shadowed. A bit of the soup dribbled, and Bartholomew leaned forward and licked it from the corner of her mouth.

A shiver ran through her and she watched the powerful muscles of his neck convulse as he swallowed hard.

Without a word, he served her another spoonful, keeping his eyes on her lips, while Marguerite watched the muscles in his jaw flex and relax. She placed her hand over his and led it to her mouth, closing her eyes and sighing with the sheer pleasure of touching him.

She heard a rasping breath escape him.

"Marguerite, you cannot know what you do to me," he said huskily.

She looked up at him. "But I can, my lord," she said. "For you have the same effect on me."

He set the crock on the table and unfolded a linen drying cloth. "Stand," he said.

Marguerite hesitated. To be fully naked with him was forbidden, yet exciting. She looked up at him, as he held the cloth before him. The chamber was in shadows but for the fire on the hearth, and was now comfortably warm.

She stood.

"God's breath," he muttered, and Marguerite saw him shudder.

She stepped out of the tub and into his waiting arms. He wrapped her in the cloth, and when she tipped her head to one side, he kissed her neck, sending rivers of pleasure through her body.

Her arms were trapped at her sides by the cloth, and Bartholomew did naught to release her. Instead he touched his tongue to her skin where he had just kissed her. He moved his lips toward her ear, touching, tasting, caressing her sensitive skin. She felt his hot breath, heard his heated groan.

His hands began to move, stroking her bare shoulders and the sensitive skin at her nape. Slowly sliding downward, his fingers touched her through the cloth. Her nipples beaded and her head fell against his chest, and she wished her hands were free so that she could touch him, too.

"You are so soft," he whispered. "So enticing."

He rubbed her skin now, drying her with the cloth, then baring her body an inch at a time. Soon her arms were free, and the cloth was loosely draped about her hips. She ran her hands up the lush velvet of his tunic and untied the laces that held it together.

Marguerite did not know if she had ever seen a man's naked chest before, but she was certain that none could rival Bartholomew's. A dark mat of silky hair swirled across it, nearly hiding the brown disks that pebbled with her touch. Marguerite pressed her lips to his breastbone, then moved across the broad expanse to touch her tongue to each of his nipples.

He groaned and grabbed the hem of the tunic, yanking it over his head. His body seemed even larger now, unclothed. The planes of his chest were well defined, sculpted from solid muscle. His shoulders were broad and his arms brawny. Marguerite could not deny herself the pleasure of touching him as intimately as he had touched her.

She traced the firm contours of his arms, then ran her fingers down the rippled surface of his abdomen, aware that he held his breath as she did so. 'Twas a heady thing to have such a powerful effect on him, and Marguerite intended to take full advantage.

She lowered her mouth to him again, pressing hot kisses along a line from the center of his chest to his navel.

''Sweet heaven,'' he rasped. He took hold of her arms and pulled her up. His mouth came down hard upon hers and his tongue forced its way between her lips.

Entirely compliant, Marguerite raised herself onto her toes and met his kiss, welcoming the invasion of his tongue and pressing her breasts into his chest. Her senses could not have been more filled with him.

Moving quickly, he surprised her by lifting her into his arms. He carried her to the bed and set her on her feet beside it, letting the drying cloth fall to the floor. Removing the combs from her hair, he pressed kisses to her jaw below her ear. ''You were made for a man's pleasure, Marguerite.''

She was fully naked now, but the heat from his body warmed her. She pressed her fingertips into his lower back, tugging him closer, not for warmth, but for the exquisite sensations caused by his hard flesh against her breasts.

If *she* were made for a man's pleasure, then certainly *he* had been made for a woman's, though she would never say such a thing aloud.

He spread her hair out over her shoulders and touched his lips to hers once again. ''Kiss me,'' he said.

Marguerite took the lead this time, teasing him with

her tongue, nipping his lips, feathering her fingers across the bare skin of his back. She felt him work at his belt, loosening his hose and braes, pushing them down his legs.

He eased her onto the bed, lowering himself over her, twining his legs with hers.

"Open for me," he whispered, pressing kisses to her throat, then to each breast, and on the wildly sensitive skin of her belly. He grasped her hands, raised his head and looked at her then, spearing her with the sensual promise of his gaze.

Marguerite could not imagine sharing this intimacy with any other man. Not with Alain, or anyone but Bartholomew. He alone had the power to entice her, tantalize her.

He dipped his head again and Marguerite's breath caught in her throat. If she'd been warm before, she was burning now. Pleasure flared with his touch, and every muscle fiber in her body tightened exquisitely. She rocked against him, desperate to ease the savage hunger that drove every move.

Intense waves of pleasure shuddered through her, shattering the tension, making her cry out with abandon.

Bartholomew moved quickly, and before Marguerite's cries turned to whimpers, he covered her with his body and positioned himself at the most intimate part of her. He took possession of her mouth, and in one beguiling stroke, sheathed himself within her.

Holding himself still for a moment, he searched her eyes, clearly astonished by the barrier he'd breached.

Marguerite was stunned by the force of emotions that struck her. She could not speak, but tipped her hips slightly, increasing the strangely pleasurable pressure within. Bartholomew made a low sound in his throat and began to move again, withdrawing only to plunge again.

Tension built as he quickened the rhythm, and Marguerite felt close to shattering again. She could not tear her eyes from his as she wrapped her legs around his hips and forced an even greater contact between them.

Suddenly, she squeezed her eyes closed as the powerful sensations overtook her again. Bartholomew's body contracted once, then again, and he gave a guttural cry of release.

For several long moments, they remained still, as their breathing returned to normal, their hearts slowed. Then Bartholomew raised himself up on his arms and hovered over her.

Marguerite's heart swelled with love. Their physical joining could not have touched her more deeply. Somehow, he'd slipped as easily into her soul as he had her body. She touched his face with her fingers, tentatively drawing a line from his cheek to his mouth.

Bartholomew kissed her palm and Marguerite thought her heart would stop.

She could not imagine loving anyone more. No matter what she eventually remembered of her past, she would never leave Norwyck. She could not bear to be separated from Bartholomew.

She gave a last shudder of delight as he withdrew from her and lay by her side, pulling her with him. He said naught, but his eyes held an expression that Marguerite had never seen before. It was intense, luminous.

Savoring the moment in silence, she tucked her head under his chin and slid her foot along his leg.

His body jerked with the stimulation, and he drew her close so that she could not repeat the action.

Her heart swelled with the knowledge that he would have no reason to mistrust her now. No two people could share such passion and still lie to one another. He would surely know if she tried to deceive him.

"You might have mentioned your virginal state."

Marguerite's heart lodged in her throat and her breath left her. He *still* believed she knew more than she'd told him. His opinion of her had not changed in the least.

Bart felt her go still. He knew his mean remark demonstrated a continued lack of trust, but he was not about to believe in Marguerite's honesty merely because she'd sacrificed her virginity to him. His own wife had done the very same thing with the consummation of their marriage—and all the while, her heart had been engaged by Dùghlas Armstrong.

Yet Marguerite had been truly innocent in her lovemaking. Her response to his touch bore no resemblance to the way Felicia had reacted.

Marguerite pushed herself out of his embrace and sat up, holding the linen sheeting over her nakedness. She reached down to the floor, picked up the drying cloth and pulled it around herself as she left the bed.

"You…" Her voice trembled, and he watched as the muscles in her throat contorted in a hard swallow. "I…realize that you were most grievously betrayed, my lord," she said, staring with moist eyes at a place somewhere beyond Bart's shoulder.

She clutched the damp linen to her, unaware that it only covered her breasts. Her body remained mostly exposed, and she dabbed absently at a trickle of moisture that ran down her leg. The linen was stained red when she took it away, but she did not notice.

Bart felt as if he'd been kicked. Or worse, as if he'd kicked her.

"Upon my soul, I have not come here to betray you, or…" Her face seemed to crumple like a discarded piece of parchment, and one tear ran down her cheek. "Or bring any h-harm to Norwyck…"

Some foolish and naive part of him demanded he believe in her. His rational side refused to be deceived again. He swung his legs over the edge of the bed and stood. "Marguerite," he said. "What differences we have need not interfere with…*this*."

A crease appeared between Marguerite's brows.

Using two fingers, he lifted her chin and looked into her wary eyes. "You enjoy my touch," he said, letting his hand drift down to her throat. "As I enjoy yours." He lifted one of her hands and placed it upon his chest, suppressing a shudder when she whimpered.

He tipped his head down and brushed her mouth with his own. Hearing her sharp intake of breath, he gave her a soft kiss that became increasingly more demanding. He wanted her desperately. Even though he'd spent himself just moments ago, he needed her again. He pierced the seam of her lips with his tongue and felt her welcome him into the hot gloss of her mouth.

His arms went 'round her waist and he pulled her against his naked body, his arousal cradled by her feminine softness.

"I want you, Marguerite," he murmured, guiding her back to the bed. "You are mine."

Chapter Thirteen

A large, florid face with pale blue eyes scowled at her. The man's pate was nearly bald, though a few strands of greasy red hair stood on end upon it. Tiny red veins tracked his bulbous nose. "Ye'll hie yer arse to Scotland as yer da ordered ye—"

"*Non!*"

"Aye, Mairi Armstrong," the man bellowed. He raised one beefy hand and slapped her. "Ye will. And ye'll be wedded and bedded the day after ye arrive. *To me!*"

Marguerite cried out and sat up in her bed, confused and appalled.

She was fully nude and damp with perspiration. Her heart thudded within her chest and her breathing was labored. Swallowing a lump of dread, she turned and saw that she was alone in the bed. Bartholomew was gone.

She recognized the man in her dream. He was Carmag MacEwen. *Her betrothed.*

Marguerite—no, she was *Mairi*—buried her face in her hands as the memories returned. Carmag had come to her in France months before, to the home of Caitir and her husband, Alain. Carmag had intended to escort Mairi to Scotland for their wedding. At the time, Alain had managed to put him off, but only temporarily.

With dread and despair in her heart, she had eventually set out from the home she shared with her cousin, Caitir, and boarded a ship bound for Scotland, the land she had not seen in years. Alain had accompanied her.

Alain! Caitir's beloved husband had drowned.

Mairi's eyes filled with tears. Nausea assailed her. Alain was dead, Caitir widowed. And their children were fatherless now. All because he'd sailed to Scotland with her and been caught in a storm.

Regret raged through her. If only she'd gone with Carmag when he'd first come for her, then Alain would not have had to escort her to her father's stronghold in Scotland. He would still be at home with his wife and children in their sunny little cottage, rather than lying at the bottom of the sea.

Mairi wiped the moisture from her eyes and dragged herself from the bed. She felt different—nay, not just different, but drastically changed—not only because of the memories that flooded her mind now, but by the intense lovemaking she'd shared with Bartholomew all through the night. What she felt for him was beyond description, though it could not have been clearer that he did not share her feelings.

To Bartholomew, Mairi was merely a receptacle for his lust.

She dropped down next to the trunk that held her borrowed clothes. She had no choice but to go to her father immediately—to his stronghold, Braemar Keep. She would have to face Lachann, and her brother, Dùghlas, knowing that her kin had used the lowest, vilest means possible to wage war against their enemy, Bartholomew Holton.

She would be forced to wed Carmag MacEwen, her father's most powerful ally, that rude and crass warrior who made her stomach turn at the mere thought of his touch.

Mairi covered her mouth with trembling fingers and fought tears. What would Bartholomew do when he learned the truth of her identity? He would believe the worst, of course—that all along, she'd known she was Lachann Armstrong's daughter, washed up on Norwyck's shore. He would think she'd somehow used the shipwreck and her strange recovery against him.

There was naught she could say that would convince him otherwise.

Mayhap 'twould be best if she said nothing about her recovered memory.

She pulled a clean chemise over her head and arms, and reached down into the trunk for a pair of woolen hose. Her hand bumped something odd, and she pulled out the sock that held the forgotten cache of jewels. Resting back on her heels, she let out a tremulous breath. She had to get this treasure back to Bartholomew before he discovered it missing. He would be only too willing to believe she was a thief once he learned she was the Armstrong's daughter.

Do not tell him, a faint voice in the back of her mind advised.

In near despair, Mairi leaned her head against the edge of the trunk. *Could* she avoid telling him? Could she remain at Norwyck as Lady Marguerite?

Alain was dead. And her stubbornness was to blame. She should have died alongside Alain, but by some grim miracle, she had survived.

Would Lachann have any reason to think she had survived the shipwreck? Nay, he would not. There was little or no communication between Norwyck and the Armstrongs—besides the occasional raid—and Mairi doubted any gossip was exchanged then.

And Carmag MacEwen… Mairi would rather die than wed the brute. If she stayed on at Norwyck, then—

The tower door was thrown open and Eleanor's bright red head popped in. "Have you been *sleeping* all this time?" she exclaimed. "I've been waiting *hours* for you!"

Mairi pulled the jewel-laden sock from the trunk and lifted it up for Eleanor to see, but the child ignored it and came to her side. "Bartie said you were not feeling well last night and we were to leave you alone," she said. "What ails you, Lady Marguerite? Your eyes look strange."

"There is naught wrong with me, Eleanor," Mairi said, brushing one hand over her eyes. "Do you see this?"

"Aye," Eleanor replied, taking the sock from her. "The Norwyck jewels."

"We must return this to your brother's chamber," she said. "This morn, and no later."

"The morn is nearly gone," Eleanor replied. "You slept so very long, and I want to go and play in the village, but Nurse Ada said I could not!"

"Mayhap later, Eleanor," Mairi said. She took a gown from the trunk and stood. "Take this sock to Bartholomew's chamber and put the jewels back where you found them. I will meet you in the great hall after I've finished dressing."

"But—"

"Do as I say, Eleanor," she said, more harshly than she intended.

The child stuck out her lower lip, but Mairi ignored it. She walked to the wash basin and poured fresh water into it. By the time she'd soaked a cloth, Eleanor had gone.

"Oh!" Little Eleanor was startled by Bart's presence in his study, and her face flushed as red as her hair. She carried a bundle hidden in her skirts, but nearly dropped it.

"Oh?" he asked, coming 'round the desk to grab her before she could turn and run away. The rule of no children in the lord's study was not a new one. Ellie knew she was trespassing.

Bart wanted to know why.

"What have you there?" he asked, indicating her awkward hold upon her skirts.

"I...n-naught, Bartie!"

She tried to turn and run, but Bart held her fast. In her struggle, a load of trinkets fell from her skirt.

"What's this?" he asked, frowning. He knelt to see what had dropped and was shocked to note that the jewels from the locked cabinet in his chamber were now scattered about upon the floor. "Eleanor!"

Tears fell down the girl's face as she chewed her lip and wrung her hands. "I—I was just coming to get the key from your drawer...."

The little minx knew where he'd hidden the key?

"To what purpose?" he asked.

She began to weep in earnest now. "T-to put the jewels b-back where I f-found them."

He refused to be moved by her tears. "And why did you remove them to begin with?"

"I gave them to Lady Marguerite," she cried, using her tears to great effect.

"What?"

She nodded, and it took a moment for her to speak. "I gave them to her because I wanted her to stay at Norwyck. I thought if I gave her—"

"You gave her the Norwyck jewels in order to convince her to stay?"

Eleanor's wailing increased as she tipped her head in assent. Bart ignored her for the moment, picking up every precious piece that had been dropped. He gathered all the jewelry—the bracelets, brooches and necklaces that had been worn by every lady of Norwyck for centuries—and locked them in his book cabinet until he decided upon a safer place.

"Aye," she cried, "but Lady Marguerite made me bring them back—"

"Enough, Eleanor," he said. He cracked his knuckles and turned to face her. "You will go to the nursery and stay there until I say you may come out."

"But, Bartie—"

"No arguments, Eleanor," he interjected. "You behaved very foolishly, and this time, you will suffer the consequences."

"But I—"

"You need to learn some sense, my young lady," he said, "and you will be doing so in the nursery for the foreseeable future. Go."

"But—"

"And be grateful I do not insist upon bread and water for the duration."

He watched her turn and run from the study, nearly knocking over Sir Walter as she went. The old knight raised one eyebrow, but walked into the study and began speaking in a grave tone, leaving Bart no time to consider what Eleanor had done.

And how Marguerite had responded.

Bart had had a spectacular morning already, and was prepared to work with his men all afternoon, too. But tonight…he had plans that included the most sensual, most responsive woman he'd ever known.

He was sweat-covered and grimy from his exertions on the training field. He unbuckled his sword belt and dropped it upon the desk.

"I've finished my investigation into the accident, my lord," Walter said. "Thom Darcet had the men mixing too much water into the mortar. It weakened the wall, and that is the reason for its collapse."

Rubbing the back of his neck, Bart paced a path to the window of his study and back. The very last thing he wanted to be thinking of was the disaster at the wall, while beautiful Marguerite lay naked and sated in the tower bed they'd shared. "Are you certain?"

Walter nodded. "Reeve Edwin Gayte was ill for a few days before the accident," he said. "And Darcet was in charge. I questioned the men who were laying stone. They all said the mortar was too watery…."

"Why did they not go 'round Darcet? Surely the man did not watch them every minute."

"They, er, did what they could while Darcet was not present, my lord."

Bart would have to dismiss the bailiff. He did not see that he had any choice. The man had made many errors over the years, but this was the worst yet.

"You are entirely justified in giving him the sack, my lord," Sir Walter said. "His harsh methods have done the Norwyck lords no good over the years."

"But my father kept him on—"

"Aye, but when your stepmother became ill, he left matters too much in Darcet's hands. He was warned many times to take care."

Bartholomew blew a breath out through pursed lips. 'Twould be a distasteful task, one he did not look forward to.

"Shall I tell him, my lord?"

"Nay," Bart said, sitting down in a large chair near the desk. He would not pass this unpleasant duty to Walter. "Send someone for him, and I'll deal with him today, now."

"Very good, my lord," Walter said as he turned to leave. "By the way…Lady Marguerite… How does she fare after being caught in the storm?"

Bart looked into the man's canny eyes. "Very well."

"I beg your pardon for speaking out of turn, my lord, but I hope you recognize that this lady has naught in common with your late wife…." Sir Walter said.

"'Tis not your concern, Sir Walter," Bartholomew replied sharply.

"I realize that, my lord," he replied. "But as a man who has cared for and cherished your family for two generations, I wish to point out that Lady Marguerite has given you no reason to mistrust her. She has been honest and—"

"And Felicia was not?" Bart asked caustically. "You saw through her duplicity from the first?"

"Nay, my lord," Walter said quietly. "I will not say that I did. But I did not trust her when first she came to Norwyck. And I *knew* she was hiding something during those months before you returned home."

Bart stood up abruptly and went to the window. He

clasped his hands behind his back. "Ah, well. Hind-sight is a wonderful thing."

"Aye. 'Tis."

When Bart heard the door close, he turned around and let out the breath he was holding. 'Twas clear Sir Walter knew and did not approve of his liaison with Marguerite, though why the man should care was beyond Bart. 'Twas not as if he intended ever to marry again, and Walter knew it.

Henry would be the next earl of Norwyck, for Bart had had enough of marriage to last a lifetime.

Still, 'twas intriguing to consider Marguerite's reason for returning the gems. Why had she not kept them? Likely because she was after a bigger prize than a mere handful of jewels.

Mairi stepped into the great hall just as Sir Walter rounded the corner.

"Ah, my lady," he said as he approached her. He gave a slight bow. "I trust you are well after your soaking yester-even."

Mairi nodded. The knight's eyes were kind, but shrewd. Would he be able to see through her lies this morn? Would he somehow know that she'd remembered everything? Would he be able to detect her sorrow? "Aye, Sir Walter. Have you heard aught of the injured men—Master Alrick and the others?" she asked, hoping her question would divert Sir Walter's attention from her.

"Naught has changed," he replied, giving her a short bow.

Ah, but all had changed, Mairi thought. However, she nodded and watched him take his leave.

Alain was dead.

She was Lachann Armstrong's daughter.

And she would have to wed Carmag MacEwen if her father ever found her.

She closed her eyes and braced herself against the grief that threatened to swallow her whenever she thought of Alain. She could not show her pain, or surely someone would notice. Nay, she had to continue as before, as if naught had changed.

She looked around the hall. Eleanor was not in sight, and Mairi wondered what mischief the child had gotten into now. She wandered past the fireplace and into the corridor beyond, looking for her. 'Twas possible she'd come to Bartholomew's study.

She opened the door and called, "Eleanor?" There were so many nooks in here for a child to hide, and Eleanor had been piqued enough when she left the tower room, 'twas entirely possible she would want to give Mairi some trouble. But 'twas Bartholomew whose head emerged from behind one of the large chairs by the fireplace.

He rose swiftly to his feet and came toward her.

Mairi's throat went dry at the sight of him. He wore a plain linen shirt, belted at the waist. A fine sheen of sweat coated his features, and there were flecks of mud on his clothes. He looked broad and powerful as he moved, and he bore an expression she did not understand.

Without speaking, he slipped an arm around her waist and lifted her slightly, meeting her mouth with his own.

He kissed her hungrily, as if they had not just spent most of the night intimately entwined. Lips, teeth and tongue possessed her, teased and tantalized her. His scent enveloped her. His arms overpowered her.

When his mouth finally slid from hers, only to rain kisses down her jaw and neck, Mairi said breathlessly, "My lord, this is unseemly! I—"

"I want you, Marguerite," he growled. "Anywhere. Anytime," he said as he loosened his hold upon her. "But I will yield to you...for now."

"Thank you, my—"

"But only after another taste," he said, dipping his head to kiss her again.

A noise from behind startled Mairi and she jumped away from Bartholomew, embarrassed to be found in his arms.

The man who had stepped forward cleared his throat. "My lord, you wished to see me?"

"Aye, Darcet," Bart said, letting go of her arm. "Come in."

With eyes downcast, Mairi slipped out of the chamber. Flustered, she returned to the hall to look for Eleanor, but the child was not in sight. Mairi wandered into the kitchen and to the pantry, but none of the servants had seen her, either.

"Mayhap you will find her in the solar with her sister," one of the maids said.

Mairi hoped that would be true. Returning to the great hall, she ran into Henry and John, just returning from the practice field.

"My lady!" John called, while Henry merely gave a curt bow. "Are you all right? We wondered last night—"

"Aye, I'm fine," she said with a quick nod, and considered what else they wondered about last night. "Thank you for asking, John."

"Bart told us you'd taken a chill—"

"Nay, John, I am fine," she said. "Just looking for Eleanor."

"That little pest is likely into something she shouldn't be," Henry said.

"I'm afraid you might be right, Henry."

"Would you like me to help you look for her?" John asked.

"I would not want to trouble you."

"'Tis no trouble, is it, Hal?" John said with enthusiasm.

"Mayhap not for you, Brother," Henry replied. "But I have other plans."

"Very well, my lady," John said, looking askance at his twin, "just the two of us, then."

Henry headed for the stairs, and Mairi and John followed close behind.

"Is that music?" John asked.

Mairi listened. To be sure, music emanated from the far end of the gallery. It sounded like the gittern, and the chords Mairi had taught Kathryn. Mayhap Eleanor was there.

They opened the door and walked inside, startling Kathryn. She quickly set aside the gittern, clearly unhappy to have been caught playing it.

"I—I—"

"Kate, d'you know where Eleanor is?" John asked.

"Nay," she said with a frown, "though mayhap she's in the nursery. I have not seen her since we broke fast."

"I shall run across to the nursery and check on her," John said. "If she is there, do you want me to send her to you?"

"Nay, John," Mairi replied as he turned to leave. "Unless she is into some mischief."

"I will see." The next moment, he was gone.

Mairi did not understand Kathryn's uneasiness at having been discovered playing her mother's gittern. 'Twas almost as if the child believed she'd been caught at something forbidden.

Yet music should never be forbidden, Mairi thought. She knew now that music was as much a part of her as her own limbs. She had learned to play the psaltery when she was no older than Eleanor, and now played most stringed instruments well, although the lute was her favorite.

Mayhap Kathryn's reaction to being discovered was because she felt she was somehow neglecting her "duties," which she took very seriously. "Your music sounds lovely," Mairi said in an attempt to put the girl at ease. "Would you like me to show you some more?"

Kate seemed unsure whether to run away or remain in the chapel. "Nay," she said. "I must go to the kitchen and see that—"

"I was just in the kitchen, Kathryn," Mairi said, picking up the gittern and sitting on the settle, "and Cook has everything in order. Why don't you take a little time here with me?"

Kathryn's lips thinned in annoyance as she looked down at Mairi.

Mairi ignored her. "Which instrument did your mother prefer? The psaltery or the gittern?" she asked as she strummed the instrument that rested upon her lap.

"The gittern."

"Ah, *that* seems to be your instrument as well!" Mairi said. "You have become very proficient in quite a short time."

Kathryn's expression softened slightly.

"There are many more chords and notes." Mairi patted the cushioned seat beside her. "Sit here, and I'll show you."

Kathryn seemed unable to keep herself from the promised lesson, and, still keeping her silence, she sat down.

Mairi handed the gittern to her and did not hesitate to show her more notes and chords. She helped Kathryn to position her fingers upon the neck of the instrument and to pluck the strings singly to add depth to the music.

"You have a natural musical ability, Kathryn," Mairi said, grateful to have something besides her own troubles to occupy her thoughts. "Your talent would have pleased your mother, I think."

Kathryn's lips pressed together tightly.

"Once you've mastered the gittern," Mairi said, "we should try the psaltery."

Kathryn started to put the instrument aside. "Nay, Lady Marguerite, I haven't the time for this—"

"Surely you could make time?"

Kathryn seemed torn between anger and yearning. She stood suddenly, leaving the gittern on the settle. "You speak to me of my mother, yet you never knew her," she said as anger won out. "How could you possibly know what would have pleased her?"

"I know th—"

"My mother was far more beautiful and had much more music in her than you will ever have!"

"Certainly that is tr—"

"And I have work to do here in the keep," she said, "things Bartholomew trusts me to take care of…."

Her chin quivered and her hands worked at the folds of her kirtle.

"Of course, Kathryn," Mairi said quietly. "Your brother knows and appreciates how much you do."

But Kathryn's expression was shuttered and mistrustful. Mairi put one hand on the child's sleeve, but Kate shook it off and ran from the solar, leaving Mairi staring after her.

Very little was right with the world. Sad and discouraged, Mairi sat down again and folded her hands in her lap. She uttered a silent prayer for Kathryn, a troubled child who clearly suffered still from the recent events that had torn her family apart. Mairi blinked back tears as she prayed for Alain, whose loss would be devastating to Caitir and her children.

And she prayed for herself, that God would understand and forgive her continued deception.

The solar door opened and Bartholomew strode in. His face was drawn and angry.

Mairi composed herself quickly and stood. "My lord, what is it?"

A muscle worked in his jaw. "'Tis Alrick. I just received word that he died a short while ago."

Tears filled Mairi's eyes again, and the back of her throat burned. She covered her mouth with her fingertips.

Bartholomew clasped his hands behind his back and strode several paces away, while Mairi struggled to control her grief. Her emotions were so raw, now that she knew of Alain's fate.

"The accident at the wall was caused by my bailiff," Bartholomew said.

"How, my lord?" she asked with as steady a voice as she could manage. 'Twas one thing to show a bit of sorrow for a poor peasant who'd lost his life. 'Twas entirely unsuitable for a lady to grieve overmuch.

Bart turned back and walked toward Mairi. "With weak mortar. The fool thought he would save on supplies if he had the men add more water to it."

Mairi sniffed and brushed away her tears. "But surely he—"

"He was a fool. Sir Walter gave him clear instructions, but he took it upon himself not to follow them."

"I am sorry, my lord," she said, placing a hand upon his forearm. "I know it must be difficult for you."

His caring and compassion had been obvious from the first, but especially after the wall had collapsed and he'd done so much for the men who had fallen or been otherwise injured.

"This kind of loss is no more difficult for me than for any other nobleman," he said, crossing his arms over his chest. "I dislike losing any of my people to such an unnecessary—"

She raised herself up on her toes and lightly kissed his lips before he could say more. "You must tell Eleanor, my lord," she said, surprised by her own action. "Alrick was a favorite of hers, and she will be sorely distressed by the news."

"Aye," he said, taking her hand.

Chapter Fourteen

Bart noted the lines of sorrow on Marguerite's face and knew that she was much too tenderhearted. She should not be so affected by the death of a man she hardly knew.

Or had the loss of her innocence affected her so? Was that why she seemed so raw, so vulnerable? How could any man know what went through the minds of women?

She comforted Eleanor, who had been granted a reprieve from her punishment, and Bart was glad of her help. Now if only Marguerite could have some effect upon Kathryn. The girl had been stubborn and difficult ever since William's death, and Bart had not known what to do, other than allow her to play at being chatelaine like her mother before her.

He hoped she would grow tired of the game sometime before Henry married and brought a wife home to Norwyck.

Marguerite dined with the family that evening, and later played the psaltery while everyone gathered near her—all but Kathryn, who sat in a far corner, sewing.

And she was present only because Bart had prevailed upon her to join them.

Everyone but Kathryn and Henry sang with the music. Even the servants who cleared away the remains of the meal joined in as they worked.

Henry left his chair and came to crouch beside Bartholomew's side while Sir Walter looked on. "Did you send out the letters, Bart?" he asked.

"Aye, Henry," he replied with a sigh as the music continued. "We should know within a few weeks whose squire you'll be...though you could remain at Norwyck and be *my* squire."

Henry frowned. "Nay, Bart," he said. "That would never do. 'Tis best to go away from home to foster with a lord who is not kin. 'Tis what you and Will did."

Bart could not argue, though he did not like it. All the generations of Holtons had done it, just like every other noble family.

John made a jest that made Eleanor laugh, gave Kathryn a smile in spite of herself and momentarily softened the sad expression in Marguerite's eyes. For a moment, Bart was touched by tenderness for the woman and her strong compassion.

But he squelched it quickly. 'Twould not do to entertain more than a basic courtesy toward her. Not when her identity was still a mystery, and not until he understood her purpose in returning the valuable Norwyck jewels. He knew what treachery women were capable of, and he had not yet figured out Marguerite's.

She was his mistress—no more and no less.

When the hour grew late, Nurse Ada came to take Eleanor and Kathryn to bed. Bart noticed that Kathryn was not pleased with the arrangement, but said naught. She followed along just as she did every night, and when the boys dispersed, Marguerite was left alone in the hall with him.

She was nervous.

Bart suppressed a smile when she picked up the psaltery and started toward the staircase. He took the instrument from her and placed one hand at the small of her back, urging her up the stairs.

He had every intention of sharing her bed again tonight, and though the thought of forcing himself upon a woman was entirely abhorrent, he knew 'twould not be necessary. For each time he'd encountered her that day Marguerite had responded to his touch, his kiss, as if her hunger matched his own.

He followed her to the first landing, where he slipped his arm around her waist and pulled her so that her back was pressed against him. He splayed his fingers across her abdomen and nuzzled her neck.

Arousal hit him now with full force. 'Twas all he could do to keep from throwing her over his shoulder and carrying her to the nearest bed and ravishing her like some Norse barbarian. But he would not.

Setting the psaltery on the stone floor, Bart turned her in his arms, took her candle and placed it on a low table, then kissed her. She made a small sound that echoed his craving, and opened her lips to his moist caress.

A deep shudder wracked Bart and he pulled her body closer. He moved his head to change the angle of the kiss, and slipped his hand down her back to pull her against the strength of his arousal.

He gave silent thanks for whatever instinct made her move against him, torturing him, yet driving him to a level of need that he had never before thought possible. Without breaking the contact of their mouths, he backed her against the wall and continued his sensuous onslaught.

"Your chamber again, my sweet? Or mine?" he murmured, nipping at her ear.

Marguerite's breath caught on a sigh.

"So be it," Bart said. "Yours." He took her hand, picked up the candle and led the way up the stairs, cursing the distance as they went.

A loud crash stopped them before they reached the tower steps.

"What was that, my lord?" Marguerite asked.

"It came from the nursery." Still holding her hand, Bart turned and hurriedly walked to the children's room.

Eleanor stood in tears next to her bed, clinging to Nurse Ada, whose face was pinched and white. Kathryn stood with her arms crossed over her chest. A clay pot lay shattered in pieces on the floor. There was no doubt in Bart's mind that she had thrown it.

He only hoped she had not aimed it at her sister or the nurse.

"What's happened?" he asked, in a voice that was calmer than he felt.

Eleanor sniffled loudly, but the nurse kept silent.

"I threw it," Kathryn said defiantly. "I threw the pot at the wall and smashed it."

Bart stepped over the broken shards and went to Kathryn. Her face was covered in tears and her chin quivered, though she gave no other sign of weeping. "Why, Kate?" Bart asked gently. "What purpose did this serve?"

"I do not need a nurse, and I do not want to sleep in the nursery!" she cried.

"All right..." Bart said tentatively. He looked at Nurse Ada for some clue of how to proceed, but the woman's expression was one of shock and disdain. He glanced back at Marguerite, whose open, compassionate face gave him courage. "Where would you like to sleep?" he asked Kathryn.

"I'll have the chamber that Mama and Papa shared."

"I have no objection, Kate," he said, "but you must realize this is a wholly inappropriate—"

"You are not my papa, Bart," she thundered. "My papa is dead!"

Bart did not know what to do. The child was irrational, and clearly had no intention of listening to reason.

"Aye, Kate," a soft, feminine voice behind him said. "And you've taken care of your brothers and your sister just as your mama and papa would have wanted."

Marguerite stepped over the broken pot and gingerly approached Kathryn, whose protruding lower lip quivered.

"You have done it better than your mama could have imagined," Marguerite said quietly. "No family could have had better attention than what you provided, Kathryn, especially after William died. And Felicia."

Bart watch as Marguerite reached Kathryn and gathered her into her arms. Kate dissolved into tears then, weeping freely and loudly.

"I hate her!" she cried. "I hate her!"

"Aye, sweetheart," Marguerite said, rubbing Kathryn's back. Tears streamed from Marguerite's eyes, too, and again Bart felt entirely helpless. "'Tis awful to be so betrayed."

"She was my sister, my friend!" Kate wept, and finally Bart understood.

Young Kate had lost her mother nearly four years before. When Felicia had come to Norwyck soon thereafter, Kathryn had taken to her like a sad-eyed puppy. 'Twas no wonder Kate had been so difficult these last months. She had anxiously awaited the return of her elder brothers, and lived for the moment she would become an aunt. For Felicia to have violated her trust so profoundly...

Bart frowned and shook his head as he watched Marguerite comfort Kate. Would the damage Felicia had inflicted never end?

He stepped over to Eleanor and lifted her into his arms, then carried her out of the chamber, and motioned Nurse Ada to follow. He closed the door and left Marguerite alone to do as she would with Kathryn.

Kathryn's weeping had finally subsided, her tears had finally dried. She slept.

She lay on the bed in the nursery, with Mairi's arms around her. The girl so desperately needed someone to understand the pain she'd kept hidden for so long!

Mairi pulled a blanket over them against the chill of the room and closed her eyes. Mayhap 'twas her own pain that made her understand Kathryn's.

Somehow, she would have to get through the days knowing that her selfish delay in returning to Scotland had made it necessary for Alain to travel with her. If she had sailed months ago with Carmag MacEwen,

Alain would still be in France where he belonged, with his wife and children.

Yet if she had sailed last spring, she would not have been caught in the storm and would never have known Bartholomew Holton. She would already be wed to Carmag, mayhap even have grown big with his child.

Mairi shuddered.

Even if it meant she would never see Caitir again, Mairi knew she could not allow her father to learn of her presence here at Norwyck. For she knew how important 'twas to Lachann Armstrong that his daughter wed the MacEwen ally.

And Mairi knew she could never do that. The man was an abomination to her.

When Carmag had come for her, months before, he had managed to get her alone one afternoon. Mairi remembered her split lip, her blackened eye, and the bruises Carmag had left upon her thighs before Alain and his brother had managed to subdue the Scottish brute.

Alain had promised to let Lachann know of his horrible treatment of her, but Carmag had laughed at the Frenchman's naiveté. Lachann did not care whom his daughter wed, as long as the marriage sealed the Armstrong's powerful alliance.

Carmag, that savage oaf of a man, might do as he wished with his betrothed. With impunity.

Mairi shuddered again. She gently combed her fingers through Kathryn's fine, blond hair and held her as she would have one of Caitir's children. Many were the times when one or another of them had needed comforting, and they'd often come to Tante Mairi for it.

Bartholomew's sister needed a friend. She needed

patience and understanding, and Mairi was determined to be the one to give it. For she had all the time in the world.

She would remain here at Norwyck as Lady Marguerite, and would *never* let Lachann Armstrong know she was alive.

Chapter Fifteen

"Will you come with me to the village this morning, Kathryn?" Mairi asked.

Kathryn had been quiet and reserved all morning, and Mairi could not tell if the child was embarrassed by the incident of the night before, or if she had just reverted to her former, unfriendly demeanor.

"I'll come!" Eleanor cried.

"Hush, pest," Henry said as he lowered his cup to the table. "She didn't ask you."

"Of course you may come, Eleanor," Mairi said. "'Tis well and good for the ladies of the castle to visit the injured and spread the lord's largesse among the people."

"I'll come," Kathryn said.

"Good," Mairi replied. "Mayhap you will help me gather the goods that will be needed in village."

An hour later, Marguerite and the girls, and several heavily laden footmen, descended the steps of the keep. Sir Walter was at the base of the stairs.

"Good morn, my lovely ladies," he said with a bow. "What have we here?"

"Mostly food, Sir Walter," Eleanor said, hugging the older man's legs. "For the village!"

Walter patted Eleanor's red curls and looked up at Mairi. She thought she saw approval in his eyes, and suddenly felt self-conscious. She also felt like a liar.

"Ah, well, 'tis the right thing to do," he said. He gave them a wink and went past them, climbing the stairs.

They walked through the baileys and out the main castle gate, making their way toward the cottages of the injured men. Stopping at each home, they dropped off foodstuffs and visited for a short while. When they reached the cottage of Alrick Stickle, they stayed awhile, helping to sew the dead man's shroud.

Eventually, they reached Symon Michaelson's cottage. They found Anne still distraught and having difficulty coping. Symon was more awake than he'd been when Mairi had last seen him, though he was pale and sweating, and sometimes moaning with pain.

The two older boys were out near the wall, doing what they could to help pile the rocks that had fallen.

Eleanor went outside to play with two of Symon's daughters, while Kathryn remained in the cottage with Mairi and helped with the smaller children. With so many of the children gone, the cottage seemed much more spacious, and Mairi was pleased to see Kathryn pitch right in with the chores that needed to be done.

"Good morn to ye," Alice Hoget said as she pushed the cottage door open and strode in. "And how is Master Symon this fine day?"

The healer walked to the injured man's bedside and set her satchel down. She placed her hand upon Symon's forehead and gave a shake of her head. "'Tis fever ye've got, Symon, and I'm going to do what I can to bring it down.''

"Do what ye must," he rasped.

"Annie, I'll need hot water and a few clean cloths."

Given a specific task to do, Symon's wife stirred herself and did as she was instructed.

"M'lady," Alice said to Mairi, "why don't you and the young lass take the little ones out for a bit o' fresh air?"

Mairi thought that was a very good idea, so she and Kathryn put on their cloaks, bundled up the three youngest children and took them outside.

"Shall we walk to the wall?" Mairi asked as she took the two-year-old by the hand and held the infant up to her shoulder. Kathryn agreed, taking charge of the little boy who was slightly older than Mairi's two, and who needed chasing.

Kathryn had said naught about her outburst the night before, nor did she remark upon Mairi's support all through the night. Yet the girl was changed. There had been a softening in her.

"Lady Marguerite!" Eleanor called. "Where are you going?"

"For a walk to the wall," Mairi replied. "Do you want to come?"

"Nay! We're playing here. May I stay?"

"Aye," Mairi replied, taking note of a few mothers who were watching over the children. "But you'll find us at the wall if you want us."

She and Kathryn turned and followed the path toward the wall. They had not gone far when they heard the sound of horses behind them.

Bartholomew was at the head of a garrison of knights riding single file. His beautiful horse was covered in Norwyck's blue and white, and Bartholomew himself was fully garbed in mail, with his sword at his side.

He was tall and proud in the saddle, and as handsome as any man had the right to be, Mairi thought. His dark eyes flashed and he pulled to the side of the lane when he saw her, motioning for his men to go on.

He dismounted beside Mairi.

"Is aught a-amiss, my lord?" she asked, in spite of her unease. She had not seen him since she had succumbed to his lovemaking on the stair, and she did not know what to expect now. Would he take her in his arms and kiss her here, in front of his sister and the villagers?

Mairi was well aware that her behavior required no better of him. She had allowed him into her bed, and into her heart...and she was determined to perpetuate her lie.

Bartholomew shook his head, keeping his eyes upon hers. "Nay. 'Tis only a patrol. I merely take my turn with the rest."

Mairi felt a pang of disappointment at the thought that he would be away from her all day as well as the night. Though it shamed her, she could not deny that she had hoped he would come to her tonight. She hugged the bairn to her breast and suppressed her wicked desires.

"When are you coming back?" Kathryn asked.

Mairi felt his eyes upon her as he hesitated a moment before replying to his sister. "Mayhap tomorrow," he finally said. "Sir Walter will remain at the keep tonight, if you should need aught.... I'll send word of our location and when we'll return."

"Will you battle the Armstrongs?"

"I would not mind meeting up with Lachann or Dùghlas today," he said, "but no...I doubt there will be any battles tonight."

His dark eyes lit upon Mairi again and she felt the heat in her cheeks at his subtle meaning.

"Then why must you go?" Kathryn asked.

"Only to keep the Armstrongs off balance," he said. "And to prevent them feeling comfortable enough to make camp in our hills. We patrol every few days to protect our land, our village."

Mairi could not imagine her father and brother engaging Bartholomew and his men in battle. Though it had been many years since she'd seen her family, she did not remember them being particularly powerful, nor did she believe her father's fighters were especially numerous or skilled.

Something must have changed in these last ten years, or Bartholomew would not be building a wall to keep his village in safety. He would not be taking knights on patrol.

Carmag MacEwen had to be the reason. 'Twas the Armstrong alliance with MacEwen that gave her father the confidence he needed to attack Norwyck. Something Carmag had said months ago came back to her. The braggart had spoken of camps, or...what? Mairi could not recall exactly what he'd said.

'Twas frightening to think of her father becoming a powerful man. He had been a nasty, uncaring parent, and a cruel husband. Mairi remembered her mother, Teàrlag, pale and meek as a mouse, whose best act of defiance had been to get her only daughter out of Scotland and away from Lachann. Mairi had been no older than Kathryn at the time. She had been more than glad to leave Scotland, and had hoped never to see Lachann Armstrong again, though she'd missed her mother sorely for the first year or so.

She looked up to find Bartholomew's eyes upon her.

"You will look after my sisters while I am gone?" he asked quietly. His eyes spoke of more, but the words were best left unsaid for now.

"Aye, my lord," she said, her heart swelling with an emotion that promised only future pain. "Of course."

Bartholomew dallied no longer, but mounted Peg, kicked his heels into his horse's sides and rode off.

Mairi and Kathryn watched him as he disappeared beyond the wall and down the hillside. Mairi hoped the heat in her cheeks would be interpreted as a rosy blush from the chilly air, and not due to her exchange with Bartholomew.

They arrived at the wall and saw Symon's sons, who, along with several other boys and men, were knocking off mortar and stacking the rocks in a pile. "Do you think they'll be able to finish the wall?" Kathryn asked.

"I'm sure they will," Mairi replied. "I see no reason why they would not. And besides, 'tis a good idea. The village will be much better protected against the Scottish raids this way."

"Aye, that's what Bartholomew says," Kathryn said. "Though the animals will be left out to graze in—"

Mairi laughed. "You sound just like your sister," she said. "Eleanor recently told me of her concerns for the livestock."

"Well, 'tis true," Kathryn countered. "There must be a way to protect the sheep, or Norwyck will lose its wealth. When I am a wife, I must think of such things.''

''Aye,'' Mairi said, touching Kate's cheek. ''You are right. Your husband will rely upon you for good, sound advice. The man whom your brother chooses for you will be a lucky one.''

They walked a bit farther, and Kathryn said, ''Will Bart find *you* a husband if you do not remember who you are, Lady Marguerite?''

Mairi stumbled, but quickly recovered herself. She had not thought of much beyond keeping her presence at Norwyck from her father. The consequences of her intimacy with Bartholomew had not occurred to her.

And she preferred not to think of them now.

Bart rode to the head of the company and tried to shake thoughts of Marguerite out of his head. Images plagued him—of her with the infant cuddled to her breast, his head tucked under her chin, her lips caressing the fine down of his hair.

Bartholomew had spent the night painfully regretting that she had seen fit to remain with Kathryn. Though he knew Kate had needed whatever comfort Marguerite had been able to give, he could not be certain his own need had not been greater. He could practically taste her, feel the smooth softness of her skin under his hands, his mouth.

Somehow, he would get through another night without her, but when he returned to the castle, there would be no impediment to spending the night in sensual bliss with her in the tower room.

''My lord,'' said one of the knights, ''is this where we split up?''

Bart surveyed the land before him. 'Twas full of

dangerous dells and dales where the Scottish enemy could easily lie in wait. "Aye," he said. "Take twenty men and head west toward the dell. I'll take another twenty and go north. Gilbert, take the rest and go toward the coast."

"Aye, my lord."

"Even if you see no one, I want reports of anything unusual—fire rings, horses' tracks...."

The knights nodded and rode toward their men, each taking his own contingent and riding away. Bart continued northward, keeping his own eye out for any signs of Armstrong intruders.

The day was long and passed uneventfully, so 'twas necessary to work at keeping his thoughts centered upon the task at hand, and not on Marguerite or the memory of her walking with the child. That recollection gave him a strange, unwelcome sensation that he refused to examine too closely.

Instead, he found his thoughts turning to the single night they'd spent together, and his boundless passion for her. Her responses that night had exceeded any expectations he might have had, and he knew that the months ahead, in Marguerite's bed, would be more satisfying than any he'd known in his life.

He had been surprised to discover Marguerite and his sisters in the village, giving whatever comfort they could to Alrick's widow and the families of the other injured men. Her actions were exactly what his own mother and stepmother would have done.

Bart could not doubt that she was a lady of gentle birth, for such activity to come so naturally to her.

Yet to whom did she belong? She was no man's wife—of that he was certain. Was she a Frenchman's daughter, as she thought? Or the sister of an English nobleman? Mayhap she belonged to a Scottish family, but until her memory returned, he would have no answer.

He could enjoy her to the limits of his abilities. And he fully intended to do so.

"Halt!" he called. Dismounting, he threw Peg's reins to one of the men, then walked ahead, studying the ground. The tracks of horses' hooves were evident. Bart did not believe there had been many, mayhap half a dozen. But there was evidence of a recent fire, too.

He wondered what Armstrong's men had been up to, for they were the only ones who would have encroached upon Norwyck land on horseback. Bart glanced around the hilly terrain. He and his men weren't far from the Armstrong border, but there was a clear demarcation that had stood for centuries, separating the two estates. The horsemen who had come over to Norwyck land had to have known they were trespassing.

But to what purpose? There had not been a raid in recent days. What had these men hoped to accomplish?

Bart remounted Pegasus and led his men on patrol along the perimeter of his land. He had to consider whether this encroachment was cause enough to attack Armstrong's village. Until now, he'd refrained from any action other than defending his own demesne.

His method was not from cowardice, but from a desire to avoid any further warfare. He'd seen so much of death and destruction that he did not care to engage his men in any more battles unless absolutely necessary.

His defensive strategy was twofold. He would get the wall erected to deter Armstrong from attacking, and he would patrol his borders often enough to keep Lachann off balance.

The Scotsman would never know when 'twas safe to attack.

Chapter Sixteen

Servants spent the afternoon making Kathryn's new chamber ready for her, then Mairi and Eleanor helped to move her small items from the nursery. Dusk came, and they supped together with Henry, John and Sir Walter, but Bartholomew did not return.

When 'twas time for bed, Kathryn was reluctant to go to her chamber alone. Henry began to mock her for moving out of the nursery too soon, and John worked to suppress a knowing smile. But Mairi would not allow either brother to tease her. Kathryn had taken the responsibility of the entire castle upon her small shoulders and would need help easing it off again.

Giving the boys a quelling glance, Mairi said, "Why don't Eleanor and I see you to your room, Kathryn?"

Kate was clearly pleased by the suggestion, but her pride would not allow her to agree to it too readily.

"Please, Kate!" Eleanor said. "I want to see you in your new bed, and try out your new mattress."

"Mayhap I can be persuaded to tell you a tale while you make yourself ready for sleep."

"Oh yes!" Eleanor cried, and Kathryn agreed to Mairi's proposal in a much more demure manner.

They went first to the nursery and got Eleanor out of her clothes. Wrapping a blanket around the shift-clad girl against the chill in the corridor, Mairi walked with the two sisters to Kathryn's new chamber, wondering where Bartholomew's room might be. Surely 'twas nearby.

The fire in Kathryn's room burned low, so Mairi stoked it, making it flare while the girls climbed into the bed together. Mairi smiled and covered them with thick blankets, then sat on the edge of the bed.

"This is a tale that I—" Mairi realized that she could not mention that her mother had told this story to her when she was a child, so she began again. "Once there was a great gray seal that lived in the North Sea…." And as the Holton girls settled down for the night, Mairi told them a story she had told Caitir's children many times.

"…and so the lonely fisherman on the Isle of May found his true love, even though she was a Selky of the sea."

Eleanor's eyes were closed by the time Mairi said the final words of the story. Kate's eyelids were heavy, too, but she resisted closing them. "Eleanor is asleep," she whispered.

"So she is," Mairi replied. "Do you mind if she stays here with you?"

Kathryn shook her head. "We're accustomed to sharing a bed."

"If you're sure…"

Kathryn yawned. "'Twill be all right. For tonight."

Mairi smiled, stroked Kathryn's cheek and stood. "Good night to you, then."

"Good night," Kathryn said. She turned to her side and pulled the blanket over her shoulder.

Mairi left the chamber and discovered Sir Walter waiting outside. "My lady," he said. "I've come looking for you."

"Oh?" she said with a sinking heart. Now he would tell her that he'd discovered her lie, and intended to tell Bartholomew she was an Armstrong. His enemy.

Walter took her elbow and led her to the solar at the end of the gallery. When they stepped inside, he lit a candelabra that sat upon a table near the fireplace.

"Lord Norwyck sent word that he would not be returning to the castle this eve," the knight said. "He gave specific instructions that you were to be informed."

Mairi blushed, realizing how Bartholomew's message must seem to him, even though she felt relieved that her secret still seemed safe.

"Th-thank you, Sir Walter," she said. "I might have worried had I not heard."

"Aye," Walter replied absently, walking toward the fireplace. He took a piece of straw, lit it with the candle and put it to the wood on the hearth. In a moment, a fire blazed. He stood up and turned to face Mairi. "My lady…" he said. A deep crease formed between his brows. "The tale you told the children, the Selky on the Isle of May… Is that not a Scottish lay?"

Mairi swallowed, but her breath would not come. She was so entrenched in her lies that they threatened to choke her.

"Easy, lass," Sir Walter said, his expression easing. "'Tis not something I'll hold against you. But I'd appreciate it if you'd be frank with me."

Mairi dropped into a chair near the fire. She took a

deep breath and let it out slowly. "My memory returned, Sir Walter," she said. "Who I am, from whence I came…"

"And?"

"France," Mairi said. "I've lived with my cousin in France these past ten years. I was returning home to be wed when the storm came up and sank our ship…along with Alain," she said with a quavering voice, "my cousin's husband."

Sir Walter shook his head somberly. "'Tis a terrible thing. No wonder you've seemed so aggrieved. Why did you not tell us?"

Mairi hesitated. "I only just remembered yesterday morn. Everything. The storm, the drowning…"

"Who is your family, then?"

She looked up at Sir Walter with watery eyes and wondered what would happen if she told him. Would he send her away? Tell Bartholomew?

Or would he understand her abhorrence of Carmag MacEwen and the Armstrongs, and allow her to stay?

"I am Mairi Armstrong," she said. "Daughter of Lachann, sister of Dùghlas, betrothed of Carmag MacEwen."

Mairi's revelation left the old man speechless for a moment, red-faced and stunned. "Armstrong," he muttered then. *"MacEwen!"* he rasped, looking directly at her. "That onion-eyed maggot? You are to wed him?"

"Aye," she replied with a quavering voice. "My father decided he wanted an alliance with the MacEwen, and so he…offered…me for—"

"The man is a pestilence in and of himself," Walter said. "'Tis no wonder the Armstrong has become so bold. With an ally like MacEwen, he'll have no short-age of men or weaponry.''

Mairi kept silent, for she had no knowledge of war-fare. She only knew that she would say or do anything to convince Sir Walter to keep her secret.

''You are truly to wed the MacEwen?'' Walter said as he took a chair across from her.

She nodded, blinking back tears.

'''Tis no wonder you wished to keep your secret, lass. I cannot blame you for it. What will you do now?''

''I…I planned to do naught,'' she said, looking up at Walter with pleading eyes. ''Only to remain here at Norwyck as Lady Marguerite…''

''And what of Lord Norwyck?'' Walter asked. ''Will you tell him?''

Mairi shook her head. ''He can never know,'' she answered quietly, ''for his hatred of all Armstrongs runs deep. He doesn't trust me now, and if he ever learned who I really am, he would think the worst—that I—I intentionally set out to deceive him….''

Walter made a low sound of frustration and rubbed one hand across his mouth and chin. He stood up and paced to the other side of the solar while Mairi sat quietly, watching. *Everything* depended upon the old knight's decision here and now. Her whole future.

''I will never wed Carmag MacEwen,'' she said quietly, but vehemently. ''I will die before I ever be-come his wife.''

Walter nodded, and turned toward the window. ''You've put me in an awkward position,'' he said.

''I'm sorry. I should never have told you,'' Mairi murmured.

He gave a quick shake of his head and gazed outside

for a few moments, deep in thought, then he paced
back to the fireplace.

"There is much that you have done since your arrival here, my lady," he finally said, standing before
the fire. "You've taken Eleanor in hand, offered Kathryn some true comfort, given John confidence—aye,
the lad was sorely lacking until you gave him the attention he needed."

The knight turned and looked at her. "And Bartholomew?" he said. "You've turned the despair in
his eyes into something altogether new and different."

In a puff of disbelief, Mairi let out the breath she'd
been holding.

"Aye, 'tis true," Walter assured her. "Of late, I've
seen a glimmer of hope there."

"He'd as soon give me to the MacEwen as look at
me, once he knows who I am, Sir Walter," she said
without bitterness as she arose from her chair. She
stepped away, wringing her hands.

"I would not be so sure, lass," the white-haired
man said quietly.

"Oh, but I am, Sir Walter," she said. "If Lord Norwyck ever discovered that I'd deceived him, he would
cast me out. And be justified in so doing."

"My la—"

"I am no less a liar than Felicia was."

"There's a world of difference between the two of
you," Walter said, "and do not let me hear you com-
pare yourself to Felicia again."

Mairi bowed her head in capitulation.

"Your father will not break the betrothal upon your
request?"

"Nay, I've tried that," she replied. "'Tis Mac-

Ewen…or death. If not by my father's hand, then my own.''

Sir Walter let out a long breath. "I'll keep your confidence, Mairi Armstrong, for you have done much good here, and 'twould serve no purpose to expose you now. But be warned, there is naught that I wouldn't do for this family. And if it ever happens that you—''

"Sir Walter…" Mairi said. She held back tears of gratitude as she spoke. "You know that I've come to…to care deeply for the Holtons, don't you?''

"Aye," he said firmly. "Your feelings for Bart are in your eyes.''

Mairi cast her gaze toward the floor in embarrassment. "Sir Walter, if I thought my presence endangered anyone here, I would leave Norwyck upon the morrow.''

"Aye, lass," Walter said, wrapping an arm about her shoulders. "I know you would.''

"But I don't ever intend for my father to discover—" A soft noise nearby startled Mairi and made them both look up. "Mice," Walter said. "We'd best get a few cats from the castle yards in here to take care of them.''

Mairi closed her eyes, not so certain that the noise had been a mouse. What if it had been one of the girls?

Sir Walter put his hand upon Mairi's head, as he would a child. "You are weary, lass. Find your bed. And may God be with you.''

The morn brought with it a chilly wind. Mairi and the girls stayed indoors, playing music, playing finger games and sewing delicate linens for the chapel. Mairi did not know where Bartholomew's brothers were, ex-

cept that they had not gone outside the castle walls
with the patrol. 'Twas likely they were out on the practice field, as was their habit.

Kathryn's mood was somber, reminiscent of days
past, when she would not accept Mairi's help with the
gittern.

Mairi did not expect the child to be miraculously
transformed, but it was difficult to see her revert back
to stubbornness after they'd made such progress.

Eleanor was restless, as usual, but somehow managed to sit still for extended intervals while they
worked on the altar cloths.

Mairi worried about Bartholomew. Had Norwyck's
men been engaged in battle? Had he been injured?
When would he return?

There was no way to satisfy her desire for answers.
Time passed slowly, broken only by the noon meal.
At least John and Henry arrived with Sir Walter for
supper, and helped to dispel some of Mairi's worry.

"They found signs of camps in the hills," Henry
said.

"And one just north," John added, "along the
coast."

"But no Armstrongs," Sir Walter said, catching
Mairi's eye.

"Camps so close?" Kathryn asked. Worry darkened
her eyes.

"They're—" Henry began, but John interrupted.

"Nay, Kate," he reassured her. "They're a good
way off. There's no danger to the castle or the village."

"Why do they make camps?"

"We don't know," Henry said.

"We only just heard about them from one of Bart's men, who came in last night."

"Why didn't Bartie come home?" Eleanor said. That lower lip protruded in a manner that was becoming all too familiar to Mairi, though she felt the same. She wondered where Bartholomew was, and when he would return. "'Twas cold last night."

"Aye," Henry said with a grin. "'Twas."

"And why are you so glad of it?" Kate asked him harshly.

"'Tis what men do," Henry replied as he dug into his supper. "Ride all day, engage the enemy, sleep out of doors…" He stopped eating for a moment to sigh. "Is that not right, Sir Walter?"

The older man suppressed a smile. "Nearly, Hal."

"When do you leave for fostering?" Kathryn asked.

"I don't know, Kate," Henry said. "But soon, though. Bart sent out letters to all the lords of Northumberland."

"Don't worry, Kate," John said with a grin. "We'll soon be rid of him."

Henry playfully tossed a crust of bread at John's head, and the children all laughed and jested until the meal ended and they dispersed.

When 'twas bedtime, the boys and Walter disappeared, and Nurse Ada arrived in the solar to get Eleanor and take her to bed.

"Nay!" the girl protested. "I want to stay with Kate! Please let me go with her to her chamber!"

"Eleanor—"

"'Tis all right, Nurse," Kathryn said with a loud sigh. "I will let you come tonight, but that's all, Eleanor. You must go back to the nursery tomorrow."

Eleanor clapped her hands with joy. "Lady Marguerite, will you give us another tale tonight?"

Mairi nodded. "Aye," she said. But not another Scottish story. She would think of something entirely different to tell these girls.

"Does this arrangement suit you, my lady?" Nurse Ada asked Mairi.

"We'll muddle along tonight, Nurse. Thank you," Mairi said with a smile, and Ada left them. Mairi turned to the two sisters. "Shall we put away our needlework and get you ready for bed?"

Before long, Mairi was tucking the girls together into the big bed. The fire in the fireplace flared comfortably, and Mairi made herself a place upon the bed. "Have you ever heard the story of Pegasus?" she asked.

"Do you mean Bartie's horse?" Eleanor asked.

"Nay, I mean the first Pegasus," she said, "a mighty horse with wings."

The girls shook their heads, and Mairi began to tell of the Greek horse, a myth that had been told for many hundreds of years. And as she spoke of Pegasus and his rider, the hero Bellerophon, Mairi could think only of Bartholomew as he rode his huge warhorse through Norwyck's hills, and wonder when he would be home.

The girls soon fell asleep, and Mairi returned to the solar. No one was about, neither Bart's brothers nor Sir Walter. Would that she had told the Pegasus tale on the previous eve! Then she would not have put Walter in the position of having to lie to Bartholomew about her identity.

Mairi was restless. Too unsettled to sleep, she tried sewing for a while, but soon put her needle down and began to pace. Surely Bartholomew would return soon. Talk of Armstrong camps nearby worried her, and she tried to remember what that braggart, Carmag, had said about his forays into English territory.

Months ago, when Carmag had come for her in France, he'd boasted of his conquests against the English lords, and how he and Lachann had made themselves wealthy men with the livestock and goods taken from under their enemy's noses. Mairi dearly hoped that if the MacEwen laird had a camp in the hills, Bartholomew would not come across it. She wanted him back at Norwyck, healthy and without battle wounds.

'Twas frightening to think how much she'd grown to need him, how deeply she cared for him and his family, especially since she jeopardized all with her lies. She knew she had no choice for the truth would cause an even more dire state of affairs.

It began to rain, and Mairi watched as the cold drops hit the windowpanes with vicious force. Bartholomew and his men would need to take cover from this weather, mayhap making a camp of their own. In that case, they would not return tonight, and Mairi would be on edge all night long.

She forced herself to stop pacing, and sat down with Kathryn's gittern. She turned the pegs to tune it, then began to play, hoping the music would relax her. She shut out the sound of the pouring rain and tried to empty her mind of all thoughts of Bartholomew.

After strumming a few chords, she played a song that required all her concentration, an intricate piece she'd learned from a French minstrel who had visited her town several months before. She bent her head over the gittern and willed her fingers to move quickly and accurately over the strings, stopping and starting again every time she made a mistake. Which was often.

She could not get Bartholomew out of her thoughts. n Still, she worked at the music, even more persistently than before, until she could stand it no more. She left the gittern on the settle and arose, just as the door flew open.

Bartholomew!

Mairi gasped when he stepped into the room, kicking the door closed behind him. He opened the buckles of his hauberk and shed the heavy garment, letting it drop where he stood. His linen shirt was wet and dirty, as were his hair and face. He looked entirely disreputable and dangerous, and Mairi took a step back as he took one forward.

His eyes burned darkly, and they never left hers as he strode across the room. When he stood before her, practically pinning her against the wall, he lifted one hand and cupped her chin.

"I have thought of naught else but you," he rasped, his tone sounding angry to Mairi's ears. "While I traversed the hills looking for the enemy, I could see little but your face in my mind, feel your naked legs wrapped around me, weigh your heavy breasts in my hands."

He lowered his mouth to hers.

Chapter Seventeen

He brushed her mouth with his lips, barely restraining himself, afraid he would crush her with the intensity of his need.

He shouldn't care.

He'd come into the solar with every intention of laying her out before the fire and having his way with her. But when he'd seen the fear in her eyes, he had softened his intent. He wanted her willing, intrigued, excited by his touch. So he held back, and touched only her jaw with his hand, her mouth with his own.

And waited for some sign that she wanted him as profoundly as he wanted her.

Her breath caught and she opened her eyes. Suddenly, her arms were about his neck and she was kissing him fiercely, pressing her body against his soiled clothing, without a care for her own.

Bart did not think twice. He pulled her to him, cupping her head, thrusting his tongue through her lips. She met it readily, and the heat of her mouth made him ache for the heat he would find when he tore off her clothes and made himself one with her.

She lowered her hands. Pushing his tunic aside, she

slid her hands up the quivering flesh of his abdomen, his chest. Without breaking the kiss, she touched his nipples.

Bart heard himself utter a groan. He had to be inside her. Immediately.

Moving quickly, he whisked her into his arms and walked toward the fireplace, where the gittern lay upon the settle. Setting her down, he moved the instrument, threw his tunic off, loosened his laces, then moved to cover her body with his own.

She was trembling, but that did not keep him from shoving her skirts up, baring her legs. He hesitated then, but she slipped her hands around his neck and pulled his head down, taking his mouth in a searing kiss.

She made a small sound as her tongue engaged his, as if she had waited hours, *days* for this moment. A stunning intensity of emotion filled him suddenly, and he moved his head so that he could look at her.

Neither of them spoke. As her eyes searched his, he shifted his braes and entered her with one smooth thrust, squeezing his eyes closed with the pleasure of their joining.

When he began to move, Marguerite matched his rhythm. For as cold as he'd felt just moments ago, he was burning now, with a frenzy he'd never known before. His muscles quivered with tension and he reveled in the sensations her body brought to his. He took her lips again and kissed her fiercely, swallowing her cries of pleasure, pouring every bit of passion into her as he reached his own crest.

Shuddering, he lowered himself and gathered Marguerite in his arms, holding her until his heart stopped pounding and his breathing slowed. He had never known such emotion, nor felt so intimate with another person…not even his own wife.

'Twas dangerous thinking.

Still, his lack of control appalled him. He'd had no intention of ravishing Marguerite the moment he walked through the door. Yet he'd been unable to control himself once she'd shown her own eagerness.

Bart lifted himself onto his forearms and met Marguerite's eyes, unfocused and dazed as they were. It did not help that her reaction to their coupling was every bit as marked as his own. He did not want to feel any connection with her beyond what they shared in bed.

Her insinuation into his family, into his village, was incidental. She was no more interested in his brothers and sisters or in the condition of the villagers than Felicia had ever been.

He pushed himself off the settle. Silently, Marguerite sat up and rearranged her skirts. She did not glance up or meet his eyes, but Bart refused to allow her to remain unnerved. He reached down and took her hand, drawing her up to her feet. Without letting go, he kissed her soundly and squired her to the door.

"Come with me," he said in a low tone.

She made no reply, but went with him as he left the solar and walked through the gallery toward his bedchamber.

Mairi felt the heat flush her cheeks as she followed him out the door—the door that had been left unbarred. Anyone could have walked in on them while they were so intimately entwined.

She could hardly believe her actions. She'd nearly accosted him when he'd come through the door. Eventually, when he took a moment to reflect upon their interval together, he would no doubt be disgusted by her indecent behavior.

Mairi swallowed her embarrassment and let Bartholomew lead her to a chamber at the far end, beyond Kathryn's new room, and far from the nursery. She had made up her mind to be his leman, and intended to fulfill the role. After all, she planned to spend the rest of her days at Norwyck, hidden from Lachann Armstrong. She would not think of any consequences now, but would force herself to live within the moment.

They stepped inside and Mairi realized 'twas Bartholomew's bedchamber. A large bed was elevated upon a dais and draped with a heavy, rich red cloth. A fire burned on the hearth, and candles set upon several tables illuminated the room. A tub of steaming water had been placed in front of the fire.

He turned and faced her, lowering his head to nip playfully at her lips. "Will you serve me?" he asked between kisses.

Mairi knew he referred to the bath, and to the custom of the lady of the house serving, or bathing, the lord, but she could form no reply as he battered her senses with his lips, and his hands.

He slipped his chausses and braes down his long legs, taking his hose with them until he stood entirely naked before her. The sight took Mairi's breath away.

He was beautiful. Mairi made a conscious effort to calm her pounding heart as she viewed his broad chest with its small, beaded nipples, and his tightly muscled abdomen, and watched as he climbed into the bath and sat down.

The tub was barely large enough to contain him.

Mairi touched his shoulder and stepped behind him. She picked up the clean washing cloth that had been left nearby and, using the soap provided, began to wash Bartholomew's back.

He groaned and leaned forward, giving her greater access. She pushed his glossy, black hair aside and ran the cloth over his neck, sliding it around to the front to touch his throat. Entirely compliant now, he tipped his head back, giving Mairi complete control.

Bartholomew's body intrigued her. She could do naught but admire the taut flesh over hard muscles, and savor the differences between them.

Finally she dropped the cloth into the water and used her bare hands to wash him, touching him without reserve or embarrassment, until he grabbed her hands and stood, with the water pouring off him. He stepped out of the tub without regard to the puddle he caused, and took Mairi into his arms.

He kissed her hungrily, as though he had not just made love to her only moments before. Mairi responded eagerly.

"Nay...slowly this time," he whispered as he took her hand again and led her to the bed. He pulled down the blankets and turned back to her. "Allow me," he said.

Drawing out his sensual onslaught, he slowly ran his hands up her bodice, lingering over her breasts as he unlaced the ties that held it together. When 'twas open, he slid it down her arms slowly, touching his lips to her shoulders, then to her arms as he bared them.

Mairi closed her eyes and shivered with the pleasure of his touch. Her skirts fell to the floor, and as she stood before him wearing only a thin shift, he spoke. "So very beautiful…"

His words, more than his kisses, made her feel lovely and desired. He slipped her shift off her shoulders, and when she was fully naked, he lay her on the bed. "I would have you in daylight, in order to see you better."

"Oh, but—"

"There needn't be any secrets between us, Marguerite," he said, nuzzling her neck, cupping one breast.

She could not heed his words now, not while his lips were on a sure course toward her nipple, and he would soon suckle there, where she craved him.

"I thought today would never end," he whispered, looking into her eyes. Mairi had felt the same, but she was incapable of speech, or of thought, while Bart seduced her again. He made love to her slowly, carefully, touching every part of her, including her heart…her soul.

He took such care that Mairi could almost make herself believe she was more to him than a convenience, a mistress to be used…and discarded when he tired of her.

'Twas still dark when Bart awoke to sounds in his chamber. The fire had burned low, but he could see Marguerite nearby, hastily donning her clothes.

"What are you doing?" he asked.

"I must return to my own chamber, my lord," she said without stopping.

"Why?"

At this, she paused. "My lord, 'twould not do for your sisters to find me here."

"My sisters never come to my chamber," he said,

but then realized he was wrong. Eleanor had not only come in, but had taken the Norwyck jewels from a locked case here.

"The servants, then," Marguerite countered. "'Twould not do for Rose to find me gone from my own bed." She raised one hand to hold her hair back as she stepped into her shoes, and the motion gave her an aura of vulnerability. Bart did not care for it.

"'Tis not her concern, or anyone else's," he said harshly as he sat up and swung his legs over the side of the bed. He picked up a heavy robe from the back of a chair and slipped it on.

"Still," Marguerite said, "I must go. 'Tis unseemly... I mean, I should not..." Flustered, she bit her lower lip and tried to think of a better way to say she did not want to be found naked in his bed.

Bart almost felt the guilt that Walter had tried to heap upon him with regard to Marguerite. 'Twas likely she was a true lady of gentle birth, from a household in France. And he had defiled her.

"Come," he said, unwilling to consider the matter further. He picked up a candle, took her arm and stepped out of the chamber into the chilly gallery.

Quickly, they made their way to the stairs and the tower room, where Bart hurriedly relit the fire. Marguerite stood watching him, clearly misunderstanding his intentions.

"Get undressed," he said. "And climb into bed. I'll come and warm you as soon as this gets going."

"Nay, my lord!"

"Aye, my lady," he said, grinning at her discomfiture. "If you'll not spend the night in my bed, then I'll finish it here in yours."

"But my lor—"

"I'll be gone before any of the servants are about, Marguerite," he said as he fanned the flame. He did not tell her how loath he was to spend the rest of the night alone in his bed, probably because his need for her surprised him. He wanted her nearby not just for the release her body could provide, but for something more. Her mere presence, holding her close…that was enough.

Chapter Eighteen

In the weeks since Bart had made Marguerite his mistress, there was a growing sense of calm in the keep and the village itself. Men resumed working on the wall under Edwin Gayte's direction, and there were no further mishaps. Every man who was injured had recovered, except for Symon, whose leg was still in splints, and one other fellow, whose arm had been broken.

Norwyck's knights had turned up naught on their patrols, other than one vague sign after a heavy rain a few weeks past, of a man traveling on foot from the vicinity of Norwyck, toward Braemar Keep. Why any Englishman would go to Armstrong's stronghold was difficult to understand, but Bart kept that information stored in the recesses of his mind.

A tendency toward complacency had come over him recently, and he worried that sharing Marguerite's bed was making him lose his edge. So he worked his knights—and himself—tirelessly. They practiced without mercy on the field every morning with swords and quintain, and patrols went out every night. He would create such a Norwyck presence in the hills that Armstrong would never have the belly to attack.

Bart glanced up from his desk when the door to his study opened.

"Ah, this is a surprise," Sir Walter said. "You're sitting."

Bart let the remark go and lifted the sheet of parchment he'd been reading. "This is a missive from Bitterlee."

"For Henry?"

Bart nodded. "Aye. Lord Bitterlee has agreed to take Henry for fostering."

Walter clasped his hands behind his back and walked to the other side of the room. "'Tis time the boy left us," he said. "What about John?"

"John will stay. He'll be my squire."

Walter gave a slow nod, as if unsure that this was the correct course, but unwilling to say so.

"It only remains to determine when Hal should leave Norwyck," Bart said.

"Do you plan to escort him yourself?"

Bart jabbed his fingers through his hair. "I would like to, but I don—"

"All has been quiet for weeks," Walter said. "'Tis winter now. Armstrong has likely closed himself up by the fire in his keep and will remain there until spring."

Bart gave a shake of his head. "Do not believe that for one moment. Armstrong will attack as soon as he thinks I've relaxed our vigilance."

"And so you wait," Walter said. "Why not attack?"

"I have no wish to lose any more men than necessary," he said. "Once the wall is finished, we will be in a better position to defend the village and the castle. Fewer Norwyck men will be lost.''

"Aye," Walter said. "But 'tis not likely that you'll get Lachann or Dùghlas by waiting here for them."

"'Tis what I've decided, Walter," Bartholomew said. "At least until spring. Mayhap I'll have a different plan then. For now, I do not wish to make war upon the Scot."

"And what about Henry?" Walter asked. "Will you wait until spring to take him to Lord Bitterlee?"

"Mayhap," he said, frowning. "Though Hal is anxious to go."

"'Tis difficult to let him go," Walter said. "But the earl of Bitterlee is a good and fair man. He recently wed, did he not?"

"Aye."

"Something you should consider." There was a harsh edge to the old knight's voice, an edge Bartholomew had not heard since he was a lad.

Bart looked up sharply. "Nay. 'Tis something I'll never again consider."

"Lady Marguerite is a likely wife, my lord," Walter said.

"My decision has naught to do with her," Bart said.

"You would rather keep Lady Marguerite as your leman, your whore?" Walter taunted.

Bart stood so abruptly, his chair fell over.

"So we *do* have a new whore of Norwyck?" Walter added, intentionally sarcastic.

Bart's jaw clenched and a vein pulsed in his temple. He tightened his hands into fists.

"Never again, old man," Bart said in a quiet, but threatening tone. "Never again say such a thing about Lady Marguerite." He towered over the old knight, and could easily have bested the man, but had too much respect for his family's retainer.

Walter did not back down. "What else should we think, my lord? The servants…even your brothers are aware of your…your recent sleeping habits."

"You should think naught!" Bart barked. "'Tis none of your concern."

"As you wish, my lord," Sir Walter said as he went to the door. "Forgive me for pointing out what you should already know."

As Walter left the room, Bartholomew stood speechless. Then, turning around, he set his jaw defiantly and kicked the chair he'd knocked over. 'Twas no one's business what occurred between himself and Marguerite. *No one's*.

He picked up Bitterlee's letter again, but tossed the parchment back to the table without looking at it.

He would not wed again. It did not matter what Walter or anyone else said about his liaison with Marguerite. She would never become his wife.

In shock, Mairi turned on her heel and hurried away from Bartholomew's study. She had just raised her hand to knock on the door when she'd heard the voices. Of course, she was not meant to hear that interchange between Bart and Sir Walter, and she had been unable to hear it all. But she had heard enough.

She was the new whore of Norwyck.

With her heart in her throat, she pulled her shawl over her shoulders and went out the first door she saw. 'Twas cold, but Mairi did not feel it as she half ran across the bailey to the barren winter garden. She kept going until she reached the shed—the place where

Bartholomew had nearly seduced her once before, a lifetime ago.

Fumbling with the latch on the door, she managed to lift it, then pushed the door in and went inside, weeping openly now.

They were foolish tears, she knew. But it hurt none-theless, facing up to the fact that she was no more to Bartholomew than his kept whore. And that everyone at Norwyck knew it.

Whatever had been her purpose in going to Bar-tholomew's study, she could not remember it now. She gave herself up wholly to her sorrow and her regret that there was no alternative to her present course of action.

If she returned to Braemar Keep, she would soon find herself wed to Carmag MacEwen. If she told Bar-tholomew that she was Mairi Armstrong, 'twas likely he would use her as a hostage in exchange for Dùgh-las, perhaps. Bart hated her brother and would like naught more than to kill him and Lachann for their grievous wrongs against Norwyck.

Yet that would set off a war much worse than any of the border skirmishes Norwyck had experienced to date. Many more men would be injured and killed if Lachann Armstrong and Carmag MacEwen joined forces, and Mairi could not tell Bart, could not warn him, without giving her identity away.

Nay, she had no choice but to remain here as Bar-tholomew Holton's whore. And hearing the word from Sir Walter's mouth was like a stinging slap in her face.

Bartholomew's lack of denial was even worse.

When she had exhausted all her tears, she wiped her face with the edge of her shawl. She would return to whatever she'd been doing when she'd overheard Bartholomew's discussion. She made her way to the shed door and stepped outside, only to see Eleanor skipping up the path. With Bartholomew.

'Twas too late to slip back into the shed, for she'd already been seen.

"Lady Marguerite!" Eleanor called, breaking into a run.

Mairi turned quickly away and wiped her face again, loath to think that any sign of her tears remained.

"You were supposed to go and get Bartie— What is it? What is wrong?" the child demanded.

"'Tis naught," Mairi replied, forcing a smile to her lips. She could not bring herself to look up at Bartholomew, who stood behind Eleanor.

"You are weeping!"

"Nay!" Mairi said hastily. "'Tis only a bit of dust in my eye."

"Let me see," Bartholomew said, coming to face her. He bent slightly at the knees, took Mairi's chin between his fingers and tipped her head back.

Mairi shrugged out of his hold and stepped away. "'Tis naught," she said, starting down the path. "Are we going into the village or not?" she asked, remembering now why she'd gone to get Bartholomew.

Something was definitely amiss. Bart had come to know Marguerite's face and all her expressions as well as his own, but this one…he'd never seen it before. And it did not bode well.

She *had* been weeping, and she had not wanted him to know it. And that bothered him more than he wanted to admit. 'Twas not that he thought she was lying to him, or keeping some dark and dangerous secret from him. He knew better. She had not had contact with anyone but the castle servants, and a few of the villagers, so he'd come to believe her purpose at Norwyck was no more nefarious than she'd said.

But something had upset her. And an instinct within him drew out a deep sense of protection. He wanted to strike out at whatever had caused her tears.

Bart considered carrying her back to the keep and into the tower, where they'd shared so many delectable hours together.

"Bartie, will you come with us to the village?" Eleanor asked, skipping alongside him while holding his hand.

"What business have you in the village?" he asked.

"Tildy's mum had her bairn last night," his sister replied. "And I want to see it."

"What makes you think I'd be interested in seeing the miller's newest child?"

"I didn't think so," Eleanor chirped. "But Lady Marguerite said you might be persuaded to walk with us to the village."

"Ah…" he said, absurdly pleased that Marguerite had intended to seek out his company.

Eleanor let go of his hand and ran to a large rock that bordered a small pond. She jumped up on it, then skipped to the next rock, holding her arms out to keep her balance. One wrong step and she would fall into the icy water. "And that's why she was supposed to go and get you in your study," the child called out, "and not be out here in the garden!"

"Eleanor, get down," Marguerite said.

Bart took several long strides and reached the little girl before any disaster befell her. He took her hand and made her jump down beside him.

"Come on," he said. "You know, I think Hal is right to call you 'pest.'"

She stuck out her lower lip and acted greatly insulted. But her mood did not last long. She was soon chattering enough for all three of them, precluding any opportunity for Bart to question Marguerite.

He wondered why she had not come to him in his study as Eleanor had said. If she had truly wanted him to walk with her, why—

God's bones, had she overheard his conversation with Walter?

Bart tried to recall the exact content of their talk, but could not. What he did remember was that she had clearly been called "Norwyck's whore."

They reached the miller's cottage and went inside. Eleanor's friend was thrilled to see her, and the rest of the family scrambled to make the cottage presentable for the lord, and to show him the new bairn.

Bart watched restlessly as Marguerite put them all at ease, cooing and praising the child, and calling it beautiful, when all Bart could see was a shriveled red bundle that let out a terrible wail when it was taken from its mother.

Yet Marguerite took the squalling thing, held it in the crook of her arm and rocked it until it quieted.

Her eyes held an extraordinary expression, and Bart found himself rubbing his chest and wishing he could slam his fist through something. Sir Walter should have known better than to engage in such talk when they could be so easily overheard.

"My lord, you honor my house," the miller said. "Pour his lordship a cup of ale, lad," he said to his eldest son.

Bart took the mug that was offered, even though he

had no wish to drink here, or to deplete the miller's stores. But 'twould have dishonored the man to refuse his hospitality.

"'Tis a fine, er…"

"Lad, m'lord," the miller said jovially. "Another lad."

"Well, my congratulations to you, Miller." He lifted the mug and drank.

"Let me see," Eleanor whispered, coming up to Marguerite and pulling her arm so that she would lower the infant.

Marguerite sat down on a stool near a rough table and leaned toward the girl. Her shawl dropped away, leaving her hair uncovered and shining in the light that came in through the west window. Her delicate fingers pulled the blanket away from the infant's chin so that Eleanor could see his entire face.

Bart watched, transfixed, while Marguerite smiled and spoke softly over the tiny down-covered head.

"He has a little dimple in his chin," Eleanor whispered.

"Aye, he does," Marguerite responded. Bart saw her throat move as she swallowed, and he had the impression that she was about to weep again, though he had no understanding of why something so simple should cause such emotion in her. "Look at his tiny fingers, Eleanor."

Bart's eyes followed when Marguerite lifted the bairn's hand, and he was surprised to see the miniature perfection of the fingers, the tiny nails. And he suddenly knew what a miracle this was, something he'd never noted before.

Marguerite turned away abruptly, but not before Bart saw a tear escape one eye.

"Let's go and play," Tildy said, pulling Eleanor away from the infant. "We can look at Willie anytime."

"Willie?" Bart looked up sharply. "You named him for my brother?" he asked the miller.

"Ah, aye, m'lord," the man replied. "I hope you're not offen—"

"Nay, I take no offense," he said, frowning. 'Twas too much. First Marguerite's tears, now this remembrance of Will. "'Tis good of you to remember William this way."

"He was a good lad, your brother, m'lord," the miller said.

Bart nodded, feeling his loss once again. Will would have made a much better lord of Norwyck. The title and responsibilities were not what Bart had had in mind when he'd gone off to fight in Scotland three years before. He had intended to do no more than return for his wife when his service to King Edward was done, and make a home in the manor house that had been part of Felicia's dowry. He'd wanted to raise Holton sons and daughters, much as his own father had done.

As Felicia's widower, Bart still retained possession of her properties, though he had no interest in ever visiting any of them. The houses were closed up and left to rot, though the fields were still tilled by the peasantry. Mayhap he would deed the manor house to Marguerite when he eventually tired of her.

Except Bart did not think he would ever tire of Marguerite.

Mairi vowed never again to allow Bartholomew to see her tears. Which would not be difficult, for she intended never to weep again. Though her situation was not of her choosing, life could be much worse. Had she washed ashore a few miles north, she would have become the wife of Laird MacEwen.

She lay next to Bartholomew as he slept. He had made love to her with a gentleness he had never shown before, and Mairi believed his feelings toward her had softened. She knew he would never speak to her of love, but Mairi would do all that was necessary to assure his satisfaction with her. She would give him no reason to discard her, never show any sorrow or regret for her position in his life.

She would be certain that he enjoyed her in their bed, so that he could not possibly want another. He had taught her much, these last few weeks, of a man's needs, and what a woman could do to satisfy them. He had also shown her the delights of her own body, and was tireless in arousing and then satisfying her.

He reached for her. "Still awake?" he murmured, nuzzling her ear.

"Umm."

"Come here," he said, pulling her closer. "Let me taste you."

She turned and faced him, breathing in his scent as his lips met hers. She cherished this closeness that they often found during the hours after they first fell asleep, times when Bart would kiss her and hold her until she dropped back into slumber.

Her feelings for him deepened every day as she observed him going about his tasks: training his knights, rearing his family, overseeing the welfare of his village. He was responsible and caring, though he would have all of Norwyck believe that he was hard and callous.

When she awoke the next morn, he was gone, as was his habit. Mairi knew he trained every day in anticipation of the battle he would eventually have to fight against Armstrong. Sir Walter had convinced him to take on even more knights, expecting that battle to come soon, whether Bartholomew wished it or not.

Mairi stayed within the warm confines of her bed for a few minutes, knowing that the floor would be cold, even though Bartholomew had stoked the fire before leaving. When she finally dragged herself out of bed and stood, she had to sit back down again, or fall down. She was as light-headed as she'd been right after the shipwreck. And nauseated.

She reached up and felt the place on her head where she'd been hit, but found only a slight soreness left over from weeks ago. 'Twas not what caused her nausea.

She swallowed several times to keep from vomiting, but finally made an awkward lunge for the basin and retched. The light-headedness persisted, and Mairi sank to the cold floor, puzzling over what was wrong with her.

And then it dawned on her. She'd watched Caitir go through this four times—once with each child, and again with the one she lost.

And Mairi knew she was with child.

As terrifying as 'twas, she was elated with the knowledge that she carried Bartholomew's bairn.

Chapter Nineteen

Bart stood at the door of the solar and watched the familiar sight of Marguerite as she plucked a few notes and hummed. Apparently unsatisfied with the sound she produced, she tried again, changing the notes to her satisfaction.

Her head was bent over the psaltery as she played, and though he could not see her face, he knew there would be a fine crease between her delicately arched brows as she worked to make her song perfect. He'd seen the look before, when she worked on one thing or another.

He'd also seen the looks of mirth, of sorrow and of pleasure upon her face. And he admired each one.

He had recently come to ponder what would happen when she remembered her name and where she belonged. He questioned whether she would leave Norwyck, leave him.

Naught at Norwyck would be the same when she was gone.

He quickly girded his heart against any such tender feelings. There was no place for them in his life, and he had long since decided to keep Marguerite relegated to his bed, and nowhere else. Tenderness—or love, the kind of which the bards and minstrels sang— had no bearing on his life, and he meant to keep it that way.

'Twas most difficult to keep his resolve during the night, when she huddled against him for warmth, and he pulled her close, wrapping his arms about her, entwining his legs with hers. But he was more asleep than awake then, and not accountable for his actions or his wayward emotions.

"My lord!" she said, looking up from the psaltery and noticing him for the first time. "You startled me."

"'Twas not my intention." His voice sounded colder than he intended, too.

"'Tis early," Marguerite said. She set the psaltery on the floor next to her. "I did not think you'd be back so soon."

"Hal and John are still on the practice field," he said, walking toward her. "My sisters are with Sir Walter in the stable, looking at the new foal."

"Aye, 'tis quiet in the keep."

"Have you any plans with my sisters for this afternoon?"

"Nay," she said, looking up at him quizzically.

"Take a ride with me," he said, holding his hand out to her. "Down the beach. The day is fine. 'Twill be one of the last before winter takes hold."

She stood. "That would be—"

Before his eyes, she lost all her color and began to fall, but he caught her up in his arms before she could hit the floor. He placed her carefully upon the settle and rubbed her hands. When she did not regain consciousness, he tapped her pale cheeks, then rubbed her hands and arms again.

In spite of his resolve to feel no tenderness toward her, he was filled with alarm when she did not respond, and was about to call for a footman to hasten into the village for Alice when Marguerite's eyes fluttered open.

"What…?"

"You fainted," he said. Frowning, he jabbed his fingers through his hair. Then he touched her forehead, her cheeks, her hands.

"That's absurd, my lord," she said, moving to sit up. "I have never fainted."

"How would you know?" he scoffed. The woman had no memory, so 'twas impossible for her to know whether she'd ever fainted.

"I—I'm just not the type," she said defiantly. "I'd know it if I were."

"Stay still a moment, Marguerite," he said. Her sudden infirmity rattled him. She might deny that she'd fainted, but he'd seen her go down with his own eyes. There was no mistake.

"I just arose too quickly, my lord," she said. "And I…I missed the noon meal. I'm hungry."

"If that's all 'tis…"

She sat up. "I assure you, Bartholomew," she said, "I am fine. Just feed me, and take me for that ride."

She took his hand and stood, more slowly this time, and walked out of the solar with him. She appeared to be all right, though it shocked him to think of Marguerite succumbing to some illness. There was still too little color in her cheeks, but she moved along with her usual vigor.

He tried to shrug off his worry. Mayhap 'twas merely hunger that had caused her to faint. Or mayhap he'd been keeping her from sufficient sleep every night.

Whatever the cause, he would keep a close eye upon her until he was certain naught was amiss.

They went to the kitchen, where Bart directed the cook to prepare a meal for Marguerite. When it was ready, he carried it to his study. They sat together on a low settle beside the fire, where Bart insisted she eat all that was there.

"I am not an invalid, my lord," she said irritably. "I can feed myself."

Her manner intrigued him. He had seen her short-tempered only once before, yet today she had not only fainted, but was somewhat surly. Her color had come back, and she was even more beautiful than ever, with a glow about her that he could not attribute to the bright sunlight shining in through the tall, narrow windows.

"Please do not take offense at my asking," he said in good humor, "but do you feel well enough to ride?"

"Aye," she replied haughtily. "I feel perfect.

Mairi had not been outside the castle walls in ages, and Bartholomew could not have chosen a better day to take her riding. Though the weather was chilly, there was no wind, and the sun shone brightly over a fairly calm sea.

She rode atop Pegasus, in the space between Bartholomew's legs. She knew she'd been an absolute termagant after the fainting episode, but had been shocked and frightened by her powerlessness. What if this pregnancy incapacitated her? She had already decided not to tell Bartholomew—at least not until he noticed the changes in her body and she would have no choice but to confess.

Because a pregnant mistress would be useless to him.

She'd heard with her own ears that he had no intention of marrying again, and she was certain he would not care to wed the nameless survivor of a shipwreck. Nay, if he ever married, 'twould be for the purpose of increasing his estates. Not to give a poor bastard child a name.

She leaned her back against his chest and forced all dismal thoughts from her mind. 'Twas a beautiful day and she delighted in the freedom she felt upon the back of Bartholomew's mighty warhorse. She felt adventurous, even reckless, as they rode down to the sand.

"Shall we return to old Jakin's hut?" Bart asked huskily.

His hot breath made her tingle, and the thought of returning to the broken-down cottage excited her. But she was still feeling contrary. Perverse.

"Nay, my lord," she said playfully, turning so that he could hear her. "I want to see something new."

With movements of his body, Bartholomew gave Pegasus his head, and soon they were galloping up the broad, flat beach, with the water on their right. Tall grasses grew on their left, and Norwyck's massive walls rose starkly beyond. The tower loomed high above it, and Mairi could see its windows glistening in the sunlight. 'Twas where she often stood and looked out at the sea that had claimed Alain's life.

Bart tightened his arms around her and leaned slightly forward, urging Pegasus on. They rode even faster, and Mairi laughed with delight. The sand and water seemed to go on forever, and when Bartholomew finally slowed Peg near a rocky rise, Mairi wondered if they still stood upon Norwyck land.

She tipped her head up to ask him, but he swallowed her question with a kiss. Suddenly releasing her, he swung down from Pegasus's back and reached up for her. He lifted her down, keeping her pinned against the horse. Then he kissed her again, teasing her mouth with his teeth, his tongue.

Mairi slid her arms up his chest to his most sensitive points and was rewarded by his sharp intake of breath. Brazenly, she skimmed one hand down, exploring the edge of his tunic, finding his braes, closing her hand over him....

He moaned. And allowed her to stroke him only twice before he grabbed her hand and put it back upon his chest.

Gratified by her success, and anxious to tease him some more, she broke away and started to run through the grass at the edge of the beach, laughing.

Bartholomew had not expected this, so she had a good head start before he came after her. Once he started running, his long legs tore up the sand and he caught up to her quickly. She was out of breath when he grabbed her from behind and gently pulled her to the ground, breaking her fall with his own body.

She found herself lying atop him and laughing in his puzzled face. She pressed against his fully aroused body, and delighted in her effect upon him.

"Marguerite..."

Her laughter stopped as she looked into his eyes, so rich and brown. Cherishing the moment, she smoothed his hair away from his forehead, and another dark lock from where it was trapped upon the dark stubble on his chin.

Then she leaned down and kissed him. She felt full and wonderful and so very alive at this moment, with the knowledge that she carried his bairn within her.

"'Tis a shame," she whispered playfully, "that the weather is too cold for further intimacy, my lord."

He shook off his dazed expression and grinned wickedly. "So you think, my lady," he said. He eased her off him and came to his feet, then pulled her up beside him. In silence, he led her to a grouping of boulders in the grass, and lay his cloak upon the ground next to one of them. Then he sat upon it, with his back against the large rock.

"Come," he said. "Sit."

She began to kneel beside him, but he guided her to his lap, so that she straddled him. His mouth caught hers in a searing kiss, and he slipped his hands under her skirts.

Mairi quickly realized what he intended when she felt his hands working at his laces. He lifted her slightly, and when she came down again, they were joined. A sound of pleasure escaped her, and she began to move. Bart's eyes closed and his head fell back.

"Marguerite…" he whispered.

"Aye, my lord," she said fervently, never letting up.

If he discovered her pregnancy tomorrow and sent her away, at least she would have today.

Bartholomew walked across the bailey toward the practice field. For the first time in his memory, he'd been reluctant to leave his bed.

'Twas nearly dawn, and Marguerite remained in

their room in the tower, sleeping soundly. With good reason.

Bart breathed deeply. Even now he could smell her alluring scent, feel her silk-soft skin under his rough hands. Her sighs of pleasure were fresh in his ears.

She had been insatiable last night. Their playful interlude on the beach the previous afternoon had led to even more hours of inventive, exhilarating lovemaking in the tower. And he still felt as if he'd not had enough of her.

Would he ever?

Was there a way to bind her to him forever?

He did not care to admit it, but he felt about Marguerite as he'd never felt for another. She was honest and true. Without memory, she was entirely guileless. Since arriving at Norwyck, she had not had the freedom to leave the estate or to engage in any plot, the way Felicia had done.

Even so, Bart felt in his bones that she was naught but honorable and virtuous, and would be so even if she knew her name. Every word she spoke, every action she took attested to her honor. She had charmed John, had taken away Kathryn's brittle edge and was managing Eleanor better than anyone yet. Even Henry respected her.

Sir Walter wanted Bart to marry her. The old man nagged him about it at every opportunity. Walter thought he could shame Bart into marriage, by calling Marguerite Norwyck's whore.

Well, the old knight might just have succeeded.

"My lord," said Sir Duncan, Norwyck's sergeant-at-arms.

Bart abandoned his thoughts and stopped to listen.

"There are reports in the village of stolen cattle."

"Confirmed?"

"Sir Walter is in the village now, with the reeve, and they're questioning the men."

"We'll ride out as soon as your company and Sir Stephan's are ready," Bart said. All had been quiet for weeks. There had been no sign of any offense against Norwyck, and Bartholomew had been concerned. Now he knew why.

They reached the stable, where Pegasus was already saddled and waiting. Bart mounted. "Have the men arm themselves for battle, but leave a large garrison here to defend the castle. I'll meet you at the west gate."

He glanced up at the tower and saw movement at the window. 'Twas Marguerite. She wore something plain and white, but her hair was loose and curled over one breast. From such a distance, he could not discern much, but he saw that her hand was pressed against the glass.

An odd sensation welled in his chest, as if his lungs had turned into overfilled waterskins. He raised his hand as if to touch hers. Taking a deep breath, he gave a slight bow, then turned Pegasus and urged the horse through the lower bailey, to the gate.

The connection he felt between them was nothing short of remarkable. 'Twas as if an invisible cord bound them together, hearts, minds and souls. Upon his return to the keep, he would see how Marguerite felt about marriage.

A crowd of men had gathered around Sir Walter and Reeve Edwin Gayte, and they all spoke at once. They were angry and upset over the loss of their livestock. When Bart arrived, all grew silent.

He remained mounted. "Sir Walter," he said. "What is your assessment?"

"My lord, from all accounts, several cattle and quite a number of sheep are missing from our southern fields."

A muscle in Bart's jaw tightened involuntarily. "How many?"

"Eight cows, my lord," Gayte said. "Twelve sheep."

"So far…" Walter added. "Several of the village men have not yet returned to report."

"A garrison will remain here to protect Norwyck while we're gone," Bart said. "I leave Sir Walter in charge."

Clearly, Armstrong knew where Norwyck was most vulnerable. The cattle were necessary for milk and cheese, but loss of the sheep meant loss of their valuable wool. A wall around the village would not protect the livestock, therefore Bart had no alternative but to show his superiority in battle. He had many more knights in his service now than Armstrong could ever hope to command. Lachann would have to think twice before assaulting Norwyck again, in any way.

Companies of mounted knights arrived in the village, and Bart dug his heels into Pegasus's sides, leading them past the unfinished wall.

He headed down into the valley, toward Braemar.

The sun had risen fully by the time they reached the lower dell, and here was where the Norwyck men found their butchered livestock. Ten cows in all. Fourteen sheep. Each with an arrow in its chest.

Bart felt sickened. The Armstrong bastards had not even bothered to take the wool or the meat. 'Twas merely an exercise to them, killing these animals, an arrogant method of showing contempt for Norwyck.

Bart did not know what made the Armstrong hate Norwyck so, but he would not allow this latest offense to stand. He had hoped a superior defense would show their enemy the futility of his attacks, but Bart's strategy had failed. Feeling more angry than he ever had, he rallied the men behind him and headed for Braemar Keep, with every intention of engaging Armstrong in battle. Since Norwyck had never attacked the Scotsman in his keep, the action would be unexpected. Besides, the Armstrong knights would be weary after their night's cowardly work, and Norwyck would have the advantage.

They rode hard for an hour, then stopped to water and rest the horses. When they resumed, 'twas yet another hour before they reached the base of the well-treed hillock below Braemar. His men halted behind him, staying under cover of the woods.

"My lord?" Sir Stephan asked.

Scotsmen with swords, along with archers, patrolled around Braemar Keep. Bedraggled cottages dotted the hillside below, making an attack impossible without involving women and children.

Much of the ground at the base of the hill was boggy and unsuitable for riding, at least for an army of horses. All things considered, a direct attack upon the keep was out of the question.

"They expect us," Bart said. "Send a few men to scout the land below the keep. But take care. There may be Armstrongs lying in wait."

"Aye, my lord," Stephan murmured.

"Duncan," Bart said. "The rest of the men should

remain hidden here, but in readiness in case of attack.''

"Aye, my lord."

Deep in thought, Bart walked Pegasus deeper into the wood. He tied his horse, then began to pace as he considered his plan.

Clearly, 'twould not be possible to win a battle today. He had many knights at his disposal, and the possibility of even more reinforcements if he chose to call for assistance. But with only the fifty men he had on hand today, he could not attack Braemar and come away the victor. Armstrong had far more men than Bartholomew would have guessed.

Nay, he would know Armstrong's weaknesses first, then firm up a plan that had already begun to take shape in his mind. In the meantime, he would do all that was necessary to protect the people and livestock of Norwyck.

And he would spend another night in Marguerite's arms before he went into battle.

Chapter Twenty

Mairi's lie weighed heavily upon her. She had come to share such a close intimacy with Bartholomew that her omission of the truth seemed even more grievous.

Mayhap she ought to tell him she was Lachann Armstrong's daughter, the consequences be damned.

She looked down at the courtyard far below and saw Bartholomew, sitting so proud and tall upon Pegasus. She knew what Norwyck meant to him, and how the betrayals of the past had affected him. She understood the depth of his hatred of the Armstrongs.

Could he possibly overlook her name? Would he show her the same kindness and consideration once he knew she was Lachann's daughter? Was there some way to ensure that he would understand she had not deceived him from the first?

Mairi did not doubt that he felt a fondness for her, but did not know if 'twould be enough to overcome the profound antipathy he felt for her sire.

And she did not know if she was brave enough to find out.

A tap at the door made her step away from the window. "Enter," she said.

Eleanor pushed the door open and strode in. Excitement made her eyes sparkle. "Bartie is going to battle!"

"What?" Mairi whispered. Light-headed again, she sat on a chair and put her head down before she could faint.

"The Armstrong took our livestock, and now Bartie is gathering his men and going to Braemar Keep!"

"How do you know this, Eleanor?" Mairi asked.

"From Hal!" she cried. "He went out to the practice field as he always does, but the men are all at the armorer's—sharpening their swords and repairing their armor."

"Where is Henry now?" she asked. Mayhap she could question him.

"Bartie will not let him go to Braemar, so he is getting ready to join the garrison that will stay here."

Mairi swallowed and raised her head slowly.

"Are you all right?" Eleanor asked, stopping for a moment to look at her. "You have no color, Marguerite."

"I—I'm just… This talk of battle shocked me, Eleanor," Mairi said. "That's all."

"Oh, aye." Eleanor resumed wandering about the chamber. She stopped at the bed and looked at it curiously.

Mairi had not bothered to straighten it yet, but Eleanor did not attach any significance to its tangled linens and blankets. "I don't like it when Bartie goes away."

"Your other brothers are still here," Mairi said, as much to reassure herself as Eleanor. "And I imagine Sir Walter, too."

Eleanor nodded. "Will you come and break your fast with Kate and me?"

The last thing Mairi wanted was food, but she agreed to meet the girls in the great hall after she washed and dressed.

Everyone was on edge all day, awaiting word from Bartholomew. Little information was available, only that Bart and two large companies of knights had gone to Braemar Keep.

Mairi knew this was what he and his men trained for every day, but when she thought of all the gruesome tales of battle she had ever heard, she worried even more. The hours passed slowly, and by suppertime, everyone was thoroughly disagreeable. Eleanor and Kathryn were the worst, arguing and bickering over everything.

"I do not want cod!" Eleanor cried as she shoved aside the trencher that held her supper.

"You do not have to eat, Ellie," Mairi said, reminding herself to stay calm. There was no point in forcing the child to eat, especially if she felt as Mairi did. "Come. If John and Kate will excuse us, we'll go to the chapel for a while."

As they left the great hall, Mairi felt little gratification for having circumvented another tantrum. She was too anxious. If her father and Carmag had truly joined forces, they might be able to overcome Bartholomew and his knights.

And she might have warned him.

They entered the chapel and lit a few candles, then knelt before the altar. Mairi bowed her head, oblivious to Eleanor. She prayed for forgiveness for her lie, and begged God to return Bart safely to her.

When she finally looked up, she saw that Kathryn had joined them. "When I am a wife," the girl said pensively, "do you suppose 'twill be any easier to await my husband's return from battle than it is now, waiting for Bart?"

"Nay, Kathryn," Mairi replied, "I doubt it." She got up off her knees and took a step toward her.

Kathryn stepped back.

"What is it?" Mairi asked.

The girl said naught, but continued to look curiously at her. 'Twas an expression Mairi had oft seen upon Kathryn's face in recent days, but the girl had become prickly of late, and Mairi did not attribute any special significance to it.

"Mayhap music will take our minds off your brother and all that is happening at Braemar," she said. She led the girls to Bartholomew's study, where Kathryn made a halfhearted attempt to play the gittern, while Eleanor whined.

When Mairi could stand no more, she ushered the girls upstairs to make ready for bed.

An argument ensued when Kathryn refused to allow Eleanor to spend another night in her new chamber. Mairi tried to stay out of the argument, but 'twas impossible. Their shouting jangled her irritable nerves, and for once, Mairi wished that Nurse Ada would come to see what the disturbance was.

"Please, Kathryn," Mairi said. "If you allow your sister to stay, I'll tell you another tale."

"I don't want another tale!" Kathryn cried. "I am old enough that I should not to have to sleep with that bairn!"

"'Tis true enough, Kathryn, but—"

"And I am old enough that you should have told me you're the Armstrong's daughter!" she shrieked.

"Bartie!"

Bartholomew's youngest sister shot into his arms like a red-haired arrow. He did not feel the impact of her body, since he was still reeling from the shock of Kathryn's words. *Armstrong's daughter?*

One look at Marguerite's guilty face and he knew. 'Twas true.

"Do you return victorious, Bartie?" Eleanor demanded. "Have you brought the Armstrong's head on a pike?"

He peeled the child from his legs even as he pierced Marguerite with his eyes. "Go to bed, girls," he said without changing his gaze. "No battle was fought or won today."

"Oh, but, Bartie—"

"Do as I say. Now," he said, his voice steady, even as a part of his very soul shriveled.

His sisters sensed his mood and climbed into the bed without another word. Bart took hold of Marguerite's arm and pulled her into the solar.

"Explain."

With hands twisting in the cloth of her skirt, Mairi spun around, presenting her back to him.

Every muscle in his body tensed. Every drop of blood ran cold, just as it had the day he'd learned of Felicia's betrayal.

With measured calm, he spoke again, but his words came from behind clenched teeth. "I told you to explain."

"M-my lord," she said. "I did n-not recover my memory right away...."

That was doubtful. "But you *have* recovered it now?"

He watched the back of her head as she nodded.

"And what Kathryn said... You are Lachann Armstrong's daughter?"

She turned and faced him. "Aye. I am Mairi Armstrong," she said.

He hardened his heart against the moisture in her eyes, the look of anguish upon her face. She had played him so easily, just as she coaxed pleasing music from the strings of her instruments. She'd nearly gotten him to ignore his instincts and admit to developing tender feelings for her.

He had come to believe she could not be deceitful, but now he knew better.

"I have lived in France with my cousin since I was a young girl," she continued. "My father recently sent for me. My cousin's husband—still a young man—was on board the ship when it..." She swallowed and seemed to struggle to keep her composure. "When it s-sank. He...he drowned."

When a single tear escaped her eye, Bart thought his lungs might burst. But he strode purposefully to the window to keep himself from going to her and taking her into his arms. She may have made a fool of him, but he would not make one of himself.

"I did not remember Alain until...well, 'twas some time after my wounds had healed."

"And your own identity? When did you remember that?"

"At the same time, my lord," she whispered.

Tension knotted in his back. Anger welled in his chest. *She had lied to him!* He had known better than to trust her, yet he'd carelessly let down his guard.

Before he said or did something imprudent, he strode out of the solar. He did not stop until he'd stormed out of the keep and stalked across the courtyard to the stable.

He dismissed the grooms and went to Pegasus's stall, where the mighty beast pawed the ground and whinnied a greeting.

"Easy," Bart said to the warhorse, though the command could have been for himself. Peg sensed Bart's tension and reared up. "Settle down," he said. He picked up some clean straw and began to rub the animal down.

He tried to think what Mairi Armstrong had been able to accomplish at Norwyck, what information she would be able to give her sire. There was naught that she could have learned about the Norwyck knights, besides their number. He had never told her of his war plans, so that was not in danger, either.

She might have learned that he had no ships with which to attack by sea. Or 'twas possible she'd learned what stores they had in order to withstand a siege.

Mayhap she'd seduced him just as her brother had seduced Felicia, for the simple purpose of finishing the task Lachann and Dùghlas started. To destroy him.

Bart threw down the straw and stared into the darkness of the stable. He had allowed himself to trust her, when it had been against his instincts to do so. He had known better.

"There you are, lad," Sir Walter said.

Bart turned his back and began to rub Pegasus again, with his bare hands.

"You'll be thinking she betrayed you, just like Felicia, eh?" Walter said.

What else was he supposed to think?

"She's not like Felicia, and well you should know it, my lord," Walter said quietly.

"Nay?" Bart said with sarcasm. "And what would you know of it?"

"I know that the lass loves you, Bart."

Bart let out a sound that was half groan, half sigh. "You'll forgive me if I do not believe you, old man. You know naught of it."

"But I do," he said. "Lady Mairi told me who she was some time ago, and explained why she could not tell you."

Bart sighed impatiently. More lies.

"She is betrothed to Carmag MacEwen," Walter said. "If she returns to Braemar Keep, her father will force her to wed the man—"

"Enough!" Bart barked. "You've betrayed me every bit as much as the Armstrong wench! Never bothering to tell me what you knew of her!" He turned sharply and strode out of the stall. He continued across the bailey until he reached a low, timbered building that housed all the visiting knights. He would sleep there tonight, and every night until he rid Norwyck of the Scot.

Silently, he took up a blanket from a pile near the door, wrapped himself in it and found a space to lie down. It had been a long, hard day, and he should have no trouble finding sleep.

Yet it eluded him. He forced his thoughts from Marguer— Nay, from Mairi Armstrong and her deception, and considered his offensive against Braemar. The men were ready. The animals killed by Armstrong men had been loaded onto wains and returned to the village for butchering. Though his people hadn't planned on slaughtering those animals, at least they would use them. There would be meat and leather, along with plenty of wool for spinning this winter.

War supplies would be loaded onto wains in the morn. Considering the possibility that Mairi may have gotten information to her father at Braemar, Bart knew he would have to act quickly. He thought about how many men he would leave at the castle for its defense, and decided what companies he would lead into the dense woods at Braemar.

He had a sufficient number of men, even if Mac-Ewen had joined the Armstrong forces....

Bart suddenly recalled a recent conversation with Sir Walter, when the old knight had recommended sending someone to the earl of Bitterlee, and other nearby Northumberland lords with requests for additional men. 'Twas obvious now that the old knight had known with a certainty that Armstrong had joined forces with MacEwen.

Bart wondered how many men MacEwen would bring. He had already seen more men at Braemar than he would have anticipated. Clan MacEwen was huge, and Carmag controlled a large portion of land east of Armstrong, all the way to the sea. If Bart could put his plan in place on the morrow—or the day after at the very latest—then 'twould not be so easy for Armstrong to rally any more MacEwen men.

MacEwen. Bart recalled the man from Falkirk. He was a hulking Scotsman with hands the size of anvils. Wearing primitive skins and a bit of wool, the giant had fought like a bloody Norse berserker, and seemed crueler and more crude than the other Scots Bart had fought.

The man's nose was bulbous and purple, and his eyes tiny, almost colorless orbs close-set in an altogether unpleasing face. He was a veritable troll, mean and repulsive.

And he was to be Mairi Armstrong's husband?

Bart felt his gorge rise at the thought. If Laird MacEwen was truly her betrothed, then Bart could not blame her for trying to avoid the marriage. But to lie to him?

'Twas unforgivable.

Chapter Twenty-One

Mairi forced herself out of bed the following morn, after a night of very little sleep. She had tossed and turned, then gotten up to pace, only to return to her bed once again to pitch about restlessly.

She could not resent Bart for his antipathy toward her. She had deceived him, and done so intentionally for her own purposes. 'Twould have been better to have told him who she was, and accept the consequences.

He had not returned to the keep all day, and Mairi spent half the time watching as supplies were carried out and loaded onto wains in the bailey.

Eleanor did not venture too far from her, but Kathryn remained distant and cool. Mairi could not understand how the girl had discovered her secret, unless she'd overheard Mairi divulge her identity to Sir Walter. 'Twas entirely possible.

"Why did you not tell us your true name, Lady Mairi?" Eleanor asked.

Mairi wrung her hands together. "'Twas wrong of me, Eleanor," she said. "I should have told Bartholomew everything as soon as I regained my memory. But I was afraid he would send me to my father.''

''Do you not care for him, then, your father?''

Mairi shut her eyes and shook her head. ''Surely God will punish me for feeling so, but my father has not laid eyes upon me in more than ten years. He cares only for making alliances…and war.''

''"Tis what fathers ought to do,'' Kathryn said. ''Make good alliances with their daughters' marriages.''

Mairi could not argue, for Kathryn was correct. 'Twas exactly what fathers did, and daughters happily complied. *Most* daughters. Mairi believed she would have acquiesced, too, had her chosen bridegroom been anyone but Carmag MacEwen.

But now that she had known Bartholomew Holton, and carried his child, marriage to the MacEwen brute was impossible. She would never submit, though she did not yet know how she would avoid it. Surely Bartholomew intended to send her to Braemar Keep, and just as surely, Mairi would refuse to go. Mayhap there was a convent where she could hide until her child was born.

Or 'twas possible she could manage somehow to return to Caitir in France. Her father would never have to know.

Kathryn and Eleanor were too young to understand Mairi's aversion to the marriage arranged by her father, and they'd spent every day of their lives preparing to be the wives of men chosen for them. Mairi's feelings on the matter were utterly beyond them.

Henry came to them after supper. He would say naught about Bartholomew's plans, or why they carried so many supplies. He said only that Bart had given orders that his sisters—and Mairi—were to remain in the keep, or very close by, until his return.

Henry was no more unfriendly than usual, but it seemed to Mairi that he looked at her with more interest than he'd done before. John had not spoken to her since her identity had become known, and Mairi surmised that he felt as betrayed as Bartholomew.

At bedtime, Kathryn refused to allow Eleanor in her bed. This time, she was adamant. In tears, Eleanor went to the nursery, where Mairi sang sweet, quiet lullabies until the exhausted child fell asleep.

As weary as the children, as well as sick at heart, Mairi climbed up to her chamber in the tower and went to bed.

"Mairi! Mairi! She's gone!"

Mairi came awake abruptly. The fire had died down, but a candle in a small lamp on the table next to the bed illuminated Kathryn's distraught face.

"Ellie is gone!"

Mairi sat up, swung her feet over the side of the bed and stood, ignoring a wave of dizziness. "Gone? Kathryn, tell me what you mean," she said.

"I...I woke up and felt afraid to be all alone," she said, as Mairi pulled a gown over her head and began to lace it. "So I went to the nursery to sleep with Ellie, but she was not there."

"Did you look—"

"Nay! She is gone!" Kathryn cried, grabbing Mairi's hand. "You must come and see!"

Mairi snatched up the lamp and followed the girl down the steps, then through the gallery to the nursery. She pushed open the door and found Eleanor's bed empty, just as Kathryn had said.

But in the center of the bedclothes was a jeweled dirk, driven ruthlessly through the mattress.

Kathryn cried out again, pressing her hand to her mouth. "They've taken her! The Armstrong laird has stolen her!"

Shaken, Mairi wrapped her arms around Kathryn and tried to soothe her. She had to find Bartholomew. Though she knew he had no interest in seeing her, he would have no choice but to deal with this latest disaster.

"Come," Mairi said, leading Kathryn out of the room. "We must find your brother."

They roused the servants, and sent a footman out to find Lord Norwyck while they waited in the nursery. Mairi did what she could to comfort Kathryn, but *she* felt no better. She blamed herself. Somehow, she should have protected Eleanor. Bartholomew had relied upon her to do so, and she had let him down. Again.

'Twas not long before they heard voices and footsteps in the gallery, and soon Bart was there.

He smelled of cold air, wood fire and horse, and Mairi could feel the heat radiating from his body. Of all the times she had needed him to hold her, she felt it most keenly now. He did not look at her, but went directly to the bed. He reached down and felt the linen, then pulled the dirk from the mattress.

Sir Walter came in then.

"The Armstrong has taken Eleanor," Bart said to him. He showed the older man the dirk.

Walter shook his head. He looked at Mairi. "What happened here, lass?"

"I'll tell you what happened," Bart roared. "A Scots bastard sneaked into my keep and took my sister!'' He shoved the dirk into his belt. ''And I will have her back!''

Anguish could not come close to describing what Bart felt when he saw the knife protruding from Eleanor's small bed. He vowed to have his little red-haired sister back, and have his revenge upon Armstrong, now. Tonight.

''Search the keep,'' he said tightly. He tunneled his fingers through his hair as his mind raced through possibilities. ''I want Norwyck turned upside down—explore every inch within the castle walls, every cottage in the village....''

He held little hope that Eleanor was still here. There could be no doubt that the bastard who had stolen her had gotten out and was well on his way to Braemar Keep. Which was exactly what Bart would do. He would ride to Braemar Keep himself and demand that Eleanor be released. If Armstrong refused...

Nay, he could not act precipitously, for Eleanor's life was at stake, and Armstrong held the advantage. But only for the moment.

Forcing himself to a calm he did not really feel, Bart resolved to go forward with his plans to ambush Lachann Armstrong and his men, for he knew that it was necessary to break up the Armstrong-MacEwen alliance, and severely diminish the number of men Armstrong had under his command. 'Twould put Bart in a much better position to negotiate.

And now he had an additional tool at his disposal. He had his own hostage.

He had no doubt that Lachann would want his daughter back, unharmed. Otherwise, his plans for Mairi's marriage to Carmag could not be carried out.

Wouldn't the Armstrong laird be appalled to learn that his hostage-taking ploy was in vain?

It gave Bart small satisfaction, in light of what his sister must be going through at this very moment.

"Damnation," he muttered under his breath. Ellie was small and frail. She would be terrified. She had never been treated roughly, and would not know whether her captor intended to kill her or let her live. If Armstrong harmed her in the least—

"My lord," Sir Walter said, "do we change strategies now?"

"Nay," Bart said. He looked at Mairi for the first time and nearly winced when he saw her tear-stained face. Dark circles rimmed her eyes, and she seemed smaller, more fragile now, as she held Kate in her arms, comforting her.

When she looked up at him and met his gaze, Bart saw her distress, her grief. She was truly horrified by Eleanor's abduction.

Bart understood clearly that in order to get Eleanor back, he would have to trade Mairi for her. And, in that moment, he was unsure whether he was willing to do so.

He'd thought of little else all day, as the men worked around him, making ready for their assault upon Braemar. How to use Mairi Armstrong against Lachann.

Keeping her hostage had been the most logical choice. If Lachann had to worry about his daughter's safety every time he raided Norwyck, the raids might stop, and Bart could keep Mairi indefinitely. But with Eleanor taken, he might actually have to make an exchange, and give Mairi up.

He cracked his knuckles and turned away.

'Twas all a fine mess. The only solution was to carry out his plan of having Norwyck knights lie in wait in the woods below Braemar Keep. Bart had men and supplies enough to last more than a week. 'Twould not be long before a large force of Armstrong and MacEwen men came outside the wall, heading for Norwyck.

If Bart's strategy worked, he would be able to dispatch the bulk of Armstrong's army, and get Eleanor back, unscathed.

He only now realized how much he hoped he'd be able to keep Mairi, too.

Looking at her, small and vulnerable, and caring for Kathryn, made it impossible for him to think. His throat went dry, and he felt as if the air in the nursery would choke him. Abruptly, he walked out of the chamber, went through the gallery and hurried down the steps to the great hall.

What if Sir Walter's words were true? If Armstrong intended to wed Mairi to Laird MacEwen, 'twas no wonder she had not immediately returned to Braemar Keep for her marriage. On the other hand, she could not very well announce to all of Norwyck that she was the daughter of their most hated enemy. She had been well and truly trapped.

Bart stepped outside of the keep and breathed deeply. Eleanor was gone, and he would have to trade Mairi to get his sister back. His most trusted advisor had withheld information from him for some protracted length of time, and Bart had several hundred knights whose lives were in his hands.

Was there no end to the grief Lachann Armstrong could cause?

As the search of the grounds commenced, Bart

walked across to the knights' quarters. The men were ready. Most were quiet—even solemn—as they passed the night before departing for battle. Some prayed; some drank and talked quietly with one another, reliving other battles.

Bart knew he would not sleep. He hoped that Eleanor would be found, safe and sound, somewhere within the castle walls. But he knew that was entirely unlikely.

As he joined in the search, there was no doubt in his mind that she was well on her way to Braemar Keep.

Once Mairi settled Kathryn in the bed in her tower room, she began to pace. There must be *something* she could do to get Eleanor back.

Obviously, Bartholomew would send word to Braemar, telling Lachann that he held Mairi at Norwyck. That would be the best way to guarantee Eleanor's safety.

Eventually, there would have to be a trade, and Mairi had absolutely no doubt that Bart would give her to Lachann in exchange for his sister. 'Twas as it should be.

But what if Eleanor managed to escape Lachann?

What if Mairi could prove her allegiance to Norwyck, and her love for Bartholomew?

She walked from the fireplace to the bed and back again. She had to *think!* There *had* to be a way for her to show Bartholomew what he meant to her. 'Twas not just that marriage to Carmag was repugnant to her.... Nay, she felt so strongly for Bart Holton that she could not give herself to another, even if he were the comeliest man in all of Britain.

The fact that 'twas Carmag MacEwen her father had chosen, or that the MacEwen had several ships to use for—

That was it! Months ago, Carmag had bragged about his ships, and how he could move so many men down the coast to attack the English lords whenever he fancied....

Was that how Eleanor had been stolen? Had she been secreted onto a ship off Norwyck's shore, then hidden away in a cavern on his beach?

Clearly, Lachann would never have taken the child through the village on a direct path to Braemar. If anything, he would have used his ally's resources to complete his dastardly task.

Mairi had to remember everything Carmag had told her about his lands and his possessions. He had boasted and bragged the entire time he'd visited in France. He must have said something that would be useful to her....

Mairi looked down at Kathryn, who was finally sound asleep. At least she would be safe here tonight, with a guard keeping watch by the tower stairs. No intruder would expect the child to be in the tower, and no one would get past the guard.

Wringing her hands with frustration at her inability to act, Mairi could only wish Eleanor safe. She did not want to believe that Lachann would harm a child, but she remembered her father all too well. He was a cold, self-centered scoundrel who thought of naught but his own desires.

She was afraid that when Lachann received word that Mairi was a hostage at Norwyck, he might be spiteful enough to call Bartholomew's bluff and harm Eleanor. Mairi did not delude herself into thinking her father would want to keep Eleanor safe in order to insure his own daughter's continued health.

Since he believed Mairi had drowned, 'twas likely her father had already figured another way to convince the MacEwen to ally himself with clan Armstrong.

There was no time for Mairi to find out. She checked on Kathryn once again, then left the tower room. When she met the guard at the foot of the stairs, he was not inclined to let her go.

"M'lady," he said, "I have orders to keep you here in the tower."

"Aye, I know that, Raulf," she replied. "But I just remembered something that Lord Norwyck should know. I must find a footman to fetch him for me."

A look of indecision crossed the guard's face and Mairi took advantage of it. "Only one of us can go. You must remain here to guard Lady Kathryn."

Mairi breathed more easily when Raulf finally agreed. She could see that he was unsure of his decision to allow her to go, so she hurried away before he could change his mind and detain her.

She could not tell Bartholomew of her plan, for 'twas too risky, too dangerous, and doomed to fail if Bart and his men escorted her. Yet 'twas her only chance to prove her allegiance and get Eleanor away from her father.

Surefooted, Mairi hurried down the steps to the great hall, walked briskly through the empty, cavernous space and went to a door near the chapel that led to the courtyard. Cloaks hung on hooks near the door, and she took one before slipping outside.

Walking quickly, she made her way toward the postern gate, grateful that there was a full moon, yet worried that someone might see and recognize her in the moonlight. There were men all about, presumably searching the grounds for any signs of Eleanor and her abductor.

Keeping herself hooded and cloaked, Mairi reached the gate and inched it open on its rusty hinges, praying that the squeak of metal would not alert anyone to her presence. Slipping through the small opening, she crept away from Norwyck's walls.

Chapter Twenty-Two

The footpath was well illuminated by the moon, but there was a frigid wind blowing over the water. Mairi hugged her cloak to herself and trudged along the sand. She followed the curve of the beach toward the north, and the caverns in which Carmag MacEwen hid his boats. If only she could get that far tonight, she would feel successful.

Naught impeded her as she headed north across the broad beach, neither the wind nor the strange night sounds that assailed her. She girded herself against any fear of the night, and continued on, walking for more than an hour. When she passed the place where she and Bartholomew had once made beautiful, passionate love, she did not allow herself to dwell upon the memory of that fine afternoon, but kept walking. Eventually she came to a sharp incline, rough terrain where the beach gave way to a steep rocky rise.

Mairi had no choice but to climb.

Halfway up she had to sit down and rest. She huddled next to a large outcropping of rock and caught her breath while her muscles relaxed. And she wondered if this was the way Eleanor had been taken.

'Twas entirely possible Mairi was mistaken. May-hap Lachann had managed to get the child out of Norwyck keep and past the village walls without being discovered. His audacity should come as no surprise, for that seemed to be his way now—to confound his opponent by attacking at odd times and in strange ways.

Mairi was so tired she did not know if she would be able to continue on. She glanced up at the sky and saw that there was barely a cloud to be seen, and the moon was still high. But there were many hours of night remaining.

She had to keep on.

Rising to her feet again, she resumed her climb up the stony hill and finally reached the top.

Her legs were tired and sore, and her hands were scraped and nicked from hanging on to the rocks as she climbed. Ignoring her little injuries, she walked on, mindful that if MacEwen had taken Eleanor and hidden her in one of his caverns, Mairi would have to reach the place before morning. She did not want MacEwen or his men to see her before she had a chance to determine where Eleanor was and how to free her.

Mairi walked along the escarpment for a while, keeping well away from the edge, and started scanning the water for any sign of boats or a quay. The sea was clearly visible, with a wedge of bright moonlight shimmering from the horizon to the shore.

Mairi could see naught down there.

Beyond weary, she did not know how much farther she would be able to walk, and worried that MacEwen's caverns were down below her even now, where she could see no sign of them. What if she went past them? What if she missed her chance to get to Eleanor?

Something up ahead caught her eye, something bright and orange. A small fire, perhaps?

New energy seeped into Mairi's muscles and bones. She moved ahead more quickly now, hopeful that she'd found her quarry. What other reason would there be for men to be camped just up the beach from Norwyck?

Stealthily, Mairi crept toward the glow and discovered a haphazard camp with a crude shelter at the edge of it, made of blankets thrown over a low branch. She prayed that Eleanor was underneath. 'Twas not much protection against the wind, but better than naught.

Mairi pulled up her hood to cover most of her face. She skirted around the camp and approached from the inland side, where some low trees and brush grew. 'Twas not a great deal of cover, but hopefully enough.

Several horses were tethered nearby, and Mairi knew then that these men planned to ride west to Braemar Keep. They would not be sailing to MacEwan's stronghold further north. Four men dozed around the fire, and another sat up, keeping watch. At the moment, he was gazing out toward the cliffs over the beach.

With her voice masked by the sound of the waves crashing upon rocks below, Mairi spoke softly to the horses as she approached. Shaking with uneasiness, she nonetheless took a moment to rub each horse, just as Bartholomew had shown her with Pegasus.

Then, in the shadows, she moved away from the horses. Mairi knew she would not be able to get inside the blanketed shelter without attracting the watchman's notice, so she would have to deal with him somehow.

A blow to the head was the most likely solution, so she searched for a likely weapon. Never once allowing herself to become squeamish over it, she crept up behind the fellow and struck him hard with a rock. Awkwardly, she broke his fall and eased him down to the ground. Then she slipped back into the darkness to wait and see if any of the other men would awaken.

After a few minutes of continued silence, she stole into the rough shelter. 'Twas even darker inside, so she shifted one of the blankets in order to see. As she did so, Eleanor sat up abruptly.

Mairi had the wherewithal to clap one hand over the child's mouth and speak quietly into her ear. "Eleanor! 'Tis me, Marguerite," she said, using the name that was most familiar.

Mairi could feel Eleanor's panic subside, and she removed her hand from the child's mouth. "Let's get away from here, Ellie," she whispered. "Come quickly."

Without another word, the two slipped out of the shelter. Mairi led Eleanor from the camp, and kept walking until they were a good distance away.

"How did you find me?" the girl whispered.

"When all of Norwyck was searched, and there was no sign of you, I remembered some talk about ships and caverns," Mairi replied, "and thought mayhap 'twas Carmag MacEwen who brought you this way, and not…Lachann."

"I tried to fight them, but I could not get away," Eleanor said. Mairi crouched down and hugged the girl to her. "I was so afraid, Mairi," she whispered. "I bit one of them and then I…I don't remember what happened after that. The next thing I knew, I was out of the castle and one of those men was carrying me up the beach.''

''I know, sweetheart,'' Mairi said softly as she stood again. ''You'll be safe again soon. We just have to go back down the beach without getting caught.''

She untied her cloak at the throat and took it from her shoulders. ''This is much too large for you, but I want you to cover up.''

''I *am* cold,'' Eleanor said, allowing Mairi to drape it over her shoulders. ''I feel like there's been ice in my bones since they took me from Norwyck.''

''If we keep up a good pace, we'll be home soon,'' Mairi said. ''But there's a rough spot not far from here and we'll have to take care climbing down.''

''Aye,'' Eleanor replied. ''I climbed it before. The man put me down and made me climb even though my head hurt and I was sleepy and cold.''

''I know you're tired now, Eleanor,'' Mairi said to encourage the girl to keep moving. ''But 'tis an easy walk then, after we get past that incline. We'll have you back in your bed at Norwyck before you know it. And you'll be able to tell your sister and brothers of your adventu—''

They'd gone only a few steps when they heard voices behind them. ''Ellie, run! All the way to Norwyck!'' Mairi urgently cried. ''Hide if you must, but don't let them catch you!''

Eleanor was covered by the dark cloak and she melted into the night, but Mairi was much more visible in her yellow gown. She ran inland, and the men followed. She managed to evade them for a time, giving Eleanor a chance to hide or to get far enough away that they would never catch her. But Mairi's fatigue eventually overcame her.

She tripped and fell, and as she did so, one of the pursuers grabbed her ankle.

"What?" the man said when he saw her clearly. 'Twas obvious he'd expected to find Eleanor lying there. "Who are ye?"

"I am Mairi Armstrong," she replied haughtily, "and I'll thank you to unhand me."

"Where's the little lass?" the leader asked, looming over her.

Mairi pulled away from her captor's grasp and shrugged.

"Well, 'tis even better," the other man said, pulling her roughly to her feet. "We were sent to fetch ye back to Laird MacEwen. When we couldna find ye in Norwyck's keep, we took the little lass—"

"You're lying!" Mairi cried. "You did not even know I was alive."

"Yer father and Laird MacEwen learned of ye not more than a week ago," he said, pulling her back toward the camp. "Come on."

Mairi kept her silence as she marched beside her captor, though she wondered how her father could possibly have known she was alive and well at Norwyck. When they reached the little shelter, the Scot pushed her into it. "Best ye get some sleep now, my lady," he said. "We've a long ride ahead of us in the morn."

A short while before dawn, Bart and his knights mounted their horses and headed for the castle gate. This was the day he would demand the return of his sister.

And he would not bargain with Mairi's life.

Mairi Armstrong belonged with him, here at Norwyck. She would be his lady, the Armstrong laird be damned. Bart cared for her, far too deeply than he'd admitted to himself, and he could not imagine his life at Norwyck without her.

While he had finally accepted that she had had no choice but to keep her identity from him, he would have no more deception between them. He would confront her with her lies, and insist upon a vow between them to engage in no further deceptions once they were husband and wife.

They passed through the gate to the edge of the village, heading toward the farthest point west, where the wall had not yet been completed. As they rode down the lane, Bart became aware of a disturbance within the ranks behind him. He turned to see Sir Walter riding forward at top speed.

"My lord!" he called.

Bart's brow furrowed automatically and he waited for Walter to reach him. They'd had enough bad news, and Bart did not look forward to hearing even more.

"'Tis Eleanor!" the steward stated loudly. "She is returned!"

A low murmur ran through the company of knights and all the villagers who were out watching them departed.

"Where? How?" Bart queried uncertainly. It seemed too easy, not having to use Mairi as a bargaining tool.

"Come," Walter replied. "You must hear what she has to say."

"Nay," he replied, steadfast in his purpose. "Now, more than ever, I would battle the Armstrong, for his audacity in stealing my sister. The men are prepared and—"

"My lord," Walter insisted, "Lady Mairi is gone, taken by Carmag MacEwen's men. You *must* come and hear what Eleanor can tell you."

Bart's puzzlement only increased with Walter's words, along with grim alarm. He could not imagine how Mairi had been taken by MacEwen while under guard with Kathryn in the tower.

Bart gave orders to Sir Duncan and Sir Stephan, who rode beside him, then he broke away from the ranks, allowing the knights to pass by. They would set up camp outside Braemar Keep as planned and bolster the men already there.

"Where was Eleanor found?" Bart asked when they were clear of the men.

"On the beach, outside the postern gate," Walter replied. "She was draped in Mairi's cloak, and crying to be let in."

"Where had she been?"

"Apparently, MacEwen's men sneaked into the keep—through the postern gate, I suppose—and took her. With all the activity in the bailey last night, preparations for the attack upon Armstrong, 'twas not difficult for them to pass unnoticed."

"*God's blood!*" Bart muttered.

"Aye. Somehow they learned of Mairi's survival and were sent to capture her."

"To be taken back to Braemar Keep?" Bart asked.

Walter shook his head. "I do not know, my lord," he replied. "Mayhap when you question Eleanor, you will be able to learn more."

"Is she all right?"

"Aye. Though she is exhausted and a bit scraped about the knees and hands," Walter said.

They left their horses near the main steps to the keep, and Bart ascended quickly. He made his way through the hall and up to the nursery, where Eleanor lay in her bed. Kathryn was there with Nurse Ada and Rose, the maid who most often tended Mairi.

"Bartie!" Eleanor cried weakly. She sat up in her bed and, when Bart came close enough, embraced him.

"Hush," he said as he cupped her head and held her close. She was much more precious to him than he'd ever realized. Nearly losing her had made him see that, and now he'd lost Mairi.

"I was so afraid, Bartie," Ellie whispered.

"Aye, but you're home now," Bart replied. "And safe."

"But those Scotsmen took Mairi," Eleanor said, beginning to weep. "She gave me her cloak and made me run away. And they took her!"

"Will her father make her wed the MacEwen laird?" Kathryn asked. She looked no better than she had the night before, her eyes red and swollen from weeping. The lines of worry had not left her face.

Bart turned. "What do you know of it?"

"I heard her tell Sir Walter that she left France only because her father commanded her to return. To wed Carmag MacEwen."

"Is he so very awful, Bartie?" Eleanor asked. "Kathryn said he was."

Bart eased Eleanor back into her bed and sat down next to her. Then he spoke to Kathryn. "Tell me what happened last night, Kate, after I left you."

Kathryn, too, sat on the edge of Eleanor's bed. "We

went to the tower room, just like you told us," she explained. "I got into the big bed, but Mairi said she couldn't sleep. I watched her for a while. She was pacing by the fire...."

Bart could easily imagine Mairi's body taut with tension as she paced the tower room.

"I suppose I must have fallen asleep," Kathryn continued, "because when I awoke again, Mairi was gone."

"Raulf was guarding the tower, my lord," Sir Walter said. "Lady Mairi told him she had to find you, and that he was to remain at his post and continue guarding Lady Kathryn."

"Which is when she slipped out," Bart concluded. "Where did Lady Mairi find you, Ellie?"

"'Twas someplace I've never been, Bartie," she replied. "High up on Scots land, over the sea."

"They took you up the escarpment?" Bart questioned.

"Aye," she replied. "One of them carried me for a long time up the beach. Then he put me down and made me climb a big hill, and it hurt my hands because I had to hold on to the rock so tight."

"It must be the ridge on the northern border," Sir Walter remarked.

"When we got to the top," Eleanor added as her tears started again, "we w-walked a long while, and I was afraid."

Bart patted his sister's hand and tried to be patient. He knew she'd undergone a terrible experience, but he was anxious to hear about Mairi, and how she had found Eleanor. He wanted to know what he would have to do to get her back.

"After a while," Eleanor finally said, sniffling, "we

got to a place where they k-kept their horses, and one man said they would stop and m-make camp until dawn.''

"That took a nerve," Walter muttered.

"They stuck some blankets up somehow and made me crawl underneath them. I fell asleep."

More tears delayed the story, and by now, Kathryn was weeping, too.

"I woke up and M-Mairi was there. She took me away from the camp and we ran as fast as we could, back toward Norwyck. But the men chased us. Mairi gave me her cloak and told me to run, or to hide."

Bart heard Walter say, "That's our girl." Nurse Ada had her hand over her heart, and Rose's eyes were huge, as if she could not believe her mistress's dire situation.

"I kept g-going, but when I heard them coming close, I huddled down by a tree stump and covered myself with the cloak. Th-they walked past me in the dark. But I heard th-them get Mairi."

Kathryn gasped, and Ada cried out in dismay.

"He said they were looking for her, anyway—not me," Eleanor said. "They only took me because they couldn't find her."

"And now she's to marry the MacEwen!" Kathryn cried. "He's a terrible man, and Lady Mairi will die before she weds him."

The room grew suddenly silent with Kathryn's proclamation. Dread gathered and coiled in Bart's belly.

"Explain yourself, Kate," he said. His voice sounded low and dangerous, even to his own ears.

"Lady Mairi said th-that she would die by her father's hand if she did not wed the MacEwen," Kathryn said shakily. She looked up at Sir Walter then, as if the old man would verify her words. "And sh-she said she would die by her own if she did."

"For listening at keyholes, lass," Walter said sorrowfully, "you certainly heard well enough."

Bart hardly heard Walter's words. He felt numb with the thought of Mairi at Braemar Keep, at the mercy of her father. Enraged at the thought of her wed to Carmag. Eleanor began to cry again, and Bart touched Walter's shoulder, steering him out of the nursery.

"Mairi said this?" he asked. "That her father would have her life if she refused to wed Carmag?"

Walter nodded. "My lord, she cares deeply for you," the steward said. "This marriage will be…" His chin dropped to his chest as he searched for the words. "Lachann will have to force her to it."

"Not if I can stop him," Bart said.

Walter looked up.

"I'll get her back, before the nuptials are said."

"There's a lad," Walter said, smiling. "I knew you would see reason, my lord. Lady Mairi had no wish to lie to you, but as you must see, she had no choice."

The nursery door opened, and Rose slipped out and could have gone down to the great hall without notice. But with her eyes cast down, she approached Bart and Sir Walter. She cleared her throat. "My lord," she said shyly.

"Aye," Bart said gently. He rarely had occasion to speak to any of the maids, and he knew it must have taken a great deal of heart for her to address him.

"What Lady Kathryn said…" she began, "about Lady Marguerite, er, Lady Mairi…" She looked up at the two men and bit her lip. 'Twas clear she had something to say, yet for some reason was uncomfortable with it. "My lord, m-might I speak to you alone?"

"Excuse us, Sir Walter," Bart said, curious now, but unwilling to waste any more time. His men were bound for Braemar Keep and Bart was anxious to join them there.

Quickly, he ushered Rose through the gallery to the solar, and once they were inside, closed the door.

"What about Lady Mairi?"

"She would never harm herself, my lord," Rose said. "Not now…"

"Go on."

"Well," the maid continued, wringing her hands before her, "I—I am not fully certain of this, my lord, for the lady took pains to hide the signs. But if I am not m-mistaken…Lady Mairi is with child."

The block of dread that lay so heavily in Bart's stomach dropped to the floor. He steadied himself with one hand against the mantelpiece.

Mairi…carrying his child?

'Twas all too easy to believe. He supposed he'd seen some of the signs himself, but had not recognized them. And now she was MacEwen's prisoner. Mairi, and their child.

Bart cleared the tightness from his throat. "Thank you, Rose, for speaking up," he said, heading for the door.

"You'll bring her back, won't you, my lord?"

"Aye," he replied as he opened the door to leave. "Be assured of it."

He would kill Carmag MacEwen himself to prevent him from putting his beefy hands on Mairi.

Chapter Twenty-Three

Though Mairi's captors treated her reasonably well during the long ride, she felt as close to despair as she ever had. She was exhausted, but fear and apprehension kept her upright in the saddle.

She was doomed to wed Carmag. She could not possibly carry out her vow to end her own life if this circumstance came to pass, for 'twould mean destroying the child she carried. The child she already loved as much as its father.

Mairi hoped Eleanor had managed to make her way back to Norwyck safely. It wasn't possible for the child to have lost her way, not with the sea at her side, but other calamities might have occurred. She might have come across a wild animal. Or fallen off the escarpment!

Swallowing hard and forcing herself to believe Eleanor had gotten safely back to Bartholomew, Mairi considered the situation that awaited her.

They rode inland, angling north and west toward Armstrong land. Mairi did not know what to expect at Braemar Keep, beyond the fact that Carmag would be waiting for her there. In due time—and Mairi did not think there would be much delay—she would have no choice but to wed the laird of clan MacEwen. Her stomach churned at the thought, yet she had no choice but to face facts, as distasteful as they were.

She could not help but hope that there would be some way to escape this marriage, however. If only she could think of something that would make her utterly unacceptable to Carmag.

She knew her pregnancy alone would not be enough. Many a woman married while she carried another man's child, and Carmag struck her as the kind of man who would not care. In truth, Mairi believed Carmag would be perverse enough to enjoy the prospect of raising a Norwyck son to be the enemy of his true father.

"We've not much farther to ride, my lady," one of her captors said. He had been respectful and polite ever since abducting her the previous night, but Mairi held no illusions about these Scotsmen. They would never bargain with her for her freedom. On the contrary, they would tie her down and drag her to her father's keep if necessary.

She wondered what Bartholomew's reaction to her disappearance would be. Would Eleanor understand enough of what had happened to explain to him that Mairi had not left Norwyck by choice? She would not have him think she had abandoned him, as Felicia had done.

Mairi may have withheld her identity from him, but she was not as false as Bart's late wife.

"There 'tis, my lady," the man said as they rode over the rise. "Braemar Keep."

There was no high stone curtain around the keep, and 'twas not as large or as impressive a fortress as

Norwyck. Yet Mairi could see from a distance that Braemar Keep was quite defensible, positioned high upon a hillock.

It looked primitive and raw, just as she remembered it.

One of her captors tossed another blanket to her, apparently noting her sudden shudder. Mairi pulled it around herself and tried not to think of what awaited her here.

During her ten years in France, Mairi had never had any communication from Armstrong—not until Carmag had arrived to take her back to Scotland to be his wife. Since the shipwreck, she'd learned of her brother and father, but had heard naught of her mother. Mairi did not even know if the woman who'd given her life still lived.

She swallowed and blinked away the tears that came when she thought of poor Teàrlag, doomed in her marriage to Lachann. And Mairi knew the same fate awaited *her*.

Many poor, drab cottages dotted the hillside around her father's stone keep. A timber church stood near the center of the village, its thatched roof in need of patching. Mairi wondered why, if clan Armstrong was so destitute, and in such sore need of provisions, her father had butchered those Norwyck animals and left them to rot.

She knew the answer before the thought had barely formed. 'Twas his pride. Lachann would never allow Bartholomew to know of his clan's dire need, but would kill the animals for the sole purpose of flaunting his Scottish potency before the English lord.

As they rode through the muddy lanes of Braemar, people stepped out of their cottages to see who passed.

Mairi recognized no one. Naught seemed familiar, not even Braemar Keep itself, where she'd lived the first decade of her life. Mairi looked up at the cold, dank keep. Few windows graced the building, and much of the stone was crumbling. It seemed that Lachann took no better care of his own dwelling than he did those of his clan. Several long, low buildings lay beyond the keep, and rows of Scotsmen with bows guarded the perimeter of her father's grounds.

It began to rain as Mairi dismounted without assistance. No one approached her as she walked toward the wooden stair to the keep, but a sudden bellow came from within. The scarred wooden door was flung open, and before Mairi had a moment to catch her breath, she stood looking at Carmag MacEwen, with her father right behind him.

Carmag was only partially dressed—he lacked shirt or tunic—and Mairi cringed at the sight of all that MacEwen flesh.

"Wife!" he roared.

Mairi made no reply, but stood still, bracing herself and wishing she had a weapon to use against him.

She had no doubt that he would attempt to force himself upon her as he'd done in France. Only this time there was no one to stop him from doing what was his right.

"Mairi Armstrong!" he shouted, heaving his massive bulk down the wooden steps to the ground.

Mairi glanced up at Lachann, who made no move toward her.

The Armstrong knights stood in place, and the people of clan Armstrong watched from the shelter of their cottages, as MacEwen reached her. Without warning, he lifted her so that she was face-to-face with him, and then mashed his lips onto hers.

Mairi gagged when he opened his mouth and tried to force his tongue between her tightly closed lips. She felt her feet dangling inches above the ground, and a painful pressure under her arms where Carmag held her.

She kicked her feet helplessly in the air, and one of her shoes finally made contact with his shin. He put her down suddenly and let out a laugh that chilled Mairi's blood. "We'll loosen these tight French lips of yours yet, Mairi Armstrong, and make you into a true Scotswoman!"

"Enough o' that, Laird MacEwen," called a man, distracting Carmag enough for Mairi to take a step away. "Can ye no' see ye've terrified th' lass?"

Mairi saw that the man who'd spoken was a cleric. And it appeared that he was the only one who cared—or had the nerve—to speak to Carmag. The villagers stayed well away from them, and her father remained at the top of the stair, eyeing her curiously.

"We will wed this eve," Carmag said, his voice loud and abrasive to Mairi's ears. "Prepare what you must, Father Murray."

"Nay, MacEwen," Father Murray countered. "There are the banns—"

"The banns be damned!" Carmag roared. "The woman was fairly given by the Armstrong, and now she's mine, vows or nay."

Father Murray stepped up and faced Carmag. "Church rules will be obeyed in this matter, Laird MacEwen," he said quietly. He was just as tall as Carmag, but not so broad, with unkempt hair as black as night, streaked with silver over his ears. His presence gave comfort to Mairi, however slight.

"Nay," said a low, rough voice that sent a shudder through Mairi. "I am her sire. The lass will wed when I bid her to wed. Not a moment after."

But Father Murray would not be gainsaid, and Mairi could have kissed his hand for it. "If ye'll not wait for the banns, then surely ye can give the lass a bit o' time, and after she has—"

"Enough!" Lachann said harshly. "She'll go to her mother for the night and be ready to wed come the morn. Take her to Teàrlag, Father Murray, and cease your womanish prattle."

Mairi, glad to be spared any sort of welcome by her father, placed her hand upon the priest's shabbily clad arm and walked on shaky legs toward the keep. She said naught, but considered the possibility that the priest might be able to help her.

He'd had a hand in getting her a night's reprieve, as well as the opportunity to see her mother.

The keep was dingy and dank. 'Twas dark, as well, and Mairi nearly tripped over a pair of dogs lolling by the wooden steps. When her eyes adjusted to the gloom, Mairi saw a large, scarred wooden table in the center of the hall, with the remnants of a meal upon it.

A few servants loitered about, eyeing her distrustfully as she walked through the hall.

"Did ye ride all night, then?" Father Murray asked.

"Nay, Father," Mairi replied self-consciously. Her voice was just above a whisper. "I slept a few hours before we set out this morn."

"Hmm," Father Murray said noncommittally. He led her to a rickety staircase and they began to climb.

"Yer mother has a chamber at the back of the keep where the sunlight is good and she can sew."

"Is she...well?"

"Nay, lass," Father Murray said, starting up the next flight, "though seein' ye will do her heart good."

"What ails her?"

"Besides bein' heartsick over her heathen husband and son?" Murray said. "She's got pains in her joints...keeps her from movin' much. And a cough that weakens her."

In silence, they climbed to the third floor, where they stopped before a scuffed oaken door. Father Murray spoke before pushing it open. "I can protect ye for a time, lass," he said. "But once yer wed to the man, I canna help ye."

"I thank you for all you've done, Father," Mairi said, her mind rushing through possibilities. There must be a way to escape this place. All she had to do was get away from the keep after dark, then head east, and she'd come to the sea. Once there, she would follow the coast until she came to Norwyck....

"The Armstrong and I have been lockin' horns for many a year, and I canna say that either of us has made much headway against the other. The laird gets his own way as often as Mother Church gets hers," Father Murray said.

Mairi nodded absently as the priest pushed open the door to Teàrlag's solar. Dull light streamed in from two long, narrow windows on one wall, showing up the layer of dust covering every surface of the room. There was a sense of neglect about the solar, except for a small area around the fireplace.

Mairi's mother sat in a chair pulled close to the fire. Her hair was partially covered by a white veil, which was all Mairi could see of the woman until she looked up. Teàrlag smiled. Her eyes moistened and tears began to fall as she set her needle and the raw cloth on her lap and held her arms out to her daughter. She was thin and frail, and one of her eyes was opaque with blindness. Her skin seemed almost transparent. "Mairi," she said. Her voice was a bit wobbly, but Mairi remembered it as if she had heard it only yesterday.

"Mother!" she whispered as she flew to Teàrlag's side. She knelt before her and took her hands, unable to speak for the emotion that clogged her throat.

"I never thought to see you again, Daughter," Teàrlag said. "Your cousin's husband told us you drowned."

"My cousin's— Alain? *Alain was here?*"

"Aye," Teàrlag said. "Washed ashore in a storm. MacEwen's people found him and eventually brought him here. But he returned to France after staying only a few days. When he left, we still thought you had perished."

"Nay, Mother," Mairi said breathlessly. "I washed ashore, too, but farther south."

"Aye, your father learned of this only recently. One of Lord Norwyck's men—a fellow called Darcet— came to Lachann with tales of Norwyck."

Mairi did not know of any Darcet, but found it difficult to believe that anyone from Norwyck would come to Braemar with the intention of betraying Norwyck. Mayhap Lachann had sent the man to Bartholomew to begin with, to learn what he could. She certainly believed her father canny enough to do such a thing.

"I've missed you all these years, Mairi," her

mother said wistfully. "A lass should have her mother as she grows up...."

"I missed you, too," Mairi said, realizing that tears streamed down her own face. She'd had a perfectly fine life in France with Caitir, but naught could take the place of her own mother's love.

"'Twas for the best, though," Teàrlag said, and Mairi detected for the first time the quiet strength and fortitude that had sustained her for all these years. "Your father is... I would not have him mold you into an Armstrong creature like your brother. If there was aught I could do for you, 'twas to get you away from here."

"Aye, Mother," Mairi said, wiping her eyes. She gently squeezed her cold, thin hands. "And I was happy with Caitir. I did not miss Armstrong at all, besides you."

"Ah, you're a bonny one to say so, but I know there was much more that I should have done for you."

"Nay, there was naught."

Teàrlag freed one hand from Mairi's grasp and caressed her daughter's head. They stayed quiet for several long minutes, and Mairi basked in her mother's attention. She considered telling her of the child she carried, but decided to hold back for now. Their emotions were raw as it was, without adding Mairi's bairn into it.

"I do not know if I can bear to see you wed to Carmag."

"I do not intend to wed the man, Mother."

Alarm sparked in Teàrlag's eyes. "How...? Mairi, if you defy the laird, he—"

"Listen, Mother," Mairi said quietly. She turned to look toward the door, to be sure 'twas closed and she would not be overheard. "I am leaving tonight. I know the way back to Norwyck, and Bartholomew Holton is a good and just lord. He will take us both in—"

"Nay, child," Teàrlag interjected with a shake of her head. "My hips, my knees...I cannot travel. I can barely get down the stairs when I must. I would only hold you back."

"I'll steal a horse or a mule—"

"'Tis impossible—"

"And get a wagon to carry—"

Without warning, the door crashed open and Lachann strutted in. He said naught, but approached his wife and daughter, walking around the chair with his arms crossed over his belly. He made a quiet sound from deep within his chest, and Mairi followed her mother's lead, waiting patiently for him to speak.

"So, ye've spent yer last months whorin' for the Norwyck laird."

His words were delivered like a slap, and Mairi felt color flood her face. But she did not reply.

"Carmag doesna' mind," Lachann said, moving to stand before the fire. "A virginal bride is a bane to her bridegroom."

Mairi swallowed and held her tongue as Lachann barked out a harsh laugh. She would not give her father any reason to suspect she would not be compliant. And tonight, she would get herself and her mother out of Braemar Keep.

There was no reason why she should not take a walk through the village later and see where her father kept his horses, and where his knights were billeted. She would take blankets, water skins and a bit of food, too, if she could find them. If not, then she and Teàrlag would make do without. After all, 'twas not such a long ride to Norwyck.

If only Bartholomew did not hate her for her lies. Mairi hoped that Eleanor had made him understand that she had left Norwyck only to free her, and not to run away to Braemar Keep the moment the opportunity arose.

Bartholomew *had* to understand that she wanted naught to do with Laird Armstrong or her corrupt brother.

"The ceremony will be short," Lachann said, striding toward the chamber door. "Carmag will wed ye, then bed ye, and ye'll be off to Castle MacEwen before his seed has dried upon yer thighs."

And with those crude words, Lachann turned and left, slamming and barring the door behind him.

"Oh, Mairi," Teàrlag cried. "He's locked you in!"

Chapter Twenty-Four

The Norwyck men were deadly quiet in the grove at the base of the hill. They were deep in Armstrong territory, and their situation was perilous. To attack now would bring down a shower of arrows upon them.

Yet waiting gave Armstrong time enough to discover their location and begin his own attack.

Bartholomew knew that this strategy—lying in wait—was untraditional, mayhap even cowardly. Knights should meet openly in battle, and not hide from the enemy until the time was ripe.

But he had too much to lose.

Mairi's life, her love, their bairn... He would not risk them for honor's sake. He would come away the victor, and use whatever method was necessary.

"My lord," Duncan said, "there is a good deal more activity in the village than we saw last eve."

Bart looked up through the trees toward the keep, but did not notice anything significant, other than a few more fires. "What do you make of it?"

"None of us can see so far, my lord," the knight replied. "I've sent men up as far as we dare, to try and spy."

"'Tis all we can do now," Bart said, moving to the edge of the wood, "without giving our position away."

He gazed up at the hill. There was no doubt that a great deal of activity was going on. Archers still patrolled, but the rest of the men were at work doing other things. Building a siege machine?

A cloud of smoke hovered over Braemar's hill, and Bart had no doubt that the villagers' fires were larger and more numerous than usual. What were they doing? Was one the smithy's fire, and mayhap the armorer's?

Women were out and about, too, and Bart wondered if Armstrong had figured some way to use them in battle. Then a new thought occurred to him.

"Is there any chance Lady Mairi was brought here without our knowing, Duncan?"

"'Tis possible, my lord," he replied. "The fog was quite dense this morn before the rain began. We might very well have missed her."

Bart cursed under his breath. If Mairi was already here...

"What of Laird MacEwen?" Bart asked. "Is he still at Braemar?"

"Aye, my lord," Duncan replied. "As far as we know."

Bart turned away and paced the ground. If Armstrong had managed to get Mairi to Braemar, and if Carmag were already here, there would be naught to stop their marriage from taking place. Naught but Bartholomew Holton and all the forces he could muster.

He turned back and gazed up at the village and at Armstrong's pitiful keep. Cookfires, women out and about, light emanating from the church... 'Twas a wedding that was planned, Bart thought. Though his eyes were good, he wished they were better, so that he might see exactly what was going on up there.

"As soon as your men return, have them report to me," he ordered.

"Aye, my lord."

Mairi sat quietly with her mother in her solar. Teàrlag was nervous, jumping at every sound, repeatedly glancing at the heavy oaken door. Mairi tried to distract her by speaking of her years with Caitir, and of the odd happenstance that had caused Alain to wash up on MacEwen's shore.

"I thought he drowned," Mairi said.

"Aye, he thought the same of you," Teàrlag repeated as tears welled in her eyes. "'Twas a terrible storm that brought down your ship."

"What is it, Mother?" Mairi asked. She thought all the emotion they had in them had been wrung out in the past few hours.

Teàrlag covered her mouth with one hand and shook her head. "I was almost glad..." Tears rolled down her cheeks. "I could rest easy knowing you'd never be compelled to wed the MacEwen..."

Gently, Mairi took her mother's cold, thin hands in her own. She knew she would feel the same if her own daughter were forced to wed such a man as Carmag. "'Twill be all right," she whispered. "'Twill be all right."

The door opened and a handsome young man swaggered into the solar, letting the door slam behind him. Mairi knew at once that this was Dùghlas, her brother. She stood.

He clucked his tongue and walked 'round her.

"Ye've grown into a comely wench," he said, looking her over. "Never would ha' thought it when ye left Braemar."

Mairi remained silent. She would not be goaded into an unpleasant discussion with this worm of a man, this seducer of another man's wife.

Keeping his hands clasped behind him, he prowled the room. "Where's yer English lover?" he asked, sneering. "Not come t' rescue ye?"

"Why should he?" Mairi replied carefully. "He has no use of a Scots mistress. Now that he knows who I am…" She shrugged, as if Lord Norwyck's whereabouts meant naught to her.

"Clever of ye to tell him the tale of yer lost memory," Dùghlas said. "Ye had it right nice fer all those weeks, did ye?"

Mairi bit the inside of her mouth to keep from responding. As comely as Dùghlas was, Mairi sensed that he was rotten to the core. He cast about, with the hope of getting a rise out of her, for the sheer pleasure of knowing he could do it.

But Mairi refused to play.

"Let your sister be, Dùghlas," Teàrlag said in a low, tense voice.

Dùghlas let out a laugh that chilled Mairi's bones. 'Twas clear that her brother had no respect or regard for their mother. Mairi could not expect him to hold any for her, either.

"Norwyck's wife said her husband returned from Scotland with no stomach for war," Dùghlas said, warming his hands in front of the fire. An ugly gleam of hate shone in his beautiful eyes. "She told me he vowed never to take up arms against a Scot again."

Mairi did not know if what Dùghlas said was true.

Certainly, Bartholomew had been reluctant to do battle
with clan Armstrong, but she thought he'd only been
prudently waiting for the opportune moment. She had
seen him on his practice field, day after day, with Norwyck's knights. Surely there had been good reason for
all that training.

And surely the man who'd told Lachann about her
existence at Norwyck would have mentioned the vast
number of knights at Norwyck's disposal.

"Aye," Mairi finally said. "He is loath to go to
battle. He and his men train daily, but I know he hopes
never to have to use that training."

Dùghlas nodded. "Lachann has been testing
him...."

Mairi knew this must be true. Her father had done
all he could to provoke Bartholomew, but had not succeeded. Mayhap she could strengthen their belief in
Bartholomew's cowardice and Norwyck's lack of pre-
paredness with a few more well-placed words. Though
she had no reason to think Bartholomew would attempt to take her from Braemar Keep, she would give
Lachann and Dùghlas no information that would further their cause.

On the contrary, she would do what she could to
confound them.

"Lord Norwyck remains distraught over the loss of
his brother and his wife."

Dùghlas smiled evilly. "Aye. 'Twas some of m'best
work. Felicia was a slut, even years ago, when I knew
her in France. 'Twas no great feat to seduce her while
Norwyck was away...."

Mairi bristled while Dùghlas continued his tale of
treachery and deception. She was disgusted.

"Lady Mairi."

As startled by the deep voice as Teàrlag was, Mairi turned to see Father Murray at the door. She felt her mother's alarm subside when she saw that 'twas only the priest.

"If ye care to make yer confession before yer nuptials, lass…"

"Aye, Father."

"Out with ye, Murray!" Dùghlas shouted. "I've no' finished with 'er yet."

"Yer pardon, Dùghlas," Murray said, though his tone was defiant.

Teàrlag remained quiet, though Mairi noted the set of her jaw and her pinched lips. 'Twas obvious to Mairi that her mother was no happier with the situation than she was. But what could they do? Dùghlas would be certain to lock Mairi in overnight, to guarantee that there would be a bride here for MacEwen upon the morrow.

She wondered if she could rely upon the priest for any assistance. He had already told her he could not help her once she was wed, but what about before?

"Will ye send fer me when yer ready?"

"Aye, Father," Mairi said quietly. Mayhap when she spoke to him outside her brother's presence, she would be able to convince him to help her get herself and Teàrlag away from Braemar.

Father Murray left the solar, and Mairi and her mother were left, once again, with Dùghlas.

"How many men has Norwyck under his command?"

"I do not know," Mairi said, which was true.

"Does he train archers? Swordsmen?"

Mairi shook her head. "I cannot say that I ever saw

any archers,'' she replied, with a silent prayer that her lie would be forgiven.

Dùghlas paced back and forth before the fire. ''Tell me of th' wall he builds.''

Mairi could see no harm in discussing this very obvious defense, and decided to embellish the facts. '''Tis nearly finished,'' she said. ''There was an accident awhile back…part of the wall fell, but they've repaired it and are near to finishing.''

''Does Norwyck think he can keep us out?''

''They'll have two wells within, Dùghlas,'' she said, ''and stores such as you've never seen. 'Tis entirely possible to withstand a long siege with such provisions.''

Dùghlas frowned and considered Mairi's words.

''And since Lord Norwyck wishes to avoid battle at all costs—''

The chamber door opened again, admitting Lachann Armstrong. He seemed different, more angry now, more volatile than before, and Mairi knew she would have to take great care as she dealt with him.

He approached her slowly, ominously, just as a predator would advance on its prey. Mairi heard Teàrlag's quick intake of breath, just before the back of Lachann's hand crashed across Mairi's jaw. The blow knocked her to the straw-covered floor and she remained there, with her head reeling, her split lip bleeding.

''Do na look at me with such holy righteousness in yer eyes. Tha' wee tap is no more than what Norwyck's whore deserves,'' Lachann seethed. ''Did ye no remember yer responsibility to yer clan, wench?''

Mairi kept her silence, though she got up on her knees, and then to her feet. Memories of Lachann's unpredictable brutality returned to her now, after years of relative peace and calm in Caitir's house. Her heart ached once again for her mother, who'd had to live with Lachann's vile temper for years. 'Twas no wonder she was so jumpy and nervous.

Mairi scooted away from her male kin, with the hope that she could evade another blow. Hazily, she heard her mother's quiet weeping, and her father's stern rebuke.

"Ye'll be off to MacEwen's castle after the marriage and Braemar will be well rid of ye," Lachann growled as he returned to the door. "And I've decided ye'll take yer mother with ye."

Mairi showed no emotion at this statement, but felt relieved, as well as alarmed, to know that Teàrlag would accompany her to MacEwen's stronghold. She did not know what lay in store for her, though 'twas bound to be unpleasant. She wished her mother would not be compelled to bear witness to her suffering.

After Lachann stormed out, Dùghlas continued his questioning, but Mairi had no more to say. She made up the answers she believed would placate her brother as she stood gazing out the filmy window. Far below, clan Armstrong made preparations for a grand wedding feast upon the morrow.

Chapter Twenty-Five

A light haze hovered over the hills that morn—not the dense fog that Bart had hoped would cover their movements, but maybe 'twould be.

Before dawn, he sent companies of knights in all directions to surround Braemar Hill. Archers would be at the forefront of each group, and swordsmen on horseback would follow. With the knights so widely spread, it wasn't possible to give one signal for attack, so Bart's men would lead. When they arrived at Braemar Keep, he would begin the attack, the sounds of battle signaling the rest of Norwyck's men to join them.

'Twas not a perfect plan, but it was as close to a simultaneous attack as he could make it, and would offer Norwyck's best chance for victory. Besides teaching Armstrong a badly needed lesson, Bart would not allow MacEwen to wed Mairi and take her away.

She was his, and no other man would touch her.

Bartholomew paced through the damp grass at the base of the hill, keeping himself well within the cover of the trees. He cracked his knuckles and took an occasional sip of ale as he waited for the opportune moment to climb the hill and take on Armstrong and MacEwen. He kept watch on Braemar's heights, even though the haze limited his vision. He kept his ears tuned to any nuance of sound that indicated Armstrong's knights were on the move.

An unearthly brightness finally began to spread from the east. The time was nearly ripe, but still Bart waited. There was no room for error, not with Mairi's life at stake. He wanted all his companies in place before making his move, but when the sound of pipers' music filtered down the hill, Bart mounted Pegasus and began his charge up the slope.

Mairi had never liked the sound of pipes, so the mournful music was more than appropriate for her march toward the village church, where she would wed Carmag MacEwen. Teàrlag remained behind when Mairi was summoned by one of the servants, so she made her way down the rotted steps of the keep, past the foul table of the great hall, and outside into the misty morn toward her dismal fate.

She had not been able to find a way out of the solar. Father Murray had not been allowed to return to her, and there'd been no one else about. Just Mairi and her mother, and a stout bar across an equally strong door.

Mairi found herself shaking. Mayhap 'twas due to the chill of the morn, but the cold seemed to go through her, clear to her marrow. She tried not to think of Carmag waiting for her at the bottom of the church steps, but trembled all the more when she remembered the sensation of his greasy mouth upon hers. Yesterday's assault was naught compared to what would follow this ceremony.

Dùghlas took her arm at the foot of the steps. His

grasp was not the least bit brotherly, but more like that of a guard with his prisoner. A large number of Armstrong men stood about, drinking ale and sampling food from tables that had been set up near the church. Mairi's vision was limited because of the mist, but it seemed that a fair number of these men were idle. They wore their swords at their sides, but did not appear ready for battle.

She wondered if these were the same men who often went raiding the lands of their peaceful neighbor to the south. Mairi hoped Dùghlas believed her tale of Bartholomew's reluctance to come to battle. 'Twould make her father and brother overconfident, mayhap careless, giving Bart the advantage when he finally answered Lachann's call to war.

She dared not hope that Carmag would be here among Armstrong's men when Bartholomew came to fight. The notion of soon becoming a widow was more than appealing.

Dùghlas tugged her arm roughly and pulled her through the cobbled lane as the pipes wailed. Mairi winced at the discordant sound. Villagers milled about quietly, distrustfully, and the few children that Mairi saw were not running and scampering playfully as children should. Instead, they hung on to their mother's skirts and watched as warily as the adults.

The impression that all was not well at Braemar intensified, and Mairi wished there were some way to use this information to stop her marriage to the MacEwen. Unfortunately, she could think of naught. Dùghlas would lead her to the church like a docile lamb to the slaughter, while all the Armstrongs watched.

And for all her trouble, Mairi did not even know if

her efforts to rescue Eleanor Holton had succeeded. There was a good possibility that she would never know if the child had made it safely back to Norwyck Castle.

When the poor church came into view, Mairi looked up to see Father Murray standing at the top of the steps, at the door. He did not see her, but was looking down in disgust at some disturbance on the ground to his right. His eyes flashed angrily and his color was high.

"Do ye come to the house of the Lord in a drunken stupor, Laird MacEwen," the priest roared, "to make the sacred vows that will bind ye to this woman fer life?"

Dùghlas laughed as Carmag MacEwen staggered 'round the steps to greet his bride. His filthy gray tunic was ripped at the sleeve, and his chausses and braes hung carelessly, indecently, about him.

Mairi glanced away with revulsion. Father Murray stormed down the steps and pulled Carmag away, chastising him as they went.

'Twas a reprieve, albeit a short one.

Mairi considered asking her brother to try to get Lachann to reconsider the marriage, but quickly realized that would be fruitless. She was no more than any nameless wench to Dùghlas, and there was no favor she could offer in return for his intercession. Besides, 'twas more than likely Lachann would not listen. He'd made up his mind long ago to bind clan Armstrong to MacEwen, and there'd be no changing it now.

As if conjured from her thoughts, Lachann Armstrong approached out of the mist. Mairi flinched in spite of herself, and Lachann appeared to enjoy his effect upon his daughter. Clearing his throat noisily, he spat on the ground near his feet. "Where's the MacEwen?" he asked.

"Off with the priest, making himself presentable," Dùghlas said.

Lachann spat again. He looked at Mairi, letting his eyes rove over her before speaking. "So, yer craven Sassenach lover willna be savin' ye from this weddin...."

How was Bartholomew to save her? She knew as well as her father all the difficulties Braemar posed to the Norwyck knights, and she was aware that Bartholomew's best strategy—his only strategy—was to lie in wait for Lachann to bring his men to Norwyck. That tactic certainly would not help her now.

"Nay, Father," she said, deciding to perpetuate the lie that Bartholomew was afraid to meet the Armstrong face-to-face. "Lord Norwyck does not care to fight. He is building a wall to protect his holding from you."

Lachann's responding laugh was low and quiet, almost feral, and Mairi shuddered with the thought that his blood ran in her veins. Yet the satisfied expression in his eyes gave her hope that his confidence would bring about his defeat, and spare Bartholomew's life.

Bart judged it time. The sun was up and his knights would be in place around Braemar's perimeter. The mournful sound of the pipes drifted down the hill from the village, and Bart knew that the sound of his knights would travel upon the mist as well, yet there was a dearth of Armstrong men on patrol. The timing would never be better.

Warning his men that Armstrong might have set a trap, he gave the signal to ride. Quickly, the men under his command moved into position. With discipline and agility, they rode swiftly toward Braemar, weapons at the ready, Bartholomew at the lead.

When they were halfway to the keep, they still had not met with any resistance. While he could not believe his good fortune, Bart pressed on, leading the first wave of the attack, and waiting for the opportune moment to signal all the other companies to battle.

A volley of Armstrong arrows suddenly thwarted their advance, but Bart closed his visor and charged on, anxious to find Mairi and get her to safety. There was confusion on the ground, and Bart knew with certainty that they'd taken Braemar by surprise. His plan had worked.

He continued to ride toward the keep, where he believed he would find Mairi, when a horseman attacked with sword in hand. He was without armor, so 'twas no difficult feat to dispatch him and move forward through the increasing number of armed men.

Another Armstrong swordsman came at Bart, and a fierce man-to-man contest was fought as Bart's opponent attempted to kill or maim him, or just unseat him.

"Behind you, my lord!"

Bart moved instantly, and the lance that was meant for his back impaled the assailant in front of him, killing him at once. With no respite, Bart battled his way up the hill. The mist still impeded his vision of the ground, but he was clearly able to see the upper floors of the keep at the precipice of the hill. If Mairi was at Braemar, that was the most likely place for Lachann to hold her.

As he made his way, with Norwyck men battling all 'round him, he dismounted and continued up the loosely cobbled path. A woman's shriek, nearly indiscernible in the cacophony of the battle, stopped him in his tracks. 'Twas Mairi.

Bart did not know how he could be so certain, but he *felt* her cry as much as heard it, just as he'd felt her hand touch his when she'd been in her tower and he'd been on the ground.

He turned toward the sound and found himself facing the village church. He knew he'd find her there, mayhap in the midst of saying her vows.

Fighting with two hands on his broadsword as he made his way, he finally reached the church steps, where Dùghlas Armstrong stood his ground, fighting a Norwyck swordsman to prevent him from climbing the stairs. "Yer too late, ye Sassenach bastard!" Dùghlas bellowed, even as he battled the Norwyck knight. "She's already wed!"

Bart found he cared less about killing Dùghlas than finding Mairi. After all these months of planning and training for his attack upon Braemar, and his revenge upon the Armstrongs, all he could think of was how quickly he could get to Mairi and carry her safely away from here, back to Norwyck Castle.

He vaulted over the side of the steps, climbing two at a time, leaving Dùghlas to his fate.

"Nay!" he heard a masculine voice shout vehemently. "There'll be no wedding in the midst of battle!"

Bart moved inside the doorway then, and saw her.

She was pale and obviously frightened. An ugly welt marred her chin, and a bloody gash split her lip. Yet she stood her ground, even though Lachann had a tight hold upon a handful of her hair, and MacEwen was pulling at her waist.

Bart was proud of her fortitude, even through his outrage at Carmag MacEwen's pawing, and the visible signs of abuse on Mairi's face. He would get her away from here.

Or die trying.

"Laird Armstrong!" the priest roared. "Ye shame the house of the Lo—"

"I'd skewer ye now, Murray," Lachann said ominously, pointing his sword at the priest, "but I need ye t' perform the ceremony. And perform it ye will! *Now!*"

Armstrong put his sword to the cleric's throat, and the man fell silent.

MacEwen did not seem to be armed, but Bart could not be sure of it. He saw no sword, but a true warrior would be able to use anything at hand as a weapon, and Carmag was that. The priest was not happy with the situation here, but Bartholomew could not assume the man would help him if it came to a battle and bloodshed inside the nave of the church.

Whatever happened, Bart knew it would have to be quick, because his presence would soon be known. He picked up a short wooden bench and flung it to the far side of the hollow chamber, startling the priest and the two men. They let go of Mairi for an instant, just long enough for her to dart away.

Bart drew his sword and met a very surprised Lachann Armstrong. It seemed the old man could not believe his eyes.

"Norwyck!"

"Aye," he said. "I've come for Mairi."

"And yer revenge, I'll wager." Lachann thrust his blade at him, but Bart easily dodged the blow.

"Nay, I want only your daughter," Bart said, parrying with Armstrong. He heard a crash behind him, and saw that Mairi had lifted a small wooden chair and shattered it over MacEwen's head, to prevent him from helping Lachann. "Stay back, Mairi," he called, anxious once again for her safety.

He positioned himself to deal with Carmag as well as Armstrong, especially after seeing Carmag pull a sharp little dirk from his belt. Bart chided himself for thinking the man would be unarmed. The priest moved about the nave, circling Bart and his opponent, somehow keeping Carmag from interfering, while he exhorted them all to take their battle elsewhere.

"Mairi," Bart called, ignoring the tall priest, "hide yourself until this is—"

Armstrong jabbed just as Carmag managed to thrust his dirk into the vulnerable part of Bart's body—under his left arm.

Enraged, Bart responded with a roar and a jab of his own, striking a fatal blow to Lachann Armstrong, spearing him through the chest. Oblivious to the blood running down his side, he pulled his blade from Laird Armstrong and turned to face MacEwen.

"Leave now, MacEwen," he said dangerously, through gritted teeth. "Take your men and go back to your lands and your castle, and I will spare your life."

"Ha!" Carmag barked. He crouched, ready to spring on Bartholomew. "Yer the one bloodied, Norwyck!"

"But you are the one who faces death, MacEwen."

Laird MacEwen's tiny eyes darted around nervously, evaluating his circumstances, while Bart stood at the ready, waiting for the Scot's answer. Or his move.

It came swiftly. MacEwen lunged and Mairi

screamed. Bart deflected the knife with his sword and immediately thrust his blade through the laird's heart. The man fell heavily as Mairi rushed from the shadows and into Bart's waiting arms.

"Are you all right, love?" he asked her.

"Bartholomew, you are wounded!" Mairi cried.

"Aye," Bart said, though he felt naught but a slight burning sensation. He dropped his sword, and with his uninjured hand, smoothed Mairi's hair away from her face.

"I should see to your wound," she said tremulously. Tears ran from her eyes, and she pressed her cheek to his chest as he wrapped his arms 'round her.

"Nay, just let me hold you for a moment."

The priest cleared his throat. "'Tis over," he said. "Yer father's inept lairdship is finished. Mayhap when Dùghlas is laird—"

"Dùghlas Armstrong will be laird of naught, priest," Bart interjected. He loosened his hold upon Mairi and led her from the place where her father lay slain. "Else he'd have stormed your church as I did battle with his sire."

The cleric's formidable brows came together, and he gave a quick nod. "I'll go outside and spread word of Laird Armstrong's death. Mayhap a few lives will be spared."

"Aye," Bart replied, without taking his eyes from Mairi's. He could not imagine ever mistrusting her. Mairi Armstrong, who'd proven her love and her loyalty so many times over... Only he'd been too thickheaded to know it, to see it.

The priest left them alone and Mairi finally spoke again. "Eleanor...did she return safely?"

"Only because of you, Mairi," he said gently.

Though her ordeal was over, the bruise on her chin and her torn lip infuriated him. He vowed that she would never suffer another injury or hardship again.

"These last hours away from you have been the longest of my life, Mairi Armstrong," he whispered, caressing her cheek. "Don't ever leave me again."

"But, my lord," she said breathlessly, "I…my sire is Lachann Arm—"

"And well I know it, sweetheart," he said, pulling her back into his arms. "But your husband will be Bartholomew Holton."

He heard her breath catch, and tipped his head to rain gentle kisses on her chin, her ear, her mouth.

"Be my lady, Mairi," he entreated, "be my wife. I love you with my heart and my soul. My life will never be complete without you."

Mairi had never thought to hear such heartfelt words from Bartholomew, and emotion clogged her throat. When she was finally able to speak, she cried, "Oh, Bartholomew…'twould be my very great honor to become your wife. I never thought…I never guessed you'd come for me."

"Never doubt that I will always come for you, Mairi Armstrong."

"Oh, Bartholomew, I love you so."

The church door swung open and a handsome young man of Dùghlas's age approached cautiously, though he moved with authority and dignity. He was unarmed, and he looked familiar.

"Mairi Armstrong?" he asked quietly.

"Aye. And you are…Cousin Aonghas?"

"It has been many a year, Mairi," Aonghas replied. He looked up at Bart, meeting his eyes. "Things have gone badly for clan Armstrong in recent years, m'lord. Lachann was…well, to say that he was imprudent would be a kindness. The clan wants naught but peace between us.''

"'Tis a reasonable desire,'' Bart replied. Mairi knew he wanted a way out of these constant skirmishes against her kin, and it seemed that Aonghas would provide it. ''Who will be laird in Lachann's stead?'' Bartholomew asked.

''I stand before you as the new laird of clan Armstrong.''

''You seem a good choice,'' Bart replied. ''We should be able to deal well together.'' She felt his arm slip 'round her waist. ''Go on ahead, Laird Aonghas. Announce to your people that a new era has begun. We'll follow in a moment.''

When Aonghas was gone, Bart turned Mairi in his arms and kissed her softly.

''A new age has begun for Norwyck, too, Mairi,'' he said. ''With our love, with the child you carry…and the others to come…there will be peace and prosperity. No more warring across our borders.''

''You knew about the bairn?'' she asked.

He nodded. ''Aye, love,'' he said, and Mairi did not recall ever seeing such intensity in his eyes. ''But not before I knew how I felt about you. You are my very life, Mairi. And I trust you with every moment of it hereafter.''

Kissing her lightly on her injured mouth, he turned her, and together they went out of the church to help Aonghas begin the peace between their people.

* * * * *

From Regency Ballrooms to Medieval Castles, fall in love with these stirring tales from Harlequin Historicals

On sale March 2003

THE SILVER LORD by Miranda Jarrett

Don't miss the first of **The Lordly Claremonts** trilogy!
Despite their being on opposite sides of the law,
a spinster with a secret smuggling habit can't resist
a handsome navy captain!

FALCON'S DESIRE by Denise Lynn

A woman bent on revenge holds captive the man
accused of killing her intended—and discovers
a love beyond her wildest dreams!

On sale April 2003

LADY ALLERTON'S WAGER by Nicola Cornick

A woman masquerading as a cyprian challenges a
dashing earl to a wager—with the stake being an island
he owns against her favors!

HIGHLAND SWORD by Ruth Langan

Be sure to read this first installment in the
Mystical Highlands series about three sisters
and the handsome Highlanders they bewitch!

Harlequin Historicals®
Historical Romantic Adventure!

SAVOR THE BREATHTAKING ROMANCES
AND THRILLING ADVENTURES
OF THE OLD WEST
WITH HARLEQUIN HISTORICALS

On sale March 2003

TEMPTING A TEXAN by Carolyn Davidson

A wealthy Texas businessman is ambitious, demanding and in no rush to get to the altar. But when a beautiful woman arrives with a child she claims is his niece, he must decide between wealth and love....

THE ANGEL OF DEVIL'S CAMP by Lynna Banning

When a Southern belle goes to Oregon to start a new life, the last thing she expects is to have her heart captured by a stubborn Yankee!

On sale April 2003

McKINNON'S BRIDE by Sharon Harlow

While traveling with her children, a young widow falls in love with the kind rancher who opens his home and his heart to her family....

ADAM'S PROMISE by Julianne MacLean

A ruggedly handsome Canadian finds unexpected love when his fiancée arrives and he discovers she's not the woman he thought he was marrying!

Harlequin Historicals®
Historical Romantic Adventure!

Steeple Hill Books is proud to present
a beautiful and contemporary new look
for Love Inspired!

HEARTWARMING INSPIRATIONAL ROMANCE

Love Inspired®

As always, Love Inspired delivers
endearing romances full of hope, faith and love.

Beginning January 2003
look for these titles
and three more each month
at your favorite retail outlet.

Steeple
Hill®

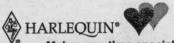

COOPER'S CORNER

Welcome to Twin Oaks—
the new B and B in Cooper's Corner.
Some come for pleasure, others for
passion—and one to set things straight...

Coming in January 2003...
ACCIDENTAL FAMILY
by Kristin Gabriel

Check-in: When former TV soap star Rowena Dahl's biological clock started ticking, she opted to get pregnant at a fertility clinic. Unfortunately, she got the wrong sperm!

Checkout: Publisher Alan Rand was outraged that a daytime diva was having *his* baby. But he soon realized that he wanted Rowena as much as he wanted their child.

HARLEQUIN®
Makes any time special ®

Visit us at www.cooperscorner.com

CC-CNM6